THE TOLLHOUSE TRIALS

C.E. Bass

Ark Dove Press

Ark Dove Press
An imprint of Ark Dove Enterprises, LLC
The Woodlands, Texas

Cover design by: C.E. Bass

I thank God for all His blessings.

I dedicate this book to my wife Amanda, whom I loved from the moment I saw her, and who has given me the patience and support during the writing of this book.

This book is for those who lost loved ones and questions what happens after we pass.

And lastly, to those priests who guide Christians correctly to lead a spiritual life in this world, to enjoy the fruits of an everlasting life.

In Christ,

C.E. Bass

CONTENTS

Title Page
Copyright
Dedication
Part I 1
Chapter One 2
Chapter Two 18
Chapter Three 33
Chapter Four 47
Chapter Five 60
Part II 70
Chapter Six 71
Chapter Seven 83
Chapter Eight 105
Chapter Nine 110
Chapter Ten 122
Chapter Eleven 130
Chapter Twelve 145
Part III 156

Chapter Thirteen 157
Chapter Fourteen 168
Chapter Fifteen 186
Part IV 198
Chapter Sixteen 199
Chapter Seventeen 214
Chapter Eighteen 218
Chapter Nineteen 228
Chapter Twenty 239
Chapter Twenty-One 253
Chapter Twenty-Two 265
Chapter Twenty-Three 276
Chapter Twenty-Four 282
Chapter Twenty-Five 295
Chapter Twenty-Six 312
Chapter Twenty-Seven 317
Epilogue 323
Memory eternal 327
Thank You 329
Acknowledgement 331
About The Author 333

PART I

"For a Christian end to our lives, peaceful without shame and suffering, and for a good account before the the awesome judgment seat of Christ, let us ask of the Lord."

- LITURGY OF SAINT JOHN CHRYSOSTOM

CHAPTER ONE

He holds the golden cross high above the crowd gathered at the banks of the Guadalupe river in the Texas Hill country. Sunshine gleaning off the rolling waters, reflecting into the priest's face. His eyes on fire from the shining sun. He prays over the river. The choir and chanters sing in unison. This is the blessing of the waters. A celebration of Theophany, the baptism of Christ.

"Can you believe these guys? This is all so dumb." He laughs.

"Be quiet Jonah. Your Mom can hear you." Said Daniel

"What is she going to do? I'm eighteen now. As an adult, I can do whatever I want. And the first thing is to never go to a church service again."

The priest continues his prayers. At the conclusion, he takes the crucifix in his hand and throws it into the river. The cross rotating in the air skips on the water. Soon, a rush of teenage boys follow the cross and dive into the river, all swimming as fast as possible to be the first to save the cross.

"Ha, ha, look at them." Jonah points at the boys swimming in the fifty degree waters.

"Jonah, be quiet. Our parents are going to ground us or whatever punishment parents have for college students."

"Daniel, come here." Jonah grabs him by the jacket and pulls him away from the crowd.

"I'm serious. Who in their right mind would believe any of this? Check out those poor altar boys. Their parents making them wear the robes and indoctrinating them with fairy tales."

A girl from choir stops singing and glares at Jonah.

Jonah mouths the word "What?" and waves her off.

"Jonah, if that's you believe, so be it. But don't make a scene here. Let the people pray and worship. OK?"

"Fine, but it's so silly... So, are we going out tonight?"

Daniel lets out a sigh of relief.

"At Justina's? Of course wouldn't miss it. The last bash before everyone heads back to college."

The procession heads toward Daniel and Jonah. Two altar boys, each carrying a burgundy banner, one with the icon of the Theophany the other of the Great Feast of the Ascension, are followed by three altar boys. The oldest carries a large cross, the younger two the golden processional fans with engraving of the Cherubim. The priest, deacon and the remaining altar boys holding large candles. Folding into the procession are the chanters, choir, and the congregation. Daniel and Jonah's parents walk past them. Both of their mothers shake their heads at them as they pass by.

"I told you, they aren't going to let us out tonight." Daniel says to Jonah.

"Dude, we are freshman in college. We are going out tonight. I don't care what they say."

"Alright, let's head back into the church."

They walk past the sign outside of the church: "Christ the Savior Orthodox Church. Divine Liturgy Sundays 10am, Vespers Saturday 5pm. All Welcome."

"No thanks. That's enough church for me. I'm headed home to take a nap and get ready for tonight's party. You want me to break you out of here?"

Daniel doesn't answer. His eye catches a glimpse of a beautiful woman rush inside.

"Daniel?" Jonah asks.

His trance broken. "Nah, that's alright. I like the music here. Plus, my Mom won't let me hear the end of it."

"You always were the momma's boy. I'll pick you up tonight." Jonah chuckles and walks off to the parking lot.

Daniel skips up the stairs and enters the church, spots an empty spot next to his mother. He hurries inside and takes it. She doesn't acknowledge him and continues staring straight ahead.

She must be mad at me.

Daniel looks around the church. The wood tones, flickering candles, the smell on incense and the calmness of the congregation in prayer brings a peace to Daniel.

To focus on prayer he brings his attention to the various icons depicting the feast days: Nativity of the Virgin Mary, Elevation of the Precious cross, Entrance of the Virgin Mary into the Temple, Nativity of Our Lord, Theophany of Our Lord, Meeting of Our Lord into the Temple, Annunciation of the Virgin Mary, Entry of Our Lord into Jerusalem, Ascension of Our Lord, Pentecost, Transfiguration of Our Lord, Dormition of the Virgin Mary. On the other side of the church are the icons of St. George slaying the dragon, the raising of Lazarus, and the Resurrection of Jesus Christ.

He stares at the Icon of the Resurrection, which

depicts Christ risen, but at the same time hallowing Hades. He breaks the gates of Hades, reaching his hands out to Adam and Eve, grabbing their wrists and lifting them out of their tombs. All the while, Old and New Testament Saints look on. It's been a fascinating icon for Daniel. And it has always given him hope that there's life after death.

"Daniel, service is over." His mom whispers to him. "Venerate the icon and don't forget to take some bottled holy water." Daniel proceeds to the icon of Christ standing in the Jordan river with Saint John the Baptist, onlookers, the holy spirit in the form of a dove above Christ and God represented by a glowing blue light above all. The first time since Genesis that the Holy Trinity is present on earth.

As they exit the church, his mom looks back at him. "Daniel, before we go, I want to introduce you to the new family."

"Mom, I need to get back to the house. I still have to pack for college."

"It will just be a minute."

"A minute, more like an hour. I really need to go. And if Dad isn't at church, why should I be here?"

"Your Dad is working today, otherwise he would be here."

"I'm sure."

The flow of parishioners empty the church. His mom sees the person she wants Daniel to meet.

"Daniel, I'd like you to meet Mrs. Hayes. They moved here from Houston."

"Hi Mrs. Hayes, it's a pleasure. How do you like it here so far?"

"It's nice. We are excited to live in a small town and

out of the city."

"Daniel, The Hayes have three children, the twins running around in the courtyard and.."

"Hi, momma."

"And this is Lydia. Our college girl. We are so proud." Mrs. Hayes says.

Daniel, lifts his head and taken by what he sees. She had a blue head covering over her black hair. The scarf framed her angelic face with big dark brown eyes, and red lips. Tongue tied by Lydia's beauty, Daniel didn't say a word.

"Daniel, where are your manners?" His mom asks.

"Um, hi, I'm Daniel. Nice to meet you." He awkwardly puts out his hand.

Lydia looks down and giggles, shakes his hand and in a fake serious voice "It's nice to meet you too."

As her hand touches his, a slight tingle runs up his arm. The warmth of her skin takes Daniel a moment to let go of her hand.

"Daniel, why don't you take Lydia over to the hall for coffee?"

"Sure. Coffee Lydia?"

"Perfect."

Standing in the courtyard, with parishioners visiting with each other and catching up on the news of the week. Lydia and Daniel find a place for themselves.

"I didn't see you in church today. Where were you standing."

"I was there. I am singing with the choir. I was behind some of the other women."

"That makes sense. So you are singer?" Daniel asks.

"Not really. I sang in the choir at my old church and really enjoyed it. I hope I can continue here."

"Your mom said you are in college, which one?"

"I'm not in college yet. I'm a senior in high school and I was just accepted into Austin university. My parents are more excited about me going to college than I am."

"Congrats on being accepted. That's an excellent school. That's where Jonah and I go. You should be excited."

"I don't know what I want to do. My parents want me to go into law or medicine. I'm not too interested in either of those."

"No, what do you want to do?" Daniel takes a sip of his coffee.

"I can't say. You will laugh."

"Try me."

"I'd rather not."

"C'mon, I promise I won't laugh. I'm really interested."

"Alright, I want to be a wife and mother. I want to get married, have children and raise them. At least three kids, four would be ideal. Sounds crazy, right?" Her nail digs a little deeper into the Styrofoam cup.

Daniel, surprised. Every girl he meets at college has career aspirations: Veterinarian, teacher, accountant, actor, writer. She's the first he's met to want to be a mom.

"Not crazy at all. Different, but not crazy. It's nice that you know what you want to do with your life."

"It's what God wants me to do. Well, all women. To be a mother first. Now you think I am this crazy religious nut?"

If you weren't so pretty, I would say yes.

"No. But you should still go to college, take classes you might like. Get your degree in case you want to do something after your future kids are out of school. Join a sorority. I hear the parties are awesome."

"Sorority? Not for me. I'm not into partying."

"Speaking of parties, there is one tonight. Would you want to go? It's a going back to school party."

"I won't know anyone there. And I'm not good around strangers."

"You will know me. I will introduce you to my friends, and in no time, you will have more friends than you can imagine."

Laughing, "You are that popular?"

"I didn't mean it that way. But come over, it's at Justina Raymond's. Her house is the big white house on Travis road. You can't miss it. It looks like one of those plantation homes you see in Louisiana."

"Let me think about it."

"Party starts at nine, but most people won't get there until ten."

"Ten? That's a short party."

Laughing, "Not really, it usually turns into an all-nighter. You should come. I promise you will have fun."

"Lydia!" her mom calling from across the courtyard.

"So embarrassing. I guess I should go. It was nice to meet you, Daniel."

"So, see you tonight?"

She takes a moment to answer the question. "Maybe. A definite maybe."

Daniel watches her walk away. Her long hair, with a slight wave touching the middle of her back cascades from underneath her scarf.

"You ready to go?"

He interrupts him watching Lydia move through the crowd, meeting her mom then heading off to the parking lot.

"She's pretty, don't you think?" His mom asks.

"Yeah, I guess so. OK, let's go."He finishes his coffee, and tosses the cup into the trash can.

On the ride home, reflecting on what Jonah had said at the river, he turns to his Mom.

"Mom, do you believe everything about Christianity?"

"What? Where did that question come from?"

"Jonah is questioning his faith and, well, I have some thoughts, too."

"Well, you shouldn't entertain those thoughts. That's just the devil playing tricks on you." Her face tightens, eyes narrow.

"It's OK to have doubts, right? Even the Apostle Thomas had doubts."

"Yes, but it's best not to let your mind wander too much. Instead of trying to find excuses to doubt, use that same energy to become more familiar with your faith. The more you learn, the more you understand."

"I guess. But Jonah."

"Listen. Jonah is just your typical college student who has been turned from his faith by some charismatic atheist professor. It's a shame. He's a good boy. With a wonderful family. It's temporary, and one day God will get him back on the right path."

"I don't know mom. Today he sounded stubborn in his beliefs."

"Changing the subject, tell me about Lydia? You two were talking for quite a while. I noticed you couldn't stop smiling when speaking with her."

"Really? I hadn't noticed."

"You were. From ear to ear. Even her mom noticed."

"She is pretty. But she's still in high school, and a little too religious for me. She doesn't want a career. Just be a mom."

"What's wrong with that? I'm just a mom. No career could give me more joy than I have being a wife and mother."

"Yeah, but girls don't think that way anymore. They all want to be something. Anyway, last thing I want is a long distance relationship. They never work. I need to explore my options." He says, spreading his arms wide.

"Daniel, put your hands back on the steering wheel. And God will set your wife in front of you. It could be today, tomorrow, or years from now. And when he does, you take her to be your wife."

"OK, I hope that happens after four years."

"You should call her."

"Mom, I said I am not interested in a relationship. And I doubt she is that interested in me. I invited her to Justina's party and she pretty much said no."

"Did she say no?"

"She said definitely maybe."

"That's a yes. She will be there."

* * *

"So you met your future wife today?" Jonah takes a drink of his beer.

"What are you talking about?" Daniel takes a drink of his.

"My mom spoke to your mom, and your mom said you spent all day talking to that new girl after church. She said you were all smiles."

"My mom doesn't know what she is talking about. She was hot, but not my type." Daniel takes another chug of his beer.

"What's wrong with her? I mean, if she's hot, who cares about her type? It's only for a night."

"She's nothing like those girls in college. She is one of those that are saving herself for her future husband."

Jonah laughs, spitting out his beer at the same time. "That will change once she's at college. She will go to a party, get drunk, meet a guy like me, and next thing, she is taking the walk of shame back to her dorm room." Jonah chugs the rest of his beer and throws his red plastic cup on the ground.

"Alright, enough playing around. It's time for the good stuff." Jonah grabs a bottle of tequila hidden in a flower pot. He opens it, takes a swig, then puts it in front of Daniel's face.

"Drink up Daniel. Who knows when the next time we can get drunk together?" .

"That would be next weekend. Are you that drunk that you forgot we go to the same college? We are in the same fraternity." Daniel takes a swig out of the bottle.

"Hey boys, enjoying the party?" Justina walks up to them, grabs the bottle, and takes a sip.

"Bottom shelf, that's nasty." She takes another swig and looks at Jonah.

"Jonah, you are looking good. College is treating you well." She grabs his arm, stroking his biceps. Then runs her hand over his chest.

"Working out? I can tell. Very nice." She steps closer, puts her hand on his shoulder and locks eyes with him. She glides her hand down his arm, to his hand, and takes the bottle. After another sip, she gives him a wry smile and quick kiss on the lips.

"Try to find me later, Jonah. See ya Daniel."

Justina walks away, back to greeting more guests.

"What was that? She didn't give us the time of day in high school." Daniel still questioning what had just happened.

"I don't know, but I'm not complaining. Man, if I could nail her, it would be a my high school dream come true."

"That's right, you had a crush on her when we were freshman. How many times did she turn you down?"

"Too many. She wasn't too nice about it, either. There was this one time it took me hours to find the nerve to call her. And when I finally picked up the phone and dialed her number, my heart pounding, and on one side hoping she picks up the phone and on the other, hoping the phone has a busy signal. Well, she answers, I can't say anything at first. She asks who was calling her, and when I finally tell her it's me, she asks "who are you?", then hangs up on me. It took me until college to ever approach a girl again."

Jonah looks over, watches Justina talk to another guy, then taking a sip of his beer. She catches Jonah looking at her and gives him a wink and a quick wave.

"She's such a tease. I promise if I get with her tonight, she will regret turning me down."

"Regret? What are you going to do to her?"

"She's going to enjoy it so much she will fall in love with me, then I will dump her and break her heart." He takes another swig.

Daniel, feeling a buzz from the tequila coming on, begins laughing at everything Jonah says.

"Good luck with that plan. It's not like Justina hasn't

been with anyone else."

"No one like me. I have a lot of pent-up emotions for her. And she will feel them all."

"Whatever Jonah, take another drink."

Jonah peers into the near empty bottle, shrugs his shoulders and follows Daniel's orders.

"So, who are you going to score with tonight?"

Daniel scours the crowd for his latest conquest. It's all the same and familiar faces from high school. Then someone catches his eye. "Lydia?"

"Who?" Jonah asks

"Lydia, the girl from church. I invited her here. I didn't expect her to show."

Jonah looks in the crowd and sees a tall, long haired brunette approaching.

"Her, dude, she is hot. If you are not interested.."

"Shut up Jonah." Daniel tucks his shirt into his jeans.

"Do you have gum or anything?" Daniel tries to smell his breath in his hand.

"Dude, you love her." Jonah jokes.

"Hi Daniel. Surprised to see me."

Daniel tries to sober up. "Lydia, I can't believe you are here."

"I had to see an example of college life, up close and personal." Lydia looks over to Jonah, who is having trouble standing without swaying.

"Hi, I'm Jonah. Daniel's best friend. Nice to meet you." Jonah puts his hand out to Lydia. She looks him over and declines the invitation.

"How are you Jonah? You seem a little happier than you did at church today."

"Yeah, it's not my kind of place. This is more of my environment. These are my kind of people. Unabashed sinners, I am happy you can join us." Jonah tries to take another swig of tequila but the bottle is dry.

"Sorry to hear that, Jonah. So Daniel, are these your kind of people? Unabashed sinners?"

"I like everyone Lydia. Even Christ hung around the sinners."

"Yes, but he did not revel in the same sinful behavior. He tried to save them from it."

"Right. But, what about the Prodigal son? He got to party, then when he came home, his father forgave him."

"That's not how it works, Daniel. And you are not in the right mind to discuss scripture."

Daniel moves closer to Lydia. "You are right, the last thing I want to do right now is discuss scripture."

The alcohol has caught up to Daniel.

"What I want to discuss is baseball."

Jonah laughs in the background.

"Baseball?"

"Yes, which base would you let me steal tonight? First, second, third or home run?"

Lydia takes a step back.

"That's disgusting Daniel. What is your problem?"

Daniel moves closer to Lydia.

"My problem is, I haven't had sex in over two weeks, and I am very horny. I bet I can show you a good time. Let me be your first." Daniel staggers as he walks toward Lydia.

Jonah laughs a little louder. "I don't think any of those lines are working, Daniel."

"Daniel, you drunken fool. Never would I sleep with you. You know, I thought you were different from these guys here. If this is what college is like, I will pass. Have a good night."

Lydia heads toward Daniel and Jonah, standing together and walks in between them, splitting them apart. Jonah falls to the ground while Daniel sways back and forth, barely maintaining his balance.

Watching her walk away for the second time today, this time, hurt, knowing he blew an opportunity.

"Forget her Daniel." Jonah speaking while sitting on the ground.

"Now help me up, I'm going to find Justina and you are going to find the easiest girl here. Screw her and forget about Lydia."

Pulling Jonah off the ground. "That's the best plan you have had all night."

❊ ❊ ❊

"Daniel, wake up. We need to go." Sitting up, she buttons her blouse.

"Lydia? Where are we going?" He looks around and tries to figure out where he's at. He realizes he's in the back seat of his car.

"Who the hell is Lydia? You kept calling me that last night. For the last time, my name is Summer."

"Of course it is." Daniel tries to sit up, but lays back down, head is splitting.

"What is that supposed to mean? "Of course it is." She pushes her hips forward so she can finish pulling up her tight jeans.

"I meant, of course, your name is Summer. How could I forget that? Thanks for a great time last night."

She leans over and gives him a long kiss. "No, thank you. You had a lot of passion last night. Whoever this

Lydia is, she sure missed a good time. Now, how about you take me home? Sooner the better. If you drive up to the house and my daddy's awake. You are in big trouble."

Daniel hurries, dresses and rushes Summer home.

* * *

"How was the party, Lydia?" Her mom takes a seat at the kitchen table, interrupting Lydia's breakfast.

"A disappointment. You would expect the boys that went to our church are better behaved."

She drops her spoon in the cereal.

"It's probably a Texas thing. I bet those guys woke up today full of regret, replaying all their words and actions and shirking at their embarrassment." She pushes her bowl away.

"Oh, honey. It's just boys being boys. No one hurt you, did they?"

"No, they were just stupid and drunk."

"Even Daniel?"

"Yes, even Daniel. At first he was cute, but the more he drank, the uglier he became. I'm so glad I left when I did."

"Well, you realize what you should do, right? Don't be mad at him, pray that he changes his ways. We all benefit from prayers."

"OK Mom, I will pray for him and his friend Jonah, and all the rest of them."

Lydia picks up her bowl, takes it to the sink. She excuses herself to her bedroom and walks over to her prayer corner. An area she set up in her room. It includes a small corner table with a candle and holy water.

On the wall above the table are icons of Christ, the Theotokos, and of Saint Lydia.

She lights a candle and silently prays for those she loves, and includes a special prayer for Daniel and Jonah to change their ways. After intense prayer, she blows out her candle and heads out of her room.

CHAPTER TWO

"Daniel, hey Daniel. Wake up. We are going to be late." Jonah throws an empty beer can at Daniel.

"Why is graduation so early?" Daniel rolls over.

"Ouch." A voice from under the sheets

"Daniel, you have company?" Jonah waits in the doorway to see Daniel's latest conquest.

Daniel pulls the sheet down just far enough so Jonah can see her face.

"Shelby meet Jonah, Shelby Jonah."

She moves her blond locks from her face. Mascara smudged under her eyes. She makes a good raccoon.

"Hey Jonah, how are you doing?" She gives him a slight wave.

"I'm OK, but better if I can get Daniel out of bed. Our parents are waiting for us. They are treating us to breakfast. Remember Daniel. You promised them we would meet up with them."

"Yeah, yeah, yeah. Sorry Shelby, I need to get ready. See you tonight?"

She grabs the sheets and wraps herself to hide from Jonah.

"If you are lucky, you will. And if you do, you will get lucky."

She walks past Jonah, heading for the bathroom.

"I told you this apartment was a great idea for our senior year. We wouldn't have slept with a quarter of the girls if we were still stuck in the dorms. So how was she?" He motions to the bathroom.

"You know I don't kiss and tell. And even if I did, I was so drunk I don't remember too much. How did you make out?" Daniel leans over to the nightstand, grabs a pack of cigarettes, takes one out, lights it, inhales then exhales the smoke out of his nostrils.

"I nailed that theater major. You know, the one that's in my finance class."

"That's right, her parents are forcing her to get a minor in business just in case acting doesn't work out. Here's a little secret, mom and dad. Your daughter will not make it in the entertainment industry." Daniel takes another drag.

"You're wrong, Daniel. She could be a star in the porn industry." Jonah says.

"Daniel, I'll let myself out. Catch you tonight. Bye Jonah." Shelby closes the door and heads back to her dorm.

"Jonah, how many girls took the walk of shame from our apartment this year?" Daniel looks out window and watches Shelby shuffle down the street.

"Who knows? Too many to count. I think we did pretty good. Remember, in high school, we couldn't even get a date. Now. Crazy."

"Yes, an epic year." Daniel stubs his cigarette out.

"Alright, let me shower and we can go get something to eat."

* * *

"We are so proud of you, boys. Graduating in four years, and with jobs lined up too. There are so many opportunities ahead of you." Daniel's mom grabs onto her husband's hand and squeezes it.

"Jonah, sorry your parents couldn't make breakfast. They got caught in traffic. But they will be here later to watch you walk and pick up your diploma."

"Thank you, Mrs. Roza. That's most important, that their investment in me paid off." Jonah takes a bite of his scrambled eggs.

"So Daniel, any special girl you plan to introduce us to today?"

Jonah laughs at the question.

"No Mom. I didn't meet any marriage material here. Every time I met someone who was close to bringing home, they failed my test."

"Oh yeah, what test was that?" She takes a sip of her coffee.

"I can't say. It's a secret. If it gets out, then girls might cheat."

"Jonah, do you know what he is talking about?"

"Yes. It's perfect. If they sleep with him on the first date, they fail." Jonah feels a fist hitting his shoulder.

"Ouch Daniel, that one hurt."

"Well, if that is true, I sure hope you used protection." Daniel's father says.

"Don't listen to Jonah. He's just trying to get you going. In any case, college is worst place for a steady girl friend. They can hold you back." Daniel takes out his after meal cigarette and lights it.

"Daniel, please don't smoke. At least not near us. And now that you are out of college, it might be a good time to quit."

"Fine." Daniel drops his cigarette in his half drank cup of coffee.

"So when you boys are back in town, you need to come by Christ the Savior. Father Ephraim has a special celebration after church for those that graduated high school, college and other work."

"What do you mean, other work?" Daniel asks.

"You remember Lydia, the choir girl, who made you smile ear to ear?"

"Kind of. What about her?"

"Well, she didn't feel college was for her, so she spent the last three years traveling eastern Europe, helping Orthodox missions get going in the former Soviet held countries. She's really doing God's work. And imagine the stories she will tell when she gets back. So exciting."

"Stories? Like I went to a town I can't spell or pronounce. Slept in a cold rat infested hostel with a bunch of other Jesus freaks and Euro trash. Tried in my best broken Russian to get people to convert to Christianity. Rinse and repeat for three years. Sounds like a blast." Jonah using his fork to play with his hash browns.

"Oh Jonah, you are worse than ever. Her mom says it was nothing like that. She helped with building several churches, worked on developing youth programs for not just Orthodox Christians, but of all faiths, and even atheists Jonah."

Daniel slips back into his seat, still in the haze of his hangover, reflects on what he accomplished over the last four years. *Just parties, girls and good grades.* He reaches for another cigarette, and his mom takes it out of his hand.

"Please, not now Daniel."

"Well, Jonah and I should get dressed for the ceremony. We will meet you after. Love you guys." Daniel gives a kiss to his mom and dad. Jonah receives a kiss from Daniel's mom and a firm handshake from his dad.

"Daniel, your mom looked good today."

"Gross Jonah, that's my mom."

"That's not what I meant. It looks like she dropped weight. Your Dad must be happy."

"Sometimes you say the dumbest things, Jonah. She could be five hundred pounds and my dad would still love her. They love being with each other."

"Are you really going to the ceremony at the church when you get back home?"

"Of course, it will make my mom happy, seeing me up in front of the congregation with the other graduates. And Lydia."

"That's right, Lydia will be there. Maybe she has loosened up while she was in Europe. You might have a chance. Especially if you talk to her sober."

"Not even going to try. Our lives are too different. I'm on the path of sinners, hers, the path of righteousness."

"Well, let her make that decision. But that would be a major conquest for you if you got her into bed."

"Not going to happen Jonah."

* * *

"Before we depart, I would like to recognize our young people and their scholastic achievements and one who just completed her mission trip to eastern Europe." Father Ephraim brings each graduate up to the solea. First the high schoolers, he tells of the universities they will attend, and how one is heading into the armed services. Next are the college graduates. Only two this year. Jonah and Daniel. Jonah reluctantly came to church at his mother's request.

"Jonah, who graduated with a bachelor's degree in finance. So if you want to increase your wealth, and you can give more to the church, Jonah might be the man for you."

"If you want to buy property, congratulations to Daniel, who graduated with a degree in real estate."

"Last but not least, let's welcome back Lydia, who went in a different direction. For the last three years working with Orthodox Christian missions and helped the former Soviet block countries restore their churches, and teach Orthodoxy to those that grew up without knowing their faith."

For the first time Daniel can remember he heard applause in the church. Then he saw her, Lydia, walking down the aisle. She was even prettier than when they first met. Except this time, she looked a little more intense, almost other worldly. Much different that the girls from college.

She takes the last spot in the row, next to Daniel. She turns to him and smiles. He can't help but smile back, and continues to smile during the whole ceremony.

Father Ephraim heads into the altar and returns with a stack of books.

"To each of our graduates, a Study Bible. I expect them to be used, placed on your desks, not as a shelf decoration with other unread books. This is the word of God." He hands each one their new Bible.

Father Ephraim says one last prayer, and the congregation departs from church.

"Daniel, please wait. I wish to speak with you before you go."

"Of course Father. Jonah, I will see you later. Lydia, it was good..."

"I will wait for you outside, Daniel. I want to speak to you, too." She says.

Daniel's heart fluttered. "OK."

The church is empty except for Father and Daniel.

Father Ephraim took over as the head priest three years ago. A young priest with a wife and one baby girl. The diocese placed him here with hopes that his youth and joy for Christ will turn Christ the Savior from a quiet, surviving church to a growing church, that welcomes visitors every week and increase the number of converts.

"Daniel, I won't keep you. I know your friends are waiting for you."

"That's OK Father. Do you need help with something?"

"No, no. I just want to let you know I am here for you. If you ever have questions about our faith, or need someone to talk with, you can call me anytime, day or night."

"Thank you Father."

"Oh, and perhaps it's time for you to come to confession. How about next Saturday after Vesper services?"

"I don't know, Father. You might be in for a long night."

"Daniel, whatever it takes. We can do it all at once or a little each week. Your mom will be here next week. Why don't you come with her?"

"I will try."

"Well, just remember I am here for you, OK?"

"Thanks, I should get going."

He walks out of the church, reaches into his coat pocket, pulls out a cigarette, and lights it. He takes a drag.

"You didn't smoke three years ago." Lydia says walking up to Daniel.

"Just one of those nasty habits you pick up at college. So how are you Lydia? I am very impressed with how you spent your last three years."

"Still trying to adjust to life back in the states. We are so blessed compared to other countries. The freedom to come to our church and worship and go back out onto the streets and speak freely about our faith."

"You must have seen and heard a lot of bad things over there." He takes another drag.

"Yes, it's a very sad situation. But one day, God willing, the churches will be restored, and Christianity will thrive again."

"You are pretty intense, Lydia."

"You have to be when you are over there. So many enemies working against you. You need to be strong and resolute. Here, we are very lazy in our faith and do nothing to protect it from the enemy."

"The enemy."

"The devil and his workers."

Daniel laughs.

"I'm serious Daniel. There are things they neglect to tell us here that I learned over there. For example, how demons are everywhere, in another realm, always tempting us, trying to keep us from Christ."

"Lydia, if you weren't so hot, I would excuse myself. Now that you are back here, I suggest you temper what you say. You will either scare people or they will think you are nuts." Daniel throws his cigarette to the ground and crushes it with his shoe.

"It seems that college has done more harm than good for you." She says.

"I had a great time in college. I am going to miss it." He grins, remembering his night with Shelby.

"So, do you still want to be a stay at home mom or has that changed?"

"Yes, I want to be married and raise a family. After Justina's party, I questioned if college was for me. I prayed on it and He answered my prayers. Within a day, I received a brochure about the Orthodox mission program. Once I read the information, I knew that's what God wanted me to do."

"It sounds like you are ready to be the wife of a priest."

"If that's what God wants. But I have a feeling I am in for something different."

"I'm different. would you go out to dinner with me?"

"A date with you?"

"Yes, why not? It's just dinner. And a movie if all goes well."

"OK, I'll take the dinner. We can skip the movie. I'm free tomorrow night."

Daniel's cheeks hurting from smiling through this entire conversation.

"Great, I will pick you up at six."

Daniel sees Jonah in the distance, just over her shoulder. He gives Daniel a thumbs up.

"Well, I've got to head back. Until tomorrow night. It looks like your mom is heading this way."

Daniel watches as his mom walks closer. Jonah was

right. She looks great, like she lost 15 pounds.

"Hi Mom, are you ready? By the way. Are you on a diet, you look great. Even Jonah said so."

"No. Not a diet. So, I saw you and Lydia talking. You had that same ear to ear smile as you did three years ago. You still have a crush on her?"

"No. But you will be happy to know I am taking her on a date tomorrow night."

"A date, with Lydia? She said yes to you?"

"Believe it or not."

"That is interesting. You two. There are odder couples."

"I thought you would be happy, Mom."

"I am. She's just different from you. What did Father want?"

"Just that he was here if I ever needed him. That was nice, but strange. He also said I am due for confession."

"We all need confession, Daniel. You should come with me on Saturday."

"I don't know, mom. Is it necessary?"

"It is, trust me."

* * *

"Are you excited about your new job? What are you going to do?" She has a bite of her steak.

"Well, on Monday, I start at H.E. commercial real estate as a broker trainee. After six weeks, I am given a portfolio of properties to manage and to market our services to new prospects."

"So you want to be the next Donald Trump?"

"I wish. But he has New York City. I'm staying right here. Austin has so much potential. Between the

University, state government, the music scene and all the new start-ups, Austin is going to be the place to be. In my senior year, I studied all the markets, and for the 90s and 2000s, Austin is projected for double digit growth. Nope, Trump can keep New York, I will take Austin.

"You sound very ambitious. It's good that you now have a plan."

"So, what about you? Planning on staying here, or are you off to save the world?"

"I'm staying with my parents for now. There are opportunities to work for several of the charities here in town, and one in Austin. I'm still deciding. And of course volunteering at the church."

Daniel can't help staring at her. She is the prettiest woman he has ever seen.

"I'm glad you are staying."

"Me too. This is a great place, Daniel."

"I've always wanted to go here. But never had the chance."

"You mean this isn't a place you take all of your dates?"

"I didn't have many dates in high school. And there was no way I could afford this place back then."

"It is very nice."

Daniel feels his cheeks hurting again.

"Are you sure you don't want to take in a movie after dinner? There are a couple of good ones playing at the theater."

"I was hoping to do something different. There is that spot that overlooks the lake. Everyone talks about it. Would you take me there?" She asks.

Daniel feels a quick burst of adrenaline, and for a

moment; lightheaded.

"Of course, that's a great idea."

They sit on top of the hill overlooking the lake, reflecting a star filled sky.

"Amazing view from here, don't you think, Lydia?"

"Truly the Heaven's declare the glory of God." She says while laying back looking straight up at the night time sky.

"What does that even mean?" Daniel asks.

"Look at all of this, that is above us. The stars and planets shine, showing God's work. People ask about where is God or proof of God. Just look above. There, in all His glory." Lydia sighs.

"You truly believe that God created all of this. The billions of stars, planets. Our planet, and everything that lives on it."

"Yes, without a doubt."

"How did he do it?"

"Haven't you ever read Genesis Daniel? It's all right there, in black and white."

"Of course I read Genesis. But I don't believe God created everything in seven days."

"Six days. He created the universe and everything in it in six days. After he declared everything very good, He rested on the seventh day."

"You've been away too long, Lydia. Aren't you familiar with evolution, the Big Bang?"

"Yes, and I disagree with those theories. All truth is in the Bible."

"You disagree with the world's top scientists?"

Lydia turns over and is face to face with Daniel.

"The scientists weren't there to observe creation, but God was, and he shared that with Moses. And Moses wrote Genesis. I will take God's word over any fallible scientist."

Daniel, struck by her unwavering faith. Deep down, he wished he could be that brave and secure knowing the truth.

"You need to do so more research. I mean Genesis is full of fantastic stories. People living hundreds of years or what about Noah and the flood? That's beyond belief?"

Lydia sits up, looks at the lake, then into the night sky. "Not really, because when God does something, it will not be something anyone else can do. When He does it, it is miraculous. Everything: creating the universe in six days, putting all those animals on the Ark, then flooding the world, destroying the Tower of Babel and dispersing the population all over the world, the seven tribulations of Egypt, the parting of the Red Seas, the destruction of Sodom and Gomorrah and turning Lot's wife into a pillar of salt, Jonah and the whale, Elijah ascending to Heaven, Isaiah seeing Heaven, the Angel visiting a young Mary telling her she will have a child, the immaculate conception, the Virgin Birth, the three wise men, the shepherds seeing the angels in the fields, Jesus healing the sick and the blind, Jesus feeding the Five thousand with five loaves of bread and two little fish, Jesus walking on water, Jesus raising Lazarus from the dead, and Christ, the Son of God, dying for our sins on a cross and rising on the third day. I believe it all from Genesis 1:1 to Revelations 22:21."

"Wow, and life after death?"

"Yes. Our souls either go to Heaven of Hell after we die and stay there until after the second coming of Christ, then Christ judges the souls and if you are worthy, your soul is joined with your resurrected body and if you aren't, then you are obliterated."

"That's pretty harsh. So who is worthy?"

"Daniel, let's lay back down and talk about other things. This conversation is getting too heavy... you must think I'm weird?"

"Different, not weird."

They continue to look up into the heavens, Daniel now in awe of what God has laid out in the sky.

"I guess my so called hotness factor is greater than my weirdness factor, otherwise you would be long gone by now."

"You are right."

They both laugh. Daniel reaches down and grabs hold of Lydia's hand. She accepts. They watch the stars in silence.

Daniel glances at her. The light from the nighttime sky shines on her face, radiating her brown eyes. He has never seen a more beautiful woman. He moves closer and tries to kiss her.

"OK, but just kissing." She says.

They kiss, he tries to move forward, she denies his advances with a laugh.

"Daniel, you are very handsome. And a good kisser. But this is as far as we are going tonight. It is time I head home."

He drives her home and walks her up the stairs to the door.

"I had a wonderful time, Daniel. Thank you."

"Me too. Do you want to go out again sometime? How about Saturday night?"

"I would love to, but I am singing in the choir at Vesper services."

"I plan on being there Saturday too. Father asked me to go to confession."

"Alright, unless you plan to confess all night, let's go straight from there."

"Go where?"

"I don't know. Come up with some place special. And is this part of the date you give me one last kiss good

night?"

CHAPTER THREE

The heat and humidity of a Texas summer morning normally keeps Daniel inside the cool air conditioned confines of his parent's home. But today is different. He sits outside in the weathered Adirondack chair, drinking coffee and smoking a cigarette, reminiscing over his date with Lydia. It was a new experience for him. Because she was different than anyone he dated before. He shakes his head thinking how much he enjoyed being with her.

What's the matter with you? You've been with a lot of women.

He watches as one squirrel chase another from one tree branch to another.

She's beautiful, smart, determined, and a good kisser.

He closes his eyes and replays the goodnight kiss. He tried to take it further, but she gently pulled his hands down, took her lips off of his and said "Daniel, this right here. The feelings. The ecstasy, the speeding heart. It's a gift from God, so let's take our time and honor and enjoy it. OK?" She smiled and gave him one last kiss and went inside.

She is really religious. She isn't changing for you or anyone. What are you going to do about that?

He takes a drag from his cigarette, blows a smoke ring into the bright blue sky.

I like it. I find it intriguing.

The squeak from from the storm door opening interrupts his internal conversation.

"So, how was your date?" His mom asks.

"Good morning Mom. It was nice. We had a good time."

"Do you think you will see her again?"

"Yes, Saturday night, after church."

"So you are going to go with me to confession?"

"I guess so."

"I like her already."

Daniel taps his cigarette out.

"Daniel, I need to speak with you about something. I wanted to wait for your dad to be here, but he is out of town and this can't wait."

"Sure Mom, what is it?" Daniel tries his best to sit upright in the slanting chair.

His mom sits down takes a deep breath.

"The weight loss you noticed. It isn't from a diet. I am losing weight because I have cancer."

Daniel leans back into the chair.

"What? Cancer?"

"Yes, the doctors confirmed it yesterday. And I'm afraid it's stage four pancreatic cancer."

Daniel's head spins. *What is stage four? Where is the pancreas? Is it curable? Does Dad Know?*

"Stage four? What does that mean, Mom?"

She tries to be strong in this moment, always trying to protect him from pain and sadness.

"Stage four means it has spread to other organs in my body, that it is terminal and there really isn't anything the doctors can do."

"Are they sure? I can't believe with all the billions

spent on research, nothing can be done."

"They want to try chemotherapy. They think it will reduce the size of the tumor and keep it from spreading. It might give me a couple of more months." Tears well up in her eyes.

Daniel stands up, takes her by the hand, pulls her up and hugs her tightly.

"Oh mom, I am so sorry, is there anything I can do?"

"Just be strong with me through this. Help your dad. And most important, pray for me."

"Of course, Mom. Are you sure you want to go to church tonight?"

"Yes, I want to pray and go to confession. I need to start preparing." She puts her hand on his cheek.

"You have turned into such a handsome young man. I am so proud of you."

The day goes at a snail's pace. Daniel tries to contemplate what his mother revealed to him. He can't understand. He needs someone to talk to.

"Hey, can you meet me? Over at the fields? Bring something to drink." Daniel hangs up the phone. He walks to his parent's room, gently pushes the door open and sees his mom sleeping.

* * *

Daniel pulls around the corner. He sees Jonah holding a bottle of whiskey hanging down by his legs, staring at the old baseball fields. He turns to see Daniel, and slightly waves to him.

"Thanks for meeting me."

"What's going on where you need a drink this bad?"

Jonah hands him the bottle, Daniel takes a drink. Lights a cigarette and tries to speak.

"What's the matter Daniel?"

"My Mom, she just told me she has cancer."

"Are you kidding? What kind?"

"Pancreatic, stage four. I guess that is bad." He takes another drag, chased by a drink.

"My uncle had pancreatic cancer. I'm sorry to tell you, Daniel, your mom is in for a real battle. She doesn't have much time, and the time she has will be miserable."

"She says the doctor wants to try chemo to help control the cancer."

"Doctors. What's one or two extra months? She will spend whatever extra time she gets in the hospital being poisoned. She will get tired, puke, feel terrible most of the time, have her hair fall out. Then she will have to go back to the doctors for blood work every week. What a miserable way to spend your last days."

Daniel drinks more, lights another smoke. Stares at the overgrown grass in the infield.

"She says she wants to fight." His voice cracking.

"We all do, but from what I saw with my uncle, she's going to lose. She needs to spend the rest of her time doing stuff she likes, spending it with family. You know, if I only had so much time left, I would take the first jet out of here to Tahiti or some Caribbean island and try to sleep with as many women money could buy." Jonah takes the bottle back and drinks.

"I'm guessing she wants to stay here with my dad, me, and be near the church."

"Why church? To pray to a god that gave her pancreatic cancer at age forty-nine? Nice god, she spent all her time in His house, and this is her reward?"

"Just stop with the atheist bull..., Jonah." Jonah's words are hitting home and it scares him.

"It's not bull. Where is the justice? Your mom is a wonderful lady. She should live forever. Meanwhile we have the worst people walking the earth until they are old men and women. You have terrible politicians, war lords, drug dealers and child molesters living until they are in their nineties and good people like your mom taken before they hit fifty. Hell, what about the little kids dying of diseases like cancer? There is no god. And if there is, this type of god is not one I want to follow. He is mean."

Daniel cries. "Stop it."

Jonah looks at Daniel, sees him crying, "Hey man, I am sorry. My anger takes over my mouth and I can't shut up."

"You make sense. I am so sad for her. She is all alone in this."

"You will be there. Your father, the priest." Jonah tries to console Daniel.

"She is doing this all by herself. We all have to do this by ourselves. I can't imagine how scared she will be, especially in the dead of night, when your thoughts of death will taunt you." He wipes the tears off his face.

"Daniel, just be there for her. Talk to her, get her mind off this, and let her enjoy whatever time she has with her family."

"I'm buzzed. I probably shouldn't drive, but I have to get her over to church. Can you take us?"

"I'm a little buzzed, too. Just go, you seem fine. It wouldn't be the first time you drove buzzed. Remember, don't go over the speed limit."

* * *

Daniel pulls up to the house, his Mom standing there, watching for him.

She looks normal, she doesn't look sick. Maybe the doctors are wrong.

He stops the car, and she opens the door, sniffing the air.

"Daniel, you've been drinking? Get out, I'm driving."

"Mom, I'm fine. It was only one drink. Get in the car. We don't want to be late for church."

"Daniel, whatever happens to me, don't let it ruin you. I need you to stay strong. Remember, this is all God's plan." She folds her hands and lays them on her small prayer book. Blue with a foil cross on the cover, it is filled with dog eared pages and strips of yellow paper bookmarking prayers for the morning, evening, before confession, and a now new strip; prayers in times of sickness.

"God has a terrible plan," he says under his breath.

"What was that Daniel?"

"Nothing?"

"This is not God's doing. We live in a sinful world, and because of it, we have diseases, war, famine, the worst of everything."

To avoid an argument and considerate of her condition, he tries to change the subject.

"I hope you don't mind. I told Jonah."

"What did he say?" She half smiles.

"That if he were you in this situation, he would take the first plane to Tahiti and hang out with as many beautiful women as possible."

"No thanks, that type of life was never a desire of mine. I pray to spend whatever time I have left with you, your dad, my closest friends, and church."

"There is nothing else you want to do?"

She takes a moment to think, while looking out the side window as the high grass and tree turn into one green and brown blur.

"I would like to see the milky way again or put my toes in the ocean one last time."

Daniel's eyes well up again.

"Honey, everything will be fine. Now, where are you taking Lydia tonight?"

"Oh crap, I forgot. I don't know if I am in the best condition to go out on a date."

"You should go. It might help take your mind off of things."

"Geez, Mom, you are talking to me like I have cancer."

"Take her out. I'm just going to go home and get some sleep."

* * *

As they approach the steps to the church, everything looks a little different to Daniel. The church is no longer a building, but something strange. Daniel can't put his finger on it. *Surreal? No, alive is a better description.*

They enter the church, venerate the icons, light candles, and stand in the back of the church. Daniel watches his mom as she holds her prayer rope, with eyes shut tightly, prays. Daniel tries to pray, but can't figure out what he wants to say.

The choir is sparse tonight, with only three singing. One of which is Lydia. He watches her and tries to decipher her voice from the other two.

The service concludes with Father Ephraim singing the last prayer.

"You should go first?" His mom whispers to him.

"No, you go first, Mom. I don't want you to have to wait too long."

"Daniel."

As she walks away to meet the priest, Daniel goes outside into the courtyard. Lights a cigarette. Takes one drag and puts it out. "I'm done with you."

Lydia sees him and walks over. Daniel, with mixed emotions, doesn't know how to react. What does he tell her? He doesn't want to break down in front of her.

"Hi Daniel, where is that smile of yours?"

"Bad day today Lydia." He can't look into her eyes.

Stepping closer.

"What happened? Are you drunk?"

"No, just had a couple of drinks with Jonah before I came over."

"Drinking before church? Daniel you..."

"My mom is dying." Daniel interjected.

"She told me this morning. I am so numb."

"Oh Daniel." Lydia hugs him, strokes his hair, and gives him a soft kiss on his lips.

Stepping back from her. "I don't feel like I will be good tonight. How about another night?"

"No, we should be together. We can go to our hill and talk or not."

"Thank you."

"Daniel, Father is waiting for you." His mom says as she exits the church.

Daniel shrugs his shoulder.

"This should be interesting. Would you mind running my mom home?"

"Of course."

Daniel gives his mom a long hug on his way into the church.

He enters the darkened church with only candles giving off light. He sees Father Ephraim at the iconostasis.

"Daniel, please come up to the front."

Daniel slowly approaches the priest.

"Hi Father." He leans down and kisses his right hand.

"Daniel, your mom told me what the doctors said. How are you doing?"

"Everything is strange, Father. Nothing is how it is supposed to be. My mom is in denial or she is stronger than imagined. The church feels different, and honestly I have so many emotions, at one moment I want to cry the next find someone or something to punch."

Father Ephraim continues to listen, letting Daniel get everything out of his system.

"Father, you knew she was sick. That's why you told me I could call you any time."

"Yes, she explained to me she went to the doctor, and they suspected cancer. It wasn't confirmed, so I didn't want to say anything to you. But I am here, for you, your Mom, your dad. I am here to help with all that is to come."

"Are you sure you can take all that on, Father? I mean, you are pretty young. Have you helped families with this before?"

"I have assisted when I was a Deacon. But no, your mother will be my first. But don't let that be a concern of yours. God will show us the way and use me to comfort her and give her the strength through the most trying times."

"My friend says this is all a waste of time. That a good and loving God wouldn't inflict on someone like my Mom with this terrible disease. A good God wouldn't let her die, while terrible people continue to walk the earth." Daniel's anger slowly building, voice raises over the whisper.

"And now what happens when she dies? That's it. She's just going to rot in the ground?"

"Daniel, I understand your anger, but trust in God. He does things His way, in His time. It makes little sense to you now, but it will, eventually."

"I don't appreciate Him using her for some sort of lesson." He says between his clinched teeth.

"God loves your mother, and He wants her home. And remember, one day, if you lead a good Christian life, you will be with her again."

"A good Christian life?"

"Yes, first thing is the reason you are here. For confession."

Daniel looks behind him, sees the exit and contemplates it. His head spinning from the change in conversation.

"I am not prepared, Father."

"Daniel, come with me. Approach the icon of Christ and confess your sins. Pretty simple."

Daniel looks at the icon, glances back at the priest, who nods his head as to say "it's OK."

He steps towards the icon. Takes a deep breath.

And like a deluge, he confesses his sins:

"I drink, I get drunk, I have sex with women, I look

at pornography, I lie, I cheat, I have been a terrible son, I am envious of others." He searches his mind.

"Father, I sin every day. If I confess every one, we will be here all night."

"If that's what it takes, Daniel, I will be here with you."

"I don't fast, when at college I didn't go to Liturgy, and today after what has happened. I question my faith."

Daniel stops. The church falls silent.

"Daniel, confession is an important sacrament of the church. The purpose is to cleanse you of your sins, to help your soul. If you should pass away without confessing your sins. He will hold you accountable. Now please kneel in front of the icon."

Daniels kneels, the priest places his stole over his head and reads the prayers of absolution over him. At the conclusion, he performs the sign of the cross over him. Daniel stands and embraces Father Ephraim.

"Thank you Father."

"I just ask that you pray for me, Daniel. Please remember, I am here for you. Anytime."

Daniel leaves church feeling a little lighter. He sees Lydia at the bottom of the steps, looking up at him with a sparkle in her eyes.

"Do you feel any better?"

"A little, I think. Are you ready to go?"

* * *

Back on the hill overlooking the lake, a somber mood fills the air. The stars muted. The lake looks like the abyss. No words spoken. Lydia waits for Daniel to speak.

"I'm trying not to. But I am questioning my faith." He says without emotion.

"Daniel, it's common for people to blame God in these situations. But at the end, they realize that God is there for comfort, not pain." She places her hand on top of his.

"On one hand, you, the church, believe there is a reason for everything. That everything has a plan, from creation to the second coming. There is good and evil, right and wrong. Then, for people like Jonah, this was all an accident. Born out of chaos. No rhyme or reason, no good or evil. Just as we are born, then die and enjoy your time while you can. My mother, given a death sentence at the age of forty-nine, confirms what Jonah believes."

As she holds his hand, she looks at him and sees a twenty-two-year-old, age five years in a moment. Clenched teeth, hardened eyes, he's transformed into something she doesn't like.

"Daniel, be patient, wait this out. The devil goes after us when we are at our weakest. This is when you have to put on your spiritual armor and defend yourself."

"Angels, demons, the devil, God, it sounds like a fairy tale. No, it's not that her dying is making me weak. It has erased the thin veil that kept me from seeing the truth." He releases her hand.

"What is the truth?"

"We have no purpose. We are a cosmic accident and my mom will have the same reward as some child rapist. I will pretend, so not worry my mom, but after they bury her, I will never step back into church again."

Lydia stands up. "Then I can't be with you, not like

this. It's time to take me home."

"Not very Christian of you Lydia?" Daniel says to her.

"I will not sit here and have my faith, my God mocked. If that is what you wish to do, fine. Go find Jonah. I'm not going to play a part in that."

Daniel jumps up. "You're right. I'll take you home."

The silence made the car ride feel twice as long. They arrive at her house and he doesn't say a word.

She begins to utter words of comfort, but closes her mouth and pats him on the shoulder. She stands on the porch watching him drive away.

Daniel, drunk, stumbles into his home from a night of drinking with Jonah. He tries to walk quietly past his parent's room.

"Daniel? Is that you?"

"Hey Dad, where have you been? Did you hear the news? Mom is dying."

He stumbles forward. His dad catches him before he falls over.

"Yes Daniel, I know. You need to get a hold of yourself."

"No, you need to get a hold of yourself, John. Are you going to be around or are you going to find a way to be gone and leave me with all of this." Daniel's finger buried into his father's chest.

"Daniel, you get one free pass. And tonight is it. Go to bed, pull yourself together and put on a brave face for your mom."

Daniel pulls his finger back and balls his hand into a fist. His father sees what is about to occur and pushes Daniel down.

"Daniel, I'm telling you for your own good. Go to bed. You will not win. Especially being drunk as you are."

Not quite understanding what his dad is saying, his voice garbled and in the darkened hallway. The faint light from the moon presents a silhouette that looks like a demon standing behind his father.

"Lydia was right. I'm an easy target for demons." Daniel falls back and passes out.

CHAPTER FOUR

Several months pass by and to keep his mind off his mother's illness and his breakup with Lydia, Daniel spends his time at work. Long days of hunting for new clients, showing properties and closing deals, chased by drinks with the boys at the firm. He wakes on Sunday mornings with hangovers and how to escape the women lying next to him. But on one Sunday morning, as the the sun rose and it's rays broke through the blinds onto his face, he wakes up.

"What is that?" He faintly hears the choir from Christ the Savior.

"What is what?" She says from the other side of the bed.

"You don't hear it? The choir?"

Laughing, "Daniel, are you still drunk? I must have taken you to heaven last night and you never came back."

Daniel lays back down. He has feelings of emptiness and regret. He looks at his watch. 6:30 AM. *Maybe I should go to church today.*

She slides over to him, and puts her head on his chest. "Let's go back to sleep, we had a long night last night."

He stares at the ceiling. Deep inside, he knows he

would be happier at church listening to Lydia sing, and talking with her about anything. *I want to smile again.*

* * *

"Hi son, your mother, she's...she's having a bad day, she could go anytime. It's time to come home."

"Alright Dad, I'm leaving now"

Daniel returns to the table where he was enjoying a liquid lunch with fellow agents from his firm.

"Hey Daniel, which chick was that? The one from last night or from the weekend?"

Daniel takes a shot of tequila and chugs his beer.

"Sorry, boys, I've gotta go home. It's my mom, she's... she's. You know... I have to run."

Daniel slams the glass on the table. Grabs his coat and heads out the door.

As he tries his best to stay in his lane, his tire leaves the road, rolling over the rumble strips. The jarring of vibrations sobers him up, but only for a moment. He lights a cigarette, opens the window and cranks up the music.

It's home without incident for him. Father Ephraim's car is in front of the house.

Daniel finds himself in the master bedroom. Father Ephraim on one side, his dad, shedding tears on the other. Each holding her hand. He looks down at his mom and she is sound asleep. In the other corner is the hospice nurse looming over the room like a vulture

"Sit down, son." His dad pats the empty chair next to him.

"Anytime." His dad tries to touch his hand, Daniel

pulls it away.

"You've been drinking? In the afternoon?" His whispers.

Daniel shrugs. "We were celebrating a record sales month."

"Hi Father, did she have a chance to speak with you? Is she good with God?" He asks.

"Yes, Daniel, she spoke with me."

They wait listening to her breathe long winded breaths. Daniel recalls reading a pamphlet on what to expect when someone was about to die. It said that it's very peaceful, but sometimes, there is something called a death rattle. The throat is so dry, and the air being pushed out by the lungs is so weak, that it creates a gurgling sound. A sound so unpleasant that the people hearing it will never forget it.

Daniel waits in quiet anticipation for the rattle. He recalls a prayer in the service "Let us die in peace without suffering or shame, and have a good account before the judgment seat of Christ."

He notices the icon of Christ above her bed. And before he was about to, for the first time in months, pray...

"Get away from me!" His mother screams in horror.

"Get them away from me. Help me!"

The hospice nurse rushes from the corner of the room and steps between Daniel and his mother. Father Ephraim jumps out of his chair.

"What's going on?" Daniel cries out.

His mother kicks her legs and flails her arms. The white sheets rising and falling like a raging sea.

"I did not do that. Stop. You are lying." She screams.

Everyone in the room is looking at each other. Daniel

catches the eye of Father Ephraim, who is frozen from the sight of a peaceful and frail women, who in a moment, is now writhing in pain as if she had her leg ensnared in an animal trap.

"Who are you? Stay away! Help, please help! I'm scared!" She weeps.

"Keep your dogs away. No!"

Her arms are flying about in awkward positions, eyelids are closed tight, tears squeeze out between them.

She continues to cry out saying "Deliver my soul from the sword and my only begotten from the hand of the dog, save me from the lion's mouth." Her mouth frozen open. The sight of her frightens Daniel. Her mouth held open, her arms contorted, back flexed in an arch. He looks at her and her eyes now open wide, pupils dilated. She stays in this frightening position for over a minute. Her body relaxes, eyes close and she whispers:

"Where have you been? you are so beautiful. Take me home." And she breathes her last breath.

The room is silent once again. All felt a peace.

Daniel kneels at his mother's side. Grabs her hand and kisses it. He looks up and sees his father push her hair back off her forehead. He leans down and gives her one last kiss. "No more fighting, sweetheart. It's time to rest."

Daniel looks over to Father Ephraim, with hand over mouth now as far back in the room as possible.

Daniel stands up. "Father, Father, isn't there something you are supposed to do, like pray for her soul or something? Don't just stand there. She expects you to pray for her."

Father Ephraim shakes himself. He finds his black

bag and fumbles for his prayer book. He opens the book to the marked page, prays, then stops. He returns to his bag and finds his robe and puts it over his cossack, places the priestly stole around his neck, grabs the holy water and the blessed oil and places it next to the bed.

"Please, Daniel, John rise and pray with me:

Father Ephraim performs the sign of the cross over Daniel's mother and prays:

"With the souls of the righteous departed, give rest to the soul of Thy servant Catherine, O'Savior, reserving it in the blessed life which is with Thee, O Lover of Mankind."

"By Thy deep compassion and many tender mercies, O Sovereign Lady. Being so inclined by nature, stand by me in this dread hour, O invincible Helper."

Father finishes the prayers, anoints her with the oil, "In the name of the Father, Son and Holy Spirit."

And continues to pray in a quiet voice from the psalter.

"Son, why don't you head home? I will wait here with Father and your mom."

"No Dad, I want to stay here with you... and her."

"No, you need to go home, sleep it off. We have a tough three days ahead of us."

"If you insist."

Daniel wants to say goodbye to his mother, but knows it's pointless.

He walks out of the room, down the hallway, and tries to keep himself together. At the den, he sees no one. For a moment, he expected to see Lydia. *Why would she be here? The way you blew her off at the lake. I can't blame her.*

Daniel steps outside and sees Jonah sitting on the

hood of his car, holding a brown paper bag.

"Daniel, come here." He gives Daniel a bear hug, squeezing him tight.

"Here, have a drink. I was heading to your office, and when I got there, your boss said you had to run. I figured this was what happened. I take it she's gone."

Daniel in shock by what he witnessed answers coldly, "Yes, she passed away ten minutes ago." Daniel looks back at the house and takes a swig of whiskey.

"Do you want a smoke?" Jonah pulls out his pack of cigarettes, opens the box and sees one last cigarette and hands it to Daniel.

He lights it up and slowly exhales. "She fought until the end, Jonah."

"I bet she was a real fighter."

"No, I mean she was fighting at the end. Scariest thing I have ever seen."

"It was probably the morphine or when you die and they say your brain is releasing a huge amount of endorphins and the synapses are going off like lightning. It's like a terrible fireworks show at the end."

"It wasn't anything like that. She was talking to people. Telling them to go away. She was so scared she was talking and screaming. She hasn't made a noise all week. And at the end she recited some bible verse. Or maybe it was a psalm. After that she calmed down, spoke to someone who brought her relief, and went away."

"I don't know what to tell you Daniel, but she is not in anymore pain. You want to go get a drink?"

"One more sip, then I have to head home. We have three days to prepare for the funeral. I know you have a problem with church, but would you come to her service, be a pall bearer? I could really use my best friend there."

Jonah comes in for another bear hug, avoiding the cigarette still in Daniel's mouth.

"Of course, I love you. I consider you my brother, which makes your mom my mom. Anything for you."

* * *

The tears have dried up. He feels guilty he isn't crying at this moment. He looks over to his father standing next to him, with the rolled up funeral program in his hand. On the solea, Father Ephraim censes Daniels' mother's casket, chanters chant prayers, Daniel looks behind him, all the faces are a blur.

Father Ephraim swings the censer back and forth, bringing a fragrant scent into the church. Daniel notices the anguish on his face.

He repeats three times in a somber tone:

"Eternal be thy memory, our sister, who art worthy to be deemed happy and ever-memorable."

The choir sings

"Memory be eternal, memory be eternal, May her memory be eternal."

Daniel hears the distinct voice of Lydia. At the moment, he realizes he misses her and needs her.

Father Ephraim finishes and walks over to the casket, opens it, takes the cross she was holding, and presents it to Daniel's father who kisses his hand and clinches the cross to his chest.

The pall bearers gather and escort the newly departed's casket down the aisle. The same aisle she walked down for so many years. For her wedding, presenting Daniel to the church, bringing him up for baptism, for communion and now, her last church service completed, she has finally departed.

At the grave side, fewer people are present. Father Ephraim continues prayers for her, blesses her casket one more time before they lower it into the ground.

"One last thing to do today Daniel, will you be alright?

"Of course Dad. Of course."

They arrive at the restaurant where close family and friends are gathered, not so much as a celebration of life, but for comfort to the family.

Daniel drinks shot after shot. He listens to his mom's friends tell him how wonderful a woman she was, and she is in a better place. He thanks them, but still rages inside at how unfair this day is.

Father Ephraim waits for one last friend to give their condolences and speaks to Daniel.

"Daniel, I know this has tested your faith, and you have fallen away, but it is time to come back to church."

Daniel smiles. "Father, what happened to you by her bedside? You froze. If I said nothing to you, you would have been useless to her."

"I'm sorry Daniel. I was shocked and surprised. I've witnessed nothing like that, only read about it."

"What are you talking about?" He takes another shot.

"Your mom, she was fighting something, and I think it was the demons."

"Demons? Come on, father. Her brain was shutting off and she must have had a bad memory flash in front of her eyes."

"We don't teach or talk about what happens at death.

But some priests believe that at the hour of death, the demons, like vultures and are waiting for each and everyone of us. In their opinion that is what your mother saw. That's who she was wrestling with."

"Father, I can't deal with this now. She is dead and in the ground. Like we all will be one day. Done. Ashes to ashes, dust to dust."

"Daniel, that's wrong, and that way of reasoning will lead you straight to hell. Please come to church. For her soul, we will commemorate her on the ninth day, and the fortieth day."

"Why those days?"

"The ninth day is in honor of the nine ranks of angels who stand before God, praying for mercy for the departed. And the fortieth day, by then, your Mom's soul should be in Heaven. But she was such a good woman. I doubt it will take that long."

"Father, I will be there. I don't know if I can believe it. But for my Mom, I will do it. Now, if you will excuse me." Daniel tries to step aside Father. But he grabs him by the shoulder.

"Daniel, come to church. Open your eyes and ears. Let God speak to you. We are all battling the demons, at this time and when we die. Even if you are not fighting back, they continue."

"I need another drink Father, please excuse me." Daniel walks past the priest.

He finds the waitress who has been filling his shot glass since he arrived.

"Another?"

"Yes, and a beer to chase it." He downs the shot.

"Hey sweetheart, just bring us a bottle." Daniel hears a friendly voice.

"Jonah, man, where have you been?"

"Pall bearers stuff. But I am here now. How are you holding up?"

"It's a long day. Glad we aren't Baptist. Couldn't imagine getting through this on fruit punch."

Jonah pours each of them a shot. They both race to the finish. Jonah pours another.

"Here's to your mom. Our Mom. May her memory be eternal." They down another shot.

"I saw the priest had you cornered. What was that about? Did he want to get paid or something?"

"Shut up Jonah. He's a good man. He wants me back at church. And something about fighting the demons. I guess that's what he said. I'm kinda buzzed. No check that. I'm kind of drunk."

"Daniel, you pick the worst time to be a drunk. If you can adjust your eyes to the far side of the room, you will see your future wife, Lydia Roza." Jonah laughs

"Lydia is here? I haven't spoken to her in such a long time. I need to talk to her."

"Why, so you can proposition her again? And make sure this isn't the liquor talking. You go over there and next thing you know, you will serve in the altar every Sunday."

"Yeah right. But you know what? I'm not scared. I can do this. I'm going over there and talk to her and be nice and sweet. Who knows, I might even ask her out on a date. What do you think about that?"

"I think you are totally wasted. But if you feel you can make it from here to all the way over there, without falling down or pulled down to a table to talk with people you don't know, go for it." Jonah pats him on the back so hard people in the table next to them turn and look.

"Ow, man, that hurt. Alright. Here it goes."

Daniel squints his eyes and tries to focus on her. *There she is, prettier than ever. Talking with, I can't tell. Everyone is blurry.* He puts one step forward, and the next, he stumbles a little but catches himself. He walks past the first table, then the second, at the third table, sits his father. "Daniel, take a seat. Some of your mom's friends want to talk with you." Daniel doesn't reply and moves on.

He passes the next table filled with teens. They remain polite and move their chairs in. He continues on. *She is so close.* A waitress steps in front of him. "Do you want another drink, Daniel? This tequila is chilled. It's very good." Daniel knows if he has one more shot, he is done for the night and won't recover until morning. "Thanks, but I'm fine for now." He tries to move past her, but she doesn't let him.

"So, I'm not supposed to do this. I could lose my job. But you want to meet me after work. My shift ends at midnight. And it looks like you can use a friend."

As he looks her over, he thinks she might fit the bill for the night. Red hair, dark red lipstick, black mascara, light blue eye shadow that sparkle when the light hits them.

"That sounds like a fantastic idea? I will see you later."

She purses her lips together and gives him an air kiss and walks by. Daniel moves forward and finds that Lydia is no longer standing there.

"Did you see where Lydia went off to?" Asking one of the other choir girls who she was speaking with.

"Hi Daniel, she said she needed to go home. I bet you

can catch her if you try."

"I'm not good at running right now." He tries to look over the tops of people's heads and through the dark windows to see if he can see her leaving.

Turning around to go back and speak with Jonah, he finds himself face to face with Lydia.

"Hi, I thought you had left."

"I was going to, but I forgot my purse. It's over at the table."

"I'm happy that you forgot it."

"It seems you might have had one too many again, Daniel."

"Well, I did bury my mother today. A little forgiveness." He reaches for a lock of hair resting on her shoulder. He feels the softness of it in between his finger.

"I've missed you so much, Lydia. Can we go outside and talk or something?"

She reaches up and takes his hand away from her hair and holds it.

"Daniel, I can talk to you as a friend, but that's as far as that will go."

"Why? We were getting somewhere. Something wonderful between us. Couldn't you feel it?"

"I could, but, and I hope you can understand this in your state. I will never compromise. No, I will never put my God second to anyone or anything. I could never date or even marry an agnostic, atheist or someone that isn't my faith." She releases his hand.

"I want to believe again, Lydia. Ever since the day she died, I have been so confused. When my mom passed...I need help with what I saw and heard."

"Maybe you should spend time with Father

Ephraim."

"Lydia, please don't make this more difficult than it is. How about we meet tomorrow for dinner?"

"I will, but on one condition."

"Name it."

"The waitress, stay away from her. Go home and sleep off your drunkenness. If you can do that, I will meet you at the food truck off of South State road. It's the only one there. Can you remember that?"

"Yes, food truck off of South. Um, South State road. I can't wait to see you again."

"Daniel." She steps closer to him so he can focus. Her eyes are caring, but holds a bit of skepticism. "I am truly sorry for your loss. But it's time for you to be strong. The drinking... it shows weakness and with your guard down, the demons are laughing, knowing how easy it is to beat you."

"My mom, she fought with them. Those demons. And she beat them."

"Of course she did. They had nothing on her. Now I have to get going. Go sober up Daniel. We will talk tomorrow." She leans over and kisses his cheek and walks away.

CHAPTER FIVE

At the wooden picnic table under a string of soft yellow lights, Daniel waits for Lydia to arrive. He sees a myriad of engravings on the old table. "Dave was here", "Texas Forever" "John 3:16" "C.B. + A.F." encircled by a heart, "Class of '92." And hash marks of those counting out the time.

"Excuse me, amigo, are you ready to order?" The cook in the truck yells out to Daniel.

"Thanks. Not yet, waiting for my date to arrive."

"A date. You are taking your date to a food truck? Lucky girl."

"It was her suggestion."

"So she's been here before. Who is it?"

"Her name is Lydia. Wavy black hair, dark brown eyes. Beautiful." He sits up as he speaks of her.

"Oh yes. Ms. Lydia. She stops here almost every day. You are the lucky one."

"I know."

He glances at his watch, and from a distance he hears the crunch of pea gravel underneath the tires of an oncoming car. He stands and sees a small SUV pull into the lot.

Without him realizing it, Daniel's face lights up and the smile from when they first met appears once again, chasing the pain and sorrow from the past week away.

She steps out of her car and walks towards him. "Hi Daniel, how are you feeling?"

My heart is fluttering, and there is so much to say to you. "I'm doing alright."

She walks up and hugs him. "You look better than you did last night. I take it because you are here you didn't go home with the waitress?"

He recalls last night's events. Snippets of his conversation with the waitress come into his mind. As he was leaving the restaurant, she came up to him and asked him if he was ready for the night ahead. "I can't. I have a girlfriend." He said.

"That's too bad." She smiled. Then grabbed his keys. And

"The next thing I knew, I was in my car, driven home by one of the other servers. With her following, to take him back to the restaurant. Thank you for stopping me from making a huge mistake."

"When you see someone about to hurt themselves, you try to help. And, for a moment, seeing you with another woman made me jealous."

"Really? I thought you despised me."

"Daniel, I never stopped... I'm starving? Rico makes the best carnitas in the hill country. You need to try them."

He steps closer to her. "You never stopped, what?"

"Nothing Daniel. I'm starving. Come on, let's order."

They sit at the picnic table. The scent of Tex-Mex spices emits from the food truck. He watches her as she eats. Taking a napkin, wiping the edges of her mouth.

"Daniel, you haven't taken a bite. What's the matter?"

Not a thing. I'm looking at you. You are so beautiful.

And I feel better when you are around. I've missed you.

"Nothing, just waiting for it to cool down." He waves his hand over the carnita.

She swallows her food. "Daniel, please eat."

"If you insist" He takes a bite. The juices from the seasoned pork seize his mouth. "You are right. These are the best."

"Hi, Ms. Lydia. I take it everything is to your liking."

"Rico, you've outdone yourself. I told my friend here you make the best carnitas, and you proved me right."

Friend. Daniel's heart sank.

"Thank you. I'm going to close up for the night. You stay as long as you like."

He walks back to the truck, untying his apron. After locking up the truck. He turns the string of lights off, but it does not matter as the bright stars in the night sky light the area for the two to see each other.

"Last night, you said you wanted to believe again. Where did that come from?"

"With everything my mom went through, especially at the end. I know there is more to life than living and dying. There is an after life. I'm embarrassed by what I said to you that night at the lake."

"Please forgive me. I should have been more understanding of what you were going through. I wasn't a very good Christian. I lacked compassion."

Daniel moves his arms across the table, palms out. Lydia puts her hands in his.

"Lydia, can we try this again? I never stop thinking about you. After my mom passed away, I walked into the den and I hoped to see you there waiting. And it disappointed me when you weren't there... and it was comforting to have you sing in the choir at her service.

Your presence throughout the day gave me strength. You are very special and I want to be with you... more than friends."

She blushes and squeezes his hands tighter. Not ready to commit. "You know what I want to do? I want to go to the beach and see the sunrise. I bet if we leave right now, we can make it to South Padre before the sun comes up."

"You don't have a response to what I said?"

"In my heart I do. I can't say it yet. But by the time we get to the beach, I am sure I have something to say. So your car or mine?"

* * *

The five hour drive takes the two from the hill country, past San Antonio and south through rural Texas, comprising small towns with populations that barely break three figures. They stop at the one gas station on the way for a coffee and snacks.

"I love road trips, don't you?" She takes a sip of the tolerable gas station coffee.

In the dead of the night the only sounds are a mix of cicadas and the occasional eighteen wheeler.

"It's been a while, but there is something refreshing about getting away." He stares at her.

"What is that look for?"

"Has your heart told you what to say yet?" He takes another sip.

"Lydia?"

She watches one of the eighteen wheelers speed pass the gas station. Dirt from the tires floats up into the street lights, creating cloud like formations. The breeze from the truck blows her hair back.

"It's close, but I'm not ready. We should hit the road. I want to see the sunrise."

Windows down bring the warm humid air into the car. Black road, cut in two by a yellow stripes, takes them south. The geography changes once they enter the Lower Rio Grande Valley, from a dusty land to lush greenery.

The conversations about their lives, dreams and wishes consume the long drive. They share stories about growing up, attending college and her mission trip. Daniel shares how he continues to leave the path of a righteous life, and when he does, he ends in failure and sin. His desire is to strengthen his Christian faith and the rest of his life, fulfilling God's commandment.

"Be fruitful and multiply. Spread the word to all the nations of the world."

She smiles, puts her arm out the window and watches her hand surf the air.

"I do need the right woman to help me with those things."

"Ha." She laughs. Brings her hand back inside the car. She turns to him and says.

"Have you found the right woman?"

"What do you think?"

"I think you need to do this on your own, without the help of the perfect woman. Because she does not exist. Do it for God. And God will help you. He is your strength. And pray to him. Prayer is powerful."

"I get it."

The car drives on, "Do you go to South Padre a lot?"

"This is my first time. When we lived in Houston,

my family took day trips to Galveston. It's nice. But I've always wanted to visit the island."

"When we get there, I want to show you something."

They head off the highway, into Port Isabel, then over the causeway. The headlights shine onto the brick sign with tropical yellow, pink and teal umbrellas over lettering "South Padre Island, Texas."

Lydia looks at the clock in the car. "6:45"

"We only have a couple of minutes until sunrise."

"Don't worry. We will be there in time." He reassures her.

"Where, the beach?"

"Just wait."

They reach a parking lot and he stops the car.

"Come on, if we hurry, we will get there right in time."

They reach the side walk on the jetty. First glimpse of daylight cracks the sky.

"Hurry." He grabs her hand and they speed up. As they come closer to what he wants to show her, she slows down. The orange yellow sun enters the sky from the sea.

"See." He points.

She sees a statue, with outstretched hands overlooking the bay, facing the rising sun.

"Is that? It looks like Christ the Redeemer."

The sun lights up the statue, showing all the features of Christ.

"Yes. That's what it is. It's called Christ of the Fisherman. It's a smaller version of Christ the Redeemer. Watch that fishing boat. It will stop before sailing and the captain will ask for a blessing."

"It's beautiful. What is the story behind it?"

"There were two brothers on a fishing boat. One was up on deck, the other below. When the one did not return from below deck, his brother went to check on him. Immediately, toxic fumes consumed him, just as they did his brother, and both passed away. Part of the settlement was a request by their mother to have this statue made and placed here."

"Lord have mercy." She watched as the sun changed from deep orange to a bright white yellow backed by the full blue sky. "Thank you for sharing this with me, Daniel."

"I thought you would like it. Are you ready to go to the beach?"

"Yes. Let's go."

The squawks of seagulls and crashing waves are the only sounds they hear as they approach the sand at the end of the wooden walkway. Lydia takes her shoes off and digs her toes into the cool sand.

"The beach is beautiful. Not a single person this time of morning." She says.

Daniel takes his shoes off. Rolls up his pant legs. "How about we take a walk into the ocean?" Daniel puts his hand out. Lydia takes it and they head toward the green-blue waters. She stops at the edge of the dry sand.

"What are you doing?" Daniel asks.

"I like when the water comes to me." At that moment, the wave crashes and rolls up the beach, ending its reach at her toes. The next one rolls in, the water a little higher, reaching her ankles. She walks further into the water, pulling her dress up past her knees. Daniel follows, the water higher than his rolled up pant legs.

He comes up behind her, taps her on the shoulder,

breaking her gaze into the sea.

"I'm ready to tell you." She says and turns to him.

"I fell in love with you and never stopped loving you. I prayed for you every night, asking God to help you find your way. To send you an angel. To open your eyes and see you are a Christian and a child of God."

The sea and gulls are now silent. Her words are sweeter than any song he's ever heard.

He puts his hands on her waist, she puts hers on his. "I've always loved you. I let the world take me away from you and what is right. But now I know. I see how my life should be. And it is with you." Goose bumps rise on his skin. He shivers. And before he can stop the words from coming out of his mouth. "Lydia, will you marry me? Be my wife?" Her brown eyes tear up, her lips smile, and she throws her arms around him. Waves crash at their waist. The sounds of the of the sea and birds in the air blend together, creating a perfect song.

"Yes. I will marry you." She whispers in his ear. She feels his arms wrap tighter around her.

"We are going to have a wonderful life together." He says.

She nods in agreement. "Yes. I am so happy."

"We need to tell everyone." She says. Then turns and runs towards the beach. Daniel runs after her. He falls into the water. Lydia stops and puts her hand out and helps him up. Drenched, he is still smiling. They continue on.

They make it half up the wide beach. Lydia falls onto the sand. Lays down and puts her hands over her eyes.

Daniel falls to her side. "Are you crying?"

"No." As she wipes tears from her eyes.

"Lydia?" He wipes the tear rolling down the side of

her face.

"It's so stupid."

She sits up. Takes a deep breath. "I can't believe we are engaged."

"It was going to happen. Deep down, from the moment I met you, I knew it. My mom knew it. Jonah. Everyone. I am sorry I wasted so much time. Keeping me from you."

"Everything is in God's time. He knew you weren't ready. But now you are."

She puts her hands a little deeper into the sand. She feels something. Pulls it from below. It's a fresh rose recently buried. She looks at it and says.

"A rose lying in the sand cries out. Pick me up.

Where are you from? A first date, proposal, a wedding bouquet?

The waves crash behind me as the sun slips into the ocean.

Do I leave you here in case she returns?

No. Pick it up, avoid the thorns, and brush off the sand.

The pedals are soft.You still have life little rose.

You are not for the seagulls dipping and rising into the orange sky, nor for the waters sliding up the sand.

See the sad bride walking along the shoreline.

You are for her heart to heal."

He takes the flower from her hand. "That's beautiful. What is that from?"

"Nowhere, it just came to me."

"You amaze me." He leans over and kisses her. She pulls him in closer. When they open their eyes, they are in front of Father Ephraim, on the solea, crowns connected by a white ribbon, on each of their heads. The icons of Christ and Theotokos behind the priest, and all of their friends and family watch as the two continue the wedding ceremony.

Father Ephraim finishes the ceremony and announces, "It's my honor to present the newlyweds. Mr. and Mrs. Daniel Roza.

PART II

"Hereafter I will not talk much with you: for the ruler of this world cometh, and hath nothing in Me."

-JOHN 14:30

CHAPTER SIX

"To Daniel and Lydia. Ten years married. Who would have thought? No, who would have thought?" The small gathering of family and friends chuckles at Jonah.

"Seriously, ten years ago, these two walked down the aisle. The love these two exuded, what they showed us all here, is that love is alive, true and beautiful. Thank you, you two, for showing there is hope for us, like myself, in finding true love. To Daniel and Lydia."

"Cheers."

Lydia and Daniel share "I love you" and kisses. Clapping in the church hall begins.

Jonah walks up to the couple and hugs them.

Jonah hands Daniel the microphone. Daniel closes his eyes and takes a deep breath. "Thank you Jonah. As you all know, I am not much for words. Except for tonight. Where I want my beautiful bride to know that, as impossible as it might seem, I love her today more than ever. Honey, you are so beautiful. A wonderful wife, an exceptional mother to our three amazing children; Liev, Simeon, and Paulina. She's a loyal servant of God. And if it wasn't for God, we would not be here today. Lydia, I love you, sweetheart."

Daniel hugs and kisses Lydia. He steps to the side, giving her an opportunity to speak. "Daniel, my love.

To everyone. I want to thank God for blessing this marriage. With God's help, we have made a good, loving life for our family and home. And we thank the church, Father Ephraim, in keeping us in your prayers. Thank you. Now Father, will you please bless this delicious food so we can eat?"

"I can't believe you fooled her this long, Daniel. For ten years, you've gotten over on her."

"Jonah, is this why you pulled me outside? I should be inside with Lydia. Plus, I haven't fooled her."

"She considers you are as much as Christian as she is. Does she know you still doubt?"

"No."

"And that you aren't the same guy when you go out of town on business trips?"

"What are you talking about? I haven't told you anything."

"We have common acquaintances. Don't worry Daniel. I won't say anything. I want to learn how you've been able to live a double life. Here, a nice Christian man. But once you leave the home, you are like one of us."

"Give me a break. I need to let loose once in a while. Business is stressful. One month I am killing it, the next month, nothing. It's not like you, in finance, always having commissions to carry me over the lean months. I have a wife and three kids to take care of. A Christian would get eaten alive by the proverbial lions in my industry. I need to network, wine and dine, pretend I like people, and other things I don't want to discuss, only to close the sale."

"So you sold your soul to the devil?" Jonah laughs.

"It feels that way sometimes. But when I make it

home, walk inside and see Lydia with the children. I feel like I escaped hell and now in my personal Heaven."

"One day, you are going to get caught. And you will have a lot to answer for."

"It's a couple more years, after I get promoted to sales manager and I don't need to do any of the client BS. I'm good. Now what about you? When can we get you to change your ways and get you back to church? There are still some good Christian single women."

"Never going to happen, Daniel. I'm fine with having my Sunday's free, not having to buy a Christmas tree, chocolate Easter bunnies, fasting, trying to understand two thousand year old writings. Nope, on Sundays, I am not ready to trade in my New York Times for the King James Bible."

"Jonah, come on, just once."

"Daniel, one thing we agreed on is we wouldn't talk about religion. Look out, Lydia is coming to steal you away from me again."

"What are you boys talking about?"

"Oh, I'm trying to get Jonah to give church another try."

"Well Jonah? You ready to come back to your family?"

"Lydia, save your breath. This isn't for me. Being a Christian and all."

"When did you decide to be an atheist? You get turned by a college professor? A pretty girl? I think by now you are grown up."

"Not at all. It was a Sunday school teacher. I was thirteen, and in Sunday school we were discussing Genesis, the beginning. I asked the teacher, Mrs. Kincaid, if she thought God created the world in six days. And do you know what she said? She said that

Genesis was a myth story. And not to be concerned with that. I asked her about Noah, and she said that was a myth story too. So I asked at what point do we trust in the Bible? And she couldn't answer. She mumbled something. Don't you remember that, Daniel? And the final blow came when I asked, "So, if there was never an Adam, then no sin, and no need for a Christ to be born and die for a sin that never happened? Right?" She had this confused looked on her face. She stuttered and said to ask the priest for clarification. Here I am, a 13-year-old that challenged and won a debate on Christianity with a middle aged woman that had been going to church for forty years. So from that moment on, I went to church to appease my parents, plus I got to be with my best friend. And lunch was pretty good too."

Lydia shaking her head. "Oh Jonah, you are so wrong. I can't believe you let an unprepared Sunday school teacher and a 13-year-old boy turn you. There are answers to all the of your questions. If you need those answers to strengthen your faith, come to our Bible study class."

"Lydia, I appreciate you trying to save me, but you should spend your time on more fruitful pursuits." Jonah gives her a pat on her cheek.

"Jonah, we love you, and we will be here for you when you are ready. Come on Daniel, let's head back inside. You owe me a slow dance."

"I love you two, too. Now go have some fun. I have a date to get ready for. Her name is Jezebel." Jonah teasing Lydia one last time.

* * *

The road winds and narrows through the Texas hill country. He has taken this drive a thousand of times. He knows every ranch, bent tree, and fallen fence post. Hands gripping the steering wheel, music blaring, thoughts about his upcoming date with his Jezebel. Her name is Tanya. *Who needs marriage? Stuck with the same woman for the rest of your life.* Now, even without believing in God, Jonah feels he lives a life with stolen blessings: Great job, growing bank account, fantastic home, money to burn, and any woman he wants. And tonight he wants Tanya.

His silver sports car grabs the road, he pushes 75 on the 55 mph road. His mind focused on tonight. *What should I wear, where should I take her, should I take her back home? Will she be a one-night stand or will I need to put work into this one to get her into bed?*

As Sunshine Curve approaches, he reaches up to grab his sunglasses out of the ceiling compartment, he remembers he left them at the anniversary party, he turns the corner, the sun larger than ever shines bright, blinding Jonah. Good thing, as he doesn't see the grill of the eighteen wheeler coming through his windshield.

For split a second Jonah heard a chorus of thundering metal crunching, cymbals of glass shattering, the cracking of his femur bones breaking, ripping through his skin and his forearms shattering. Then a quick scent of his blood, darkness, now death.

"Jonah, hey Jonah, it's me, Daniel. Can you hear me?" Daniel waves at Jonah sitting upright in his hospital bed.

He turns to Lydia. "I don't think he can hear me. His eyes are wide open, but no response. Is this typical?"

"Jonah, it's Lydia. Th nurse called and said you

opened your eyes. We rushed down here to see you. We've missed you."

"I don't know Lydia, he's been asleep for over a month. The doctors told us it can take time to come out of the coma. I wonder if he knows we are here?"

"Hard to say. I would like to think so."

Daniel walks towards the bed. "Jonah, take your time. Get your strength back. Me, Lydia, your folks, the staff, even Father Ephraim, have been dropping by while you were asleep, praying for you."

Jonah blinks his eyes and turns towards his night stand where he sees a cross and an icon of a guardian angel standing with a little boy.

"Priest, get me the priest Daniel." His voice crackles through his dry throat.

Daniel and Lydia startled. They look at each other. "Lydia, call Father. Please tell him to get down here."

Lydia walks into the hallway "Hi Father, it's Lydia, Jonah is awake, he's calling for you."

Father Ephraim walking down the hospital corridor. If he looked into the hospital rooms, he would witness the sick, diseased and those realizing their mortality, sitting upright, hoping to talk to him or anyone with a white collar. They understand their time is near and are unprepared, but don't understand what to do next. They need an advocate.

At the end of the corridor is Lydia waving at him to hurry. Father quickens his pace, Lydia leads him into the hospital room. He enters and sees Jonah wide awake. The expression on Jonah's face changes as soon as he sees Father. First happiness, then pained.

"Jonah, Jonah, the Lord has brought you out of the darkness. You are with us again."

Jonah tries to speak, but for a moment cannot utter any words.

All three in the room tell Jonah not to rush it and take time. He tries again.

"Father, the demons. You never told us about the demons."

"What Jonah? Demons?" Father looks back at Lydia and Daniel with a questioned look.

"The demons, I saw them. They were there, horrible looking. They were ferocious. And terrible, accusing me of the sinful things I've done. And they kept coming at me, one after another, surrounding me. I couldn't do anything. I didn't know how to defend myself."

"Jonah, when was this?"

Jonah sits up straight. "After the truck crashed into me."

Lydia and Daniel hold each other and listen to Jonah's account.

"Everything went dark and silent. Out of nowhere the ghouls or demons showed up. They surrounded me and attacked me. Laughing, taking turns tormenting me with all the things I did. I tried to look past them, because I thought I saw."

Jonah stops talking.

"Saw what Jonah?" Father asks

"I... I saw him."

"Who?"

Jonah points to the guardian angel in the icon.

"My guardian angel. Standing over the terrible demons. He tried to defend me but couldn't. The demons had too much to accuse me of. The demons they showed me all broken and mangled in the front seat of my car. They chanted, "You're dead, you're dead.

Your soul is with us."

Jonah tears up and reaches out for Father Ephraim.

"Father, they took me to hell where there is so much pain, anguish, and fear. I had to get away from them. I was at a loss. But something spoke to me and I turned to one of the ghouls and said, "Lord Jesus Christ, have mercy on me a sinner. Then I was released into blackness. Now, I am awake. Father? I need your help?"

"What is it Jonah?"

"Help me so that I will never to return to that place again and see those terrifying demons."

Lydia crossed her self and Daniel followed. Father Ephraim clasped his hands in joy. "Jonah, of course, of course. Get your body healed and I..."

"No father, I want to start now. What if I die again? Please help me."

Father Ephraim looked down at Jonah, whose expression was like that of a child wakening from a nightmare. His eyes full and pleading. "Jonah, let me gather some items from my car. I will be right back OK. I am here for you."

Jonah nods.

"Daniel and Lydia, can I meet you in the hallway?"

Daniel and Lydia follow the priest. "Is this the first time Jonah has spoken of this?"

Yes. This was the first time he has spoken since he woke up from his coma. Lydia and I drop by at least once a day, pray for him, talk to him and sit in silence and wait."

"There was something that I overheard the EMT tell the doctor on the first night, but I thought little of it until now."

"What is it Lydia?" Father asks

"The EMT said that Jonah's heart stopped in the ambulance. They said he wasn't breathing, no heart beat for three minutes. They were about to call it, but wanted to wait until they arrived at the hospital and had the right equipment. Suddenly, Jonah's hearts started, and he breathed."

"Father, did he go to Hell?" Daniel asked.

Father Ephraim nods his head. "What he describes is very familiar to what some of the ancient fathers witnessed and wrote about at the hour of death. Prior to his accident, Jonah was very solid in his convictions. He was a hardened atheist, and for him to wake up, ask for me and talk of demons and hell. I would say that what you heard is true."

"So what now, Father?"

"Me and him, with the help of God, are going to save his soul. It's going to be a long evening."

"Yes, Father, we will be available if you need us to come back and help."

"Thank you. Now you two have a blessed night. Pray for me. I will talk to you tomorrow."

Father turns and walks into Jonah's hospital room. Opens his briefcase, puts on his robe, and takes out an icon of Christ and places it at his bedside next to the icon of the guardian angel.

"Daniel, come on, we should go. Let them be." Lydia pulls Daniel away from the doorway.

The days and weeks go by and Jonah becomes stronger, not only physically, but spiritually. His thirst for the Lord and his eagerness to save his soul have Father Ephraim at the hospital every day and sometimes he comes back at night.

The priest returns home from his visits with Jonah.

He has trouble falling asleep after his conversation with him. His wife tries to take his mind off his troubles with stories of the day's event with the children, talk of updating their home or a movie. But even watching one of his favorite Spaghetti Western movies, his mind wanders back to the first night Jonah spoke to him about the demons and his trip to hell.

"I need to do better. I need to be a better priest," He turns to his wife as the credits roll.

"You are a wonderful priest. You can only do the best with what you are given."

"No, I need to do a better job of preparing those in our congregation for the next life. I preach to them on how to live a good Christian life today, but maybe they miss the point as to why?"

"What can you do to change that?"

Father Ephraim sits up, turns off the TV and stares at himself in the screen's reflection. "I need to do a better job of teaching them. Not only on Sunday's but other days throughout the week."

His wife wraps her arms around his shoulders, "Ephraim, you work so hard as it is. You visit the sick, poor and those in prison. You manage the church, prepare your sermons, meet with benefactors, and all the paperwork the Diocese requires. How can you find any more time in your week to help?"

"I will manage my time so this can happen. This is important. There needs to be a shift in understanding. I can't stress enough that people need to properly repent. Not in their dying days, but today. They could end up like poor Jonah, who suddenly died and never confessed his sins." Father gets up from the sofa and runs his hands through his hair and wonders if he can do anything to change the approach of the church.

"You might be right Ephraim, the church assumes the parishioners understand things already. It makes sense to take one step back."

"The problem with today's culture is that everyone is afraid to speak of death. Funerals are now celebrations of life. They burn the body to save a couple hundred of dollars. This is all wrong. We need to mourn at our funerals and pray for those who passed away. And when we remember those who have gone, it leads us to repent."

"There is a lot going against you, Ephraim. Society does not want to face their mortality. You may lose parishioners if you go this route."

"The people need to know. But right now, a terrified young man sitting all alone in his hospital room waiting for me to return because he has so much to tell me."

The priest kisses his wife goodbye and heads back to the hospital.

* * *

He walks down the hospital corridor to Jonah's once again. As he passes by several rooms, he hears, "Father, father, help me too." The priest slows his pace and stops, waits and listens for the voice again. Nothing, silence. He turns, walks back and peaks into the hospital room. It's an elderly man alone with a tube inserted into his veins, his eyes are closed. He is in a deep sleep. Father walks away until he hears bells and chimes. Nurses from either direction run into the man's hospital room.

The priest reacts the same and rushes into the room.

One nurse is looking at her watch "Time of death 9:13 pm". Father runs to his bedside. Says his bedside prayer and asks God to forgive the man's sins. The nurses tell the priest there is nothing he can do and for him to leave the room. Father complies and heads towards Jonah's room.

They continue their conversation. Jonah tells Father his sins and after how he wants to change his life and dedicate it to Christ. A monk perhaps?

Father Ephraim lets him continue to confess, he tells him "Jonah, one step at a time, not only does your body, but your soul needs time to heal."

"You will be where God wants you to be in due time. So use this time to your advantage. Study the church fathers, learn about the faith. But I don't feel a monk is your calling."

"How about I help around the church, and on Sunday's work in the altar?"

"That's a start, but there is still work to be done."

CHAPTER SEVEN

Father Ephraim sits across the desk from the reporter from the Orthodox Weekly, cheerfully answering questions from the young female reporter. He speaks of his life growing up in a Catholic household consisting of his parents, and five brothers and sisters in lower Rio Grande Valley. He speaks of his conversion to Orthodoxy. It happened while he studied the Orthodox faith at the university and learned her rich history. He delved more into the teachings and one night in the library, he heard the calling to become an Orthodox priest.

He spoke of meeting his wife Michelle when attending Seminary. She worked at the small coffee shop in town. He laughed, telling how he never drank coffee until he saw her through the store window. He speaks of being blessed with a wonderful family and a lively and growing church.

"Father Ephraim, Christ the Savior, is one of the few churches that is growing, year after year, over the past ten years. What's amazing is that you are doing this in a small Texas town. Do you want to share your secret?"

"Sophia, thank you for the question. It isn't a secret. Ten years ago, one of my parishioners, who was an atheist at the time, had something miraculous happen to him. In my dealings with him, I understood I had to become a better priest, realize what the community was lacking, and focus on one consistent message."

"What message would that be, Father?" Sophia, with pen and paper at ready, waits for his answer.

"With the time that God has given us, that time is used to save our souls, which will save ourselves when we pass away from this place."

"That's it. It seems pretty simple. Don't people understand that?"

"You would think. But I don't fault Christians for not knowing. I fault myself, other priests, the Bishops, and Arch Bishops. I believe that they, we all get caught in the trap of believing those that come to church, are as knowledgeable about scripture and our faith as we are. But we need to realize that is not the case. Most have never read their Bible from Genesis to Revelations, study scriptures daily, and read what the church fathers said about the importance of confession, repentance, and of alms giving."

Sophia thinks for a second. "So you are a Fire and Brimstone Orthodox priest?"

Father Ephraim laughs at the suggestion. "No, no, no. Our loving Lord has told us how we can be in his house after we pass from this life. And to avoid the torments of the demons."

"Demons Father?"

"Yes, demons. Those evil spirits that work for the devil."

Sophia was startled by the revelation of demons. "I'm sorry, Father, but aren't demons just made up characters for scary movies?"

Father Ephraim smiles. "That's what today's society would like you to believe. Worse, that is what the devil wants you to believe. And the demons have no fear and will attack anyone for as long as it takes to win the soul."

"Do you care to elaborate? Something I can give to my readers."

Father Ephraim nods for a moment. "There was a priest who traveled the desert. After a long day of traveling, singing psalms he found a cave to stop in and rest. And as soon as he laid down, he saw a multitude of demons coming from all directions. And he saw one was bigger and scarier than the others. This one moved around and questioned the other demons to see if they helped their assigned human to fall. The ones that didn't, enraged the leader, and were expelled, sent away to be torn apart. Then, one of the worst of the ghouls was a most evil spirit. He was full of joy and laughter as he spoke of how, after fifteen years of nightly temptations to a certain monk, he could move that monk to sin and fornicate. After the demon told the story, all the other demons were laughing and celebrating. And the priest, after he awoke from the vision, traveled into town and found that this happened. So yes, there are demons. They have been with us since Adam and Eve were escorted out of the Garden of Eden."

"And you teach your parishioners how to ward off evil spirits?" Sophia asks.

"Sophia, I understand you are skeptical. This results from the church trying not to scare people away. To hide what the church fathers have said about the things we want to avoid. Good vs evil, the devil, demons, life after death, and the soul. And the hard work we have to do in this brief life, to ensure we have wonderful after life. What we do at Christ the Savior is prepare the soul to be ready."

"Ready for what?"

"Ready for the eternal life. Our parish is growing because people are thirsty for having a good after life. They know this time here is temporary. And deep down, they know they need to do something to be ready. And we offer that. Word of what we are doing here is spreading throughout the community. We have converts from the big Protestant and Catholic churches. We have several catechumens each week. Atheists, and agnostics are finding their way here and converting too. They want a church that is truthful about the soul after death, and does not have a superficial attitude about, death. We do not hold back here, which is refreshing to most."

"There is a rumor that one of your parishioners actually died and went to hell. Is that true?"

"You can ask him yourself. He is preparing the church hall for tonight's Bible study. His name is Jonah."

Sophia stands up and thanks the priest for the opportunity to speak with him. Father points Sophia to the hall.

As she walks into the hall, Sophia sees a man putting out chairs and tables. He has the look of someone who has spent time away from everyone. A desert Father. Long brown hair with strands of gray. A beard and crows feet by the eyes. With a slight smile, he seems to enjoy the menial task at hand. Sophia hesitates to enter the hall.

"Jonah, excuse me Jonah."

Jonah looks across the hall and sees Sophia. He guesses she is recently out of college. Pretty, a girl he would have hit on in his former life.

"Yes, may I help you?"

"Hi, I'm Sophia from the the Orthodox Weekly. The story I am writing is about the growth of Christ the Savior. Father Ephraim told me to speak to you to clarify something.

"I would be happy to help. Please take a seat." They both find a place to sit amongst the semi-circle of chairs Jonah put out.

"Yes, Jonah. You don't have to answer the questions if too painful?"

"You are going to ask about my death?"

"Yes, what happened?"

Jonah looks down at the floor. He takes a hard swallow. His pulse races. He raises his head, making eye contact with Sophia. "It was terrifying, and it is hard to describe. My best friend and his wife are celebrating their tenth wedding anniversary with me. I leave to get ready for a date. On my way home, I turn the corner and hidden in the sunset is the front of an eighteen wheeler. Soon as it hit me, I died."

Sophia adjusts in her chair. She checks her phone, making sure she is recording the conversation.

"And what happened... once you died?"

Jonah leans forward. "At my death, I was alone in darkness for a moment, then the sounds of the most horrible creatures filled the void. I looked into the darkness. The sounds grew closer, and in an instance demons attacked me and took me straight to Hell. I still have a hard time describing how scary the demons were and how horrible hell is. It's been over ten years and when my guard is down, visions of that place are set in front of me."

"So you believe you were in hell?"

"Yes, the doctors say I was dead for at least three minutes. During that time I saw a glimpse of the punishment for unrepentant sinners after they die. I will do anything to never go there again. With my strength in Christ and the help of Father Ephraim, I have changed. I have died to this world. I eradicated everything that kept me from living a spiritual life: love of money, adultery, drinking, lying. All of it."

With a slight tilt of her head "That's quite a story Jonah. It's different from many reports of people dying and coming back to life. Most report a tunnel, seeing loved ones, then being pulled to go back. That didn't happen to you?"

"I can't speak to their experience. But I have a theory."

Sophia stiffens in the chair. "I would like to hear it."

"The devil is deceptive, and like it or not, we are in constant battle with evil. My thought is, the devil shows these people a tunnel, their loved ones who passed on and a warm feeling. The reports of this experience come from all walks of life. Christians, agnostics, atheists, Muslims, Jews, good people, and bad people."

"Yes, that's true."

"This is where the deception comes in. The devil makes all these people feel like they were going to Heaven, so when they come back to earth they can spread the false testimony that you can live anyway you wish and you will go to Heaven."

"You make it sound as if it is difficult to get into Heaven. Are you sure your experience wasn't the result of alcohol, drugs, or the medicine they gave you?"

Jonah shows a slight smile through his beard. "Sophia, it is easy to go to Heaven once you free yourself from a sinful life. And you can check the hospital records. I was dead for over three minutes. Are there anymore questions? I need to finish preparing the room for Bible study."

She turns off her recorder, packs her note pad and stands up.

"Thank you for sharing your story with me, Jonah."

She shakes Jonah's hand and walks out towards the exit. Watching her go, not a sinful thought entered his mind.

Father Ephraim approaches Sophia as she is leaving the hall.

"Father, thank you for spending time with me today. I think I have enough to tell the readers about Christ the Savior. But before I leave, do you mind if I take some pictures of inside the church?"

"Please, the church is open. You have a safe journey home."

Sophia enters the church and walks into the narthex. Similar to other Orthodox churches, this space is separate from the nave of the church. She takes pictures of the candle stands. Where burning candles representing the prayers for the healing of a sick loved one or the soul of a recently departed. Some candles have burned down to their wick about to be extinguished by the sand, while others are newly ignited run bright. On the right side of the entrance into the church is an icon of Christ, on the left side of the Theotokos (The Virgin Mary holding baby Jesus.) Sophia approaches each icon, crosses herself and kisses each one. Her first photo is a picture of the narthex with candle light filling the room.

She enters into the nave and takes several pictures

of the altar area, the iconostasis, which separates the church from the altar. The camera captures more images, focusing on Christ, John the Baptist, the Last Supper. On the walls are various icons of the feast days. She turns and faces the back of the church and takes another picture. As the hour is turning, sun beams enter the church through the stained glass windows. As the minutes go by, the sun beams create a prism on several of the icons. Sophia, excited by the what she is seeing, takes several more photos. She sees a magnificent prism reflecting on the last icon on the back wall. The icon is larger than most. She points her lens at the icon and focuses. Taken aback by what she sees, she captures the image and walks across the church to view the icon up close.

The icon is old and weathered. The color has faded on the corners. Standing in front of the icon, she is uncomfortable from what it depicts. Christ sitting on a throne, surrounded by what she believes are saints, the holy apostles, The Virgin Mary, Adam, and Eve. Below, three levels which depict angels and other holy men. She shutters at the image of a snake winding through the icon. It starts at the bottom corner, through the center and ends at the image of Adam, where it is biting his heel. The snake has many bands along it's body, creating segments. Inside each segment is a dark angel or demon holding scales, naked people, and angels. Near the tail of the snake demons stabbing the people with pitch forks, others have bound the people by ropes and other frenzied demonic hordes hovering around the outside of the serpent.

This is the most complex icon she has ever seen. At the bottom of the icon is a brass placard with writing in

Russian. Sophia took an introductory course in Russian and makes out the writing "The Last Judgment." She snaps one more photo of the icon and departs from the church.

"Sophia, have a safe journey back home." Jonah waves to her. Sophia, still startled by what she saw, gives him a blank stare.

"Are you alright?" Jonah asks

Sophia waves back to Jonah. "I'm fine. Thank you again."

Sophia starts her car and drives away.

* * *

"The Fire and Brimstone Orthodox Priest and how to scare people into church." The headline in the Orthodox Weekly read. Father Ephraim sees the picture of himself, Jonah, and the icon of the Last Judgment. He continues to read on.

"As some priests within our communities have preached acceptance and diversity to try and increase the size of their church congregations, Father Ephraim of Hill Country Texas has reverted to the tried-and-true method: Scare everyone into believing they are going to hell. A tactic reserved for rural Baptist churches in the deep south, Father Ephraim has borrowed. He has taken the message of Love that Christ has for us all to one of being fearful of our Lord and Savior.

To further frighten those to continue to come to church, Father Ephraim keeps on staff a man by the name of Jonah who believes he died and continued straight to Hell. And an icon, titled "the Last Judgment," which shows the controversial and disputed teachings of the trial of the soul after death. Father Ephraim includes the fear of death in all of his sermons, revealing how parishioners should use their time here to prepare themselves for eternal life. Which means confession, attendance of Divine Liturgy, taking part in Communion, tithing, giving alms, fasting and prayers. In today's forward thinking society, many believe Father Ephraim's way of running his parish is hurtful, detrimental and goes against current wisdom. Which some believe have chased people away from not only the Orthodox church by Christianity as a whole.

I reached out to Deacon Lazarus of Holy Saints Orthodox church in Buffalo, NY. In speaking with him regarding Father Ephraim's teachings, he called Father Ephraim a heretic, and fell into a trap by the evil one. He found his teaching on Gnosticism. In addition, that Father Ephraim's fire and brimstone tactics will do more harm to the souls of those in his parish. I reached out to Metropolitan Symeon to comment on Father Ephraim and what Deacon Lazarus had to say. At the time of this publication I have not received comment."

Father Ephraim scrolled to the comments section at the bottom of the article. He was shocked to see the first screen filled with so much hate and vitriol that he could do nothing more than to exit out of his screen.

His cell phone rang. "Hi, Metropolitan Symeon, your Eminence. It is so good to hear from you."

His voice strained. Even though he has lived in the United States for over thirty years, he still has a heavy Russian accent.

"Father Ephraim, have you seen the Orthodox Weekly this morning?"

"Yes, I just finished reading the article."

"What happened? This was supposed to be a good article. One that talked about the growth of your congregation. You have so much success, so many wonderful programs for the youth. I don't understand?"

"I don't know either. But I found out that she grew up in Buffalo and attended the same church where Deacon Lazarus is at."

"Yes Deacon Lazarus. I have had several emails from him concerning you. I believe his intention is to stir up trouble. This is not the first time he has gone after a priest that he believes is going against the church teaching."

"Well, I've never heard of him, and he should pay attention to his own church. Not a mission church two thousand miles south of him."

"I agree. But he is very disruptive and has been causing much trouble in the northeast and is making a name for himself amongst the progressives in our church."

"And the Metropolitan in the northeast is letting this happen? Can't they remove him?"

"It is very tricky. He is very popular and has quite a following. The church is having a difficult time in that region and removing him could be detrimental."

"That should not be a concern of the church. It will be just a momentary loss, but once he is gone, the church can't help but flourish."

"Unfortunately, that is not what others are thinking. In fact, they plan to elevate Deacon Lazarus to priest and he will head Assumption Church in Syracuse. They are very thrilled."

"Well, good for him. I pray he will spend his time and energy on his new church."

"I doubt it. He is very motivated to move up and has his sights on becoming an Archbishop. He speaks of a dream and in it, he was told that is what he has to do. After he awoke, the first thing he did was break off his engagement with his girlfriend of eight years."

"Wow, well, I can't worry about him. I'm sure I'm going to need to answer questions here. I should prepare for it. Unless there is anything else I can do for you, I will speak with you next week."

"That is all, Father. May the Lord give you strength."

Father Ephraim puts his phone down on his desk, rubs his face, and strokes his beard.

He remembers his first service after declaring to his wife how he must work on becoming a stronger priest. How he stumbled over his words at the start of his sermon. Unsure, but once he opened his mouth saying "But God said unto him, Thou fool, this night they will require thy soul; then whose shall those things be, which thou has provided?" Luke 12:20.

And he said "I ask you, when you hear this, who are they? Our Lord did not say "I". So who is they?"

The congregation stirred and the ones who dozed off came to attention, became straight and concentrated on the question at hand.

"We can find the answer in 1 Peter 5:8 "Be sober, be vigilant; because your adversary the devil, as a roaring lion, walketh about, seeking whom he may devour."

"We are in a battle, a battle with the evil one that has been raging since he tempted Eve. Our problem is we have become so secularized that we didn't realize we were fighting anyone. Which makes this an easy battle for the devil and his demons. In Luke 12:20, Christ is speaking of the demons who will wait for all of us the moment we die, and Peter warns of the evil one prowling around trying to take as many souls as possible. By looking at our weaknesses and tempting us through whatever is appealing to our senses. And the more we give into these temptations, we sin. And the more we sin, the easier it makes for the demons. From here on out, my focus at Christ the Savior is to be your shepherd, your helper, a guide of how to save your soul, not only here in this time, but more importantly for your eternal life. I won't fool you. This is going to be hard work. Not just for you, but for me as well. As I am held accountable for your salvation."

Father recalls looking out into the congregation. The reaction wasn't what he expected. He saw smiles, nods of agreement, and several older women who shed tears of joy. He lost some parishioners, but as time went by, he gained more than he lost.

"Father, Father Ephraim," Jonah runs into his office.

"Yes Jonah."

"It's Daniel he needs you... He called me and wants you to go to his home. It's his dad."

❋ ❋ ❋

Rushing to the front door, they find it cracked. Father Ephraim walks in, Jonah following behind. They step into the bedroom. Just as it was with his mother, but this time it's Daniel sitting at the bedside of his dad and has the comfort of Lydia by his side.

Father Ephraim looks down at Daniel's dad. He is quiet and peaceful.

"Daniel, how is he?"

"His heart is barely beating. It just happened. We were talking earlier, me him and Lydia. He was joking about how when he passes away he better not find my mom with George Washington. He said she always had a thing for him. Winner of the Revolutionary war, First President, Father of the country and all. We were all laughing, then he showed a moment of pain on his face, then fell asleep."

"Is he on any medication?"

"No, he stopped a couple of weeks ago and he told the hospice nurse every day since then no drugs. No morphine or anything that would prevent him from fighting."

Father, more confident than the night Daniel's mother passed, took out his oil and holy water, put on his robe and pulled out a copy of "The office at the departure of the soul" and began reading it over Daniel's father.

The hospice nurse enters the room and takes his vitals.

Father begins the service:

"O Holy God, Holy Mighty Holy Immortal One, have mercy upon us.

Glory to the Father, and to the Son, and to the Holy Spirit, now, and ever, and unto ages of ages. Amen.

O all-holy Trinity, have mercy upon us. O Lord, wash away our sins. O Master, pardon our transgressions. O Holy One, visit and heal our infirmities, for thy Name's sake."

Father asks for all to join in reciting the Lord's prayer:

All joining in, even the hospice nurse:

"Our Father, who art in heaven, Hallowed be thy

Name. Thy kingdom come. Thy will be done. On earth, as it is in Heaven. Give us this day our daily bread. And forgive us our trespasses, As we forgive those who trespass against us. And lead us, not into temptation; But deliver us from the Evil One."

Father Ephraim continues to read Psalm 50:

"Have mercy upon me, O God, after thy great goodness; according to the multitude of thy mercies, do away mine offenses. Wash me thoroughly from my wickedness and cleanse me from my sin. For I acknowledge my faults, and my sin is ever before me. Against thee only, have I sinned and done this evil in thy sight; that thou mightest be justified in thy saying, and clear when thou art judged...."

The hospice nurse looks up at Daniel. "It's almost time. Do you wish to say your last good byes?"

First Lydia walks over to the bed, leans over Daniel's father, whispers "I love you" in his ear and kisses his forehead.

"... Turn thy face from my sins, and put out all my misdeeds. Make me a clean heart, O God, and renew a right spirit within me. Cast me not away from thy presence, and take not thy Holy Spirit from me. O give me the comfort of thy help again and establish me with thy free Spirit."

Jonah, with prayer rope in hand, kneels next to the bed. "No more need to struggle, John. You will soon be with the Lord. I love you, brother." With his hand, he combs the elder Roza's hair off his forehead and kisses it.

"When Israel passed on foot over the deep, as it had been dry land, and beheld their pursuer Pharaoh engulfed in the sea, they cried aloud: Let us sing unto

God a song of victory."

"Like drops of rain my evil days and few, dried up by summer's heat, already gently vanish: O Lady, save me."

"Through thy tenderness of heart and thy many bounties, by nature inclined thereto, O Lady, in this dread hour intercede for me, O Helper Invincible!

"Great terror now imprisoneth my soul, trembling unutterable and grievous, when forth from the body it must go: Comfort thou it, O All-undefiled One..."

Daniel leans down, hugs his father and whispers words into his father's ear. Meanwhile, Father Ephraim continues with his prayers, his voice rising louder and stronger.

"... The assembly of the crafty, gaping, has compassed me round about, and seek to bear me away and bitterly torment me. Crush thou their teeth and jaws and save me, O Pure One."

"For as an organ of speech I am altogether extinguished, and my tongue is bound, and mine eye closeth. In contrition of heart I entreat thee: O my Deliverer, save me."

"Turn not from me thy many bounties; shut not the bowels of thy love toward mankind, O Pure One: but intercede for me now, and in the hour of judgment remember thou me."

"Christ is my strength, my God, and my Lord, the august church doth sing in God-befitting wise, crying aloud and out of a pure mind keeping festival unto the Lord."

"Appoint thou now a washing for sin, a stream of tears, O Good One, receiving the contrition of my heart. In thee have I set my hope, O Good One, when thou deliverest me from frightful fiery torment; for as much as thou art the Fountain of Grace, O Birth-giver of God."

"O Refuge which maketh not ashamed, and infallible unto all who are in need, Lady all-undefiled, be thou my defender in the hour of trial."

"Stretch forth, O All-pure One, thine all-honourable hands, like unto the wings of a holy dove, under whose protection and shelter cover thou me, O Lady."

"Glory to the Father, and to the Son, and to the Holy Spirit."

"O Conqueror and Tormentor of the fierce Prince of the air, O Guardian of the dread path, and Searcher of these vain words, help thou me to pass over unhindered, as I depart from earth."

"Now, and ever, and unto ages of ages. Amen."

"Lo, terror is come to meet me, O Lady, and I fear it; lo, a great ordeal hath seized hold upon me, wherein be thou my helper, O thou Hope of my salvation..."

"... To the holy and honourable arms of the holy angels transfer me, O Lady; that covered with their wings, I behold not the ignominious and revolting and gloomy forms of devils."

"Now, and ever, and unto ages of ages. Amen."

"O All-honourable Abode of God, grant unto me the heavenly, the super sensual abode, after that thou hast kindled my expiring and unradiant light by the holy oil of thy mercy."

"Arise, O my soul, O my soul, why sleepest thou? The end draweth near, and thou must speak. Arise, therefore, from thy sleep, and Christ our God, who is in all places and filleth all things, shall spare thee."

"The devil, when he beheld the healing of Christ thrown open, and the health which flowed therefrom unto Adam, being sore smitten as it were with a calamity, wailed and cried unto his friends: What shall I do unto the Son of Mary? The Bethlehemite, who is in all places and filleth all things, doth slay me..."

Daniel watches as his Father's eyes stare past him. The grip on Daniel's hand loosens. Tears well up in Daniel's eyes and fall to the floor below. Behind him, he hears those in the room sob. His stomach sinks. *He is about to leave us. I don't want him to go.* He continues to caress the back of his hand. *I hope you can feel this and bring you some comfort.*

"... The night of death, gloomy and moonless, hath overtaken me, still unready, sending me forth on that long and dreadful journey unprepared. But let thy mercy accompany me, O Lady."

"Lo, all my days are vanished, of a truth, in vanity, as it is written, and my years also in vain; and now the snares of death, which of a truth are bitter, have entangled my soul, and have compassed me round about."

Each breath he takes is softer. Daniel can't tell if he is breathing.

"... Not one have I found who grieveth over my affliction, or who comforteth me, O Lady: For all my friends and acquaintance have now abandoned me. But do thou, O my Hope, in no wise forsake me."

"Out of the flames thou didst shed forth dew upon the Godly Ones, and with water didst kindle the sacrifice of the Righteous One. For thou doest all things which thou willest, O Christ. Thee will we exalt unto all the ages."

"Vouchsafe that I may escape the hordes of bodiless barbarians, and rise through the abysses of the air, and enter into Heaven; and I will glorify thee forever, O holy

Theotokos."

"O thou who didst bear the Lord Almighty, banish thou far from me when I come to die, the chieftain of bitter torments who ruleth the universe; and I will glorify thee forever, O holy Theotokos."

"Glory to the Father, and to the Son, and to the Holy Spirit."

"When the last great trumpet shall sound unto the frightful and dread Resurrection of the Judgment Day, and all shall rise from the dead; then remember thou me, O holy Theotokos."

"Now, and ever, and unto ages of ages. Amen..."

Tears stream down Daniel's face, his words break, his whispers grow louder "Oh dad. How much I will miss you. You have been a great dad, father-in-law, husband and grand dad. You have helped so much throughout my life; making me a better man so I can be a good husband and father. Like St. Paul, you have fought the good fight, your reward is at hand. Go rest, be with mom, be in the comfort of the Lord. I love you Dad. One day, we will all be together again."

At that moment, John Roza closed his eyes and gave his last breath. They all wept.

While holding back his tears, Father Ephraim continued with prayers.

"O Lord God Almighty, the Father of our Lord Jesus Christ, who willest that all men should be saved, and should come unto the knowledge of the truth; who desirest not the death of a sinner, but that he should turn again and live: We pray thee and implore thee, absolve thou the soul of thy servant, John, from every bond, and deliver him from every curse. Pardon his transgressions, both of knowledge and of ignorance, both of deed and of word, which he hath committed from his youth up, and hath cleanly confessed or hath concealed, either through forgetfulness or through shame. For thou alone loosest those things which are bound, and guidest aright the contrite, and art the hope of the despairing, and mighty to remit the sins of every man who putteth his trust in thee. Yea, O Lord, who lovest mankind, give thou command, and he shall be released from the bonds of the flesh and of sin; and receive thou in peace the soul of this thy servant, John, and give it rest in the everlasting mansions, with thy Saints; through the grace of thine Only begotten Son, our Lord and God, and Savior Jesus Christ: with whom also thou art blessed, together with thine all-holy, and good, and life-giving Spirit, now, and ever, and unto ages of ages. Amen..."

"... Therefore we pray unto thee, the Father who is from everlasting, and immortal, and unto thine Only begotten Son, and unto thine all-holy spirit, that thou wilt deliver John from the body onto repose, entreating, also, forgiveness of thine ineffable goodness if he in any wise, whether of knowledge or in ignorance, hath offended thy goodness, or is under the ban of a priest, or hath embittered his parents, or hath broken a vow, or hath fallen into devilish imaginations and shameful sorceries, through the malice of the crafty demon: Yea, O Master, Lord our God, hearken unto me a sinner and thine unworthy servant in this hour, and deliver thy servant, John, from this intolerable sickness which holdeth him in bitter impotency, and give him rest where the souls of the righteous dwell. For thou art the repose of our souls and of our bodies, and unto thee do we ascribe glory, to the Father, and to the Son, and to the

Holy Spirit, now, and ever, and unto ages of ages. Amen"

Father Ephraim finishes and anoints Daniel's father with holy oil.

"He looks so peaceful, Daniel." Lydia holding onto him.

"He does."

"He was ready, that's why. Right, Father?" Jonah speaking from the corner of the room.

"That's right Jonah. Daniel, your Father prepared for his eternal life. He confessed all of his sins. He loves our Lord, and he was ready. Now, he will have a good account and be with your mom and all the saints." Father removes his robe and packs his bag. Before closing it, he grabs the Psalter.

"Now, you must take turns reading the Psalter until your dad leaves. And once he is released from the funeral home, you must continue reading." He hands the book to Daniel.

"Lydia and I will take turns."

"Don't forget about me Daniel, it would be a blessing if I could read as well."

"Of course Jonah."

For the next hour, they read the Psalter until people from the funeral home picked his body up. Jonah insisted on escorting Daniel's father to the funeral home and continued to read the Psalter. He read over him on the ride over, into the funeral home, until the point he could no longer follow him.

✻ ✻ ✻

The next two days were the Trisagion service in

the evening, then the funeral service the following morning. Daniel did not cry at his father's funeral. He was at peace, knowing his father was on his way to be with the Lord. His last prayers were given at the graveside. Father Ephraim, along with a few from the choir, and mourners left, leaving only Daniel and Lydia.

"It was a beautiful service Daniel." Lydia standing with her arms wrapped around Daniel.

"Yes it was, it's just us now. I pray I can be as peaceful when I go as he was. That was his last and most important lesson he taught me. I love you Dad."

Daniel kissed the gravestone and held Lydia's hand as they walked back to the limousine.

CHAPTER EIGHT

Standing at the top of the stairs, Daniel looks out onto the church grounds. Everything appears altered. The blues of the skies and green of the grass are muted. A new feeling has emerged. One of loneliness, increased responsibility and, after putting a flower on top of his father's casket, his mortality.

"Hi Daniel, how are you? It's been awhile since your father's passing." Father Ephraim asks walking out of the church.

Daniel rubs his eyes and focuses on the rhododendrons. The red blooms aren't as brilliant today.

Daniel walks down the steps and heads for the flowers. Father Ephraim follows.

Daniel reaches down and picks a flower off the plant. He brings it in close. It reminds him of all the beautiful flowers that surrounded his father's casket and the one he laid on his gravestone. He holds it up, and the color is vivid red once again.

"Father, why was my dad's passing so easy compared to my mom's?

Father Ephraim smiles. "It's because he did the work. He confessed his sins, he gave alms, he volunteered. His entire focus changed from today to eternity. It was very difficult for him at first, especially confession. But after each confession, he trusted me more. He felt better, like a weight lifted off his chest. And with that, they had nothing on him."

"Who is that, father?"

"The demons. Let's just say your dad took the expressway to Heaven. He isn't the first. I witnessed many painful bedside deaths, similar to your mother's. But once people got it, understood the message, they are passing in gentle peace. And it is beautiful."

Daniel sighs. "It seems you are the only one leading the church this way. I've heard other priests try what you are doing, but fail when the some in the parish bully them to keep quiet. We are very fortunate to have you."

"It is difficult being priest these days, Daniel. Especially a priest that keeps the Word. We are fighting evil from the outside, secularists, emerging church leaders, purpose driven leaders and other heretics trying to define who God is to justify their immoral behavior, gain attendance and sell books. Then there are those in the congregation who are stuck worshiping material things. It's good they are here trying, but many leave once they are uncomfortable. Then my bosses; many who are from different countries and gravitated to pushing the state's so-called morality. When I was a new priest, the head priest tried their way, and it was a complete failure; spiritually and financially. The people who come to church and see a priest trying to straddle both worlds, lose faith, and walk away searching for an honest church."

"Are you still having issues with that Deacon from New York? Deacon Lazarus?"

With hands clasped behind his back, Father Ephraim

looks down and kicks a small rock ahead.

"He is no longer Deacon. He's been elevated to priest. And yes, he continues to pester the head of the diocese to remove me."

"Well, it better not happen. I can't imagine how much that would hurt the church if you were removed."

"Thank you. I think I'm fine for now. And it's something I can't control or worry about, anyway. If it happens, well, as we say, it's God's plan."

"How is your job? I've noticed you've missed church quite a bit since your father's memorial."

"Yes, I am traveling a lot. Especially between Austin and San Antonio, business is booming. So many companies moving into the area."

"Just make sure you spending time in the right places. You don't need to make every sale. And if you stay away too much from home, from your church, you lose sight of what is important, which allows for more temptations. Be careful."

A light grin appears on Daniel, then vanishes.

"I will try, Father. So, um, how is Jonah doing? I haven't seen him since I arrived."

"He's over at the monastery, helping the nuns clear out brush on the property and will be back here tomorrow. Jonah's been a blessing helping at the church. And his story has brought over many converts, especially atheists."

As they turn the corner of the church, they see a car winding down the long drive into the church. A late model black sedan, dust and dirt from the driveway kicking up behind the car.

"I think it is the Metropolitan. I wasn't expecting him for another couple of weeks."

The Metropolitan makes it to the small parking lot. Walking towards Father Ephraim and Daniel, he waves, "Hi Father." As if the priest and Daniel had not seen him make his entrance.

"Come Daniel. Let me introduce you to him."

Daniel follows Father over.

"Hi Metropolitan." They exchange the kiss of peace on each cheek.

Daniel leans down and kisses the hand of the Metropolitan.

"Metropolitan, this is Daniel, one of our parishioners here. He has been with us for over a decade. He has a wonderful wife, Lydia, and three adorable children. We were just finishing up here."

"It is nice to meet you, Daniel." The Metropolitan speaks in his Russian accent.

Daniel can't help but notice the Metropolitan has two ways about him. One of peace and the other, ready for battle with a watchful eye. His gray beard spilling from his face to half way down his chest, accented by his black eyebrows. His hair is in a wavy black and gray pony tail. He could have descended from the monastery on Mt. Athos.

"Daniel, I need to speak with Father Ephraim alone. Will you please excuse us?"

"Of course, I was heading home. Father, thank you for everything."

"Father Ephraim, have you heard the news?"

"No, what are you talking about?"

"Father Lazarus, he is moving to Texas. He is taking over the large church in Dallas."

"How did that happen? Why did you bring him down here?"

"It's been going on behind the scenes. Several of the prominent members of the church and on the Parish Council were from Buffalo and Syracuse. They adore Father Lazarus from their time at those churches. Once their priest retired, they assured Father he would be his replacement."

"That's not how it works. You can tell them no."

"I tried, but they were threatening to take the church away and align themselves under the Antiochian church. There are over five hundred families there. I can't let them leave. That is not fair to the people. But, with Father down here under my jurisdiction, I can show him the errors of his way and help set him straight."

"I pray you are right."

"One other thing, he wants to meet you."

"What? Why?"

"He wants to meet all the priests in Texas. He thinks it will be helpful for him to get an idea of Orthodoxy in Texas, to make sure he understands the culture here. It will be good for you two to meet."

"Yes. That would be beneficial. Feel free to set it up."

"It's already done. He will be here on Sunday. He plans on serving with you at Divine Liturgy.

"I am truly being tested." Father jests.

"Father Ephraim, everything is going to be fine."

"You're right. It will give him an opportunity to meet the people of the parish and understand our message. Maybe being up close and personal with our church, he will change his opinion of us."

"You have a wonderful community here Father, I'm sure he will come around once he has served here."

CHAPTER NINE

Daniel enters two addresses into his navigation system, the first stop at the headquarters of Hill Country Kitchen and Cookware, then CATI Riverwalk hotel. He has two routes to choose from his home. South on Highway 35 or the take the back roads and enjoy the scenic drive. The scenic drive adds twenty minutes to his drive, he opts for the back roads.

TAP TAP TAP

Daniel looks up from his GPS. It's Lydia holding his wallet.

Daniel rolls his window down.

"Hey sweetheart. You're going to need this. Why don't you come out of the car and give me one more hug and kiss before you go?" Lydia, with mussed hair, wearing a faded church camp t-shirt and shorts.

Daniel jumps out, wraps his arms around her and gives her a tight squeeze. Lydia turns a quick kiss goodbye to a short make-out session.

"Wow, what was that about?" Daniel surprised

"Something to remember me by when you are traveling. I love you."

"Maybe I should stay. I could make up time." Daniel half joking.

"No, I don't need you getting another ticket. I will

wait for you when you get back. Now go sell that cookware store."

Daniel slides back into his car, starts it up, and drives off. Lydia blows him a kiss goodbye.

Winding down the Hill Country roads, not another car in sight. He pushes the speed to over seventy miles per hour. With the moon roof open, his favorite classic rock songs play as he speeds down the road. "Time to destination one hour" his GPS notifies him. "Challenge accepted." Daniel pushes the pedal down, increasing speed to over eighty miles per hour.

He turns the radio off, practicing his presentation to the fields, ranches, cattle, and scrub brush as he races down the road. *I don't want to over rehearse. Need to be fresh.* The local route breaks and the San Antonio skyline comes into view. Daniel enters the highway, where the beauty and peace of the country is overtaken by the dirt, heat, and chaos of the city.

"You have reached your destination." His English accented GPS informs him.

"Fifty-One minutes, I win again." He smiles as he checks himself in the rear view mirror.

* * *

He pushes the number fourteen on the elevator. The elevator creeks as it speeds up fourteen flights. Daniel snickers at the wood-paneled wall and red carpet that decorates the elevator.

He looks over the door and watches the brass arrow move as he passes each floor. Eleven, twelve, fourteen. The elevator stops, shakes, and the door opens. He walks down the hallway that reminds him of an old 1930s movie. Each door with a frosted window with black letters announcing which business, lawyer or accountant was behind it.

Now at the door marked "1467 HCKC". BUZZ, BUZZ, he presses down on the doorbell. He feels the camera above the door check him out. CLICK the door unlocks, Daniel steps into the office.

It still amazes him at how modern the office is. Well-dressed professionals, most in their twenties, occupying cubicles and conference rooms. Boxes of kitchenware stacked in the corner waiting for the staff to try them out, hoping to be ordered and put on their shelves.

A pretty woman a year removed from college walks up and introduces herself. "Hi, I'm Kelly. You must be Daniel with H.E. Commercial Real Estate? Ms. Iris is expecting you." Kelly motions for Daniel to follow her. Daniel obliges. He glances at her backside. He immediately shifts his eyes to find something more innocent. They reach the door. She knocks and hears a faint, "Come in." Before they enter, Daniel reaches down to his left hand and removes his wedding ring, and drops it in his pocket.

"Daniel. Come in, come in. Thank you for meeting me on such short notice. Please take a seat." Daniel sits down in front of her paper-strewn desk.

"Kelly, thank you. So Daniel, as I explained in my email. We recently received an influx of investment capital by a venture group here in town. They are expecting ten new store openings this year, followed by fifty next year and after. The skies the limit."

"Iris, that is great news. As you know, I represent

some of the top retail properties in the Southwest. Where were you thinking of opening your next stores?"

"Our goal is to own the Texas market and build on that. So, we are looking at Austin, Dallas metro, and Houston metro. We want the stores in high end neighborhoods."

"Iris, I spent last week working on this proposal for you. Do you want to review this now, or wait for the staff meeting?"

Iris leans back in her chair and looks at Daniel. She gives him a quick smile.

"For this project, Daniel, it's only me and you. Once we pick the locations, I will bring in the rest of the team. How I see this playing out is you will identify the locations in each area, then we will travel and visit them first hand."

"You want me to go with you? I have colleagues in each area that live and work in those towns. They'll be better at giving you a first hand look."

"Daniel, I trust you. You did such a good job with me, with us, when I was only one store. You get me, you understand the concept. I need you with me. Wouldn't you agree I would be your biggest client?"

"Definitely."

"And, with our projected growth, you would never have to cold call businesses again. And unless something horrible happens, like a nuclear war, you are set for at least the next ten years. No more time wining and dining clients only to lose out and start over. What do you think?"

Memories of days at the desk cold calling businesses, getting hung up on, stood up at dinner, or deals falling through flood his mind.

"Iris, that all sounds great. As long as you know my limitations, I am 100% dedicated to Hill Country Kitchen, becoming the number one cookware retailer in the country."

"That's what I wanted to hear. Now I have several meetings I need to attend this afternoon. Where are you staying?" Her green eyes smile.

"Oh, at the CATI. First time there."

"They have a nice restaurant right on the Riverwalk. How about we meet tonight around seven and you can walk me through the proposal?" She stands up from her desk, already knowing Daniel will say yes.

"That sounds great. I will see you later." He puts out his hand and shakes hers.

* * *

"Honey, I did it. I landed the cookware store account. This will be huge for us."

Daniel hears Lydia scream with excitement on the other end of the phone. In the background , he hears Paulina their youngest yell, mimicking her mother.

"I knew you could do it. So no more late nights wooing clients or burning yourself out by hunting down new accounts?"

"Yep, it looks like those days are finally over. However, because they want to expand all over the Texas and nationwide, I will have to travel a lot and show them the locations."

"That's alright. It will give you a chance to get to know the state outside of Austin. Maybe you can find a great place for the two of us to vacation to."

Paulina screams and giggles louder in the

background. "Well, in about ten years." Lydia says.

"I am so glad you are alright with the traveling. I thought you would be upset by it."

"No, never. Do what you have to do. Keep them happy. It's not like you are going away for months on end. We will be fine."

"I love you so much. You are the best." Daniel wishing he was back home, hugging and kissing her.

"Me too. So, what are your plans tonight?"

Daniel waits for a moment.

"I have a dinner meeting with Ms. Iris to go over the proposal in further detail."

He hears her laugh.

"You don't actually call her Ms. Iris, do you? She is our age."

"Not to her face. I guess it's the Texan in me."

"Is her husband, the chef, going to be there?"

"No. I guess they divorced last year. No one knows why. He seemed like a good guy."

"That's too bad. You know God hates divorce."

"I know."

"Well, don't pry. Keep things on the business level."

"Agreed. I need to get ready. I love you and I will talk to you tomorrow."

"Love you too. Bye."

* * *

At the outdoor table for two, Daniel takes a sip of his cold bottled water. He reviews his proposal one last time.

"Hi Daniel, this is a wonderful spot, isn't it?"

She looks down at him, with her long butterscotch-blond hair hanging down past her chin, with a slight curl inward framing her open blouse.

He can't help but notice the black laced bra peering through the shirt opening. He stands up and pulls out the chair for her to sit.

"Thank you, Daniel, but that wasn't necessary."

"My apologies, just the way my parents raised me."

She takes a quick peek at the menu, verifying they still offer her favorite drink. She places the menu back on the table, looks Daniel over. Not saying a word.

Daniel, feeling her eyes on him, reaches for the proposal and puts it in front of her. She pretends not to notice and continues to stare at him.

"Are you ready to order?"

The waiter stands at their table with pen and order book in hand.

"I'll have a French 75." Says Iris

"And for you, sir?"

"I will take a bottle of whatever light beer you have. If Texan, the better."

"Beer drinker?" Iris relaxes her gaze.

"I'm not a big drinker. I used to be, but I have recently taken it easy."

"Why is that?"

"It was effecting my, um, job performance."

"That makes sense. I like a nice drink after work. Helps me unwind. But the days of staying out late and partying are over. I think that led to my divorce. Actually, it is what led to it."

"I'm sorry to hear that."

"Between my business growing and his restaurant taking off, there was a lot of alcohol present to cure the ills that come with success. He was a mean drunk, said a lot of hurtful things. And for me. It got out of hand. I was... I don't mean to bring this up. Let's talk shop." She takes the proposal and flips through the pages. She starts at the back page with the financials. She smiles at what she sees.

"You're sure about these numbers, Daniel?"

"Yes, we can lock you into these interest rates and financing for short and long-term lease agreements. And we have several standalone locations with options to buy. Not only are you making money off the retail, but you own the land. And with all areas of Texas becoming more in demand, property is an excellent investment."

They continue to drink and pour over the proposal. Iris becomes more animated after each drink, telling Daniel of how she thought of the Hill County concept while working in housewares at the mall department store. She overheard two older women discuss how there wasn't a housewares store that understood the Texas woman. That they would even settle for something that targeted the Southern woman. That night she ran into the store, bought an $.88 one hundred page notebook and used ten pages to draft the concept and business plan for her store. She took the proceeds from the sale of her car and savings for a down payment on a house to buy the inventory and rent for her first store in downtown Fredericksburg.

"Yes, I remember when you called me. I couldn't understand what you were saying. You were so excited by the vacant space I was representing." They both laugh.

"Well, it was the perfect spot, I didn't want to lose it. And either you were a customer focused agent or poor, but you high-tailed it over and we had the paperwork completed by midnight."

They continued to laugh about past times and discuss the future of her company and how Daniel will be a big part of their success. At one point, he thought she was going to ask him to join the company. But instead, she asked,

"So Daniel, I have to ask. Why aren't you married? Don't mind me saying this, but you are a handsome man."

Daniel adjusts in his seat. He recalls his training when his sales manager, prior to calling on their first account, said, "Daniel. Here's a tip. Never wear your wedding ring on sales calls to women. You're a young, good-looking guy, and if one of these women thinks they have a chance with you, the better possibility to close the deal." This unwritten sales technique allowed Daniel to flirt with his clients, take them out for drinks, get close to them, but never more than the occasional touch on the arm or leg. But now, here he is. He can tell she has an interest in him. If he tells her the truth, he could lose the deal. If he doesn't, how long can he keep up the charade?

"I told you this before Iris, it's personal, and I'd rather not talk about it." He peels the label off the beer bottle.

"By the way, I see how you look at me and the younger girls in the office. I know you aren't gay. So were you hurt? Who hurt you?" She leans forward and grabs his hand. She strokes his thumb with hers.

"It's not that. It's complicated." He continues to let her hold his hand. His heart beats faster. He looks into her eyes, green with a slight hint of hazel. His eyes move to her lips, then down to her chest.

"Daniel, we will work a lot together. And sometimes when people work closely, things have a good chance of happening. Can you handle something like that?"

Daniel releases her hand and sips his beer. "Of course, can you?"

She laughs. "I'm a big girl. Now if something starts but goes south, we won't let it affect our business relationship, agreed?"

"Of course." Daniel's head buzzing. *Did I agree to have a relationship with her?*

"The Riverwalk is amazing. I could come and people watch all day. Families, friends, lovers. All types here. And the music. You can't find any better Tejano music than the Riverwalk." She finishes her drink.

"Hungry yet?" Daniel asks

"Not really. I had a late lunch. You know what I would want to do? Is to see what the rooms in the CATI are like. I hear every room has a river view." She looks back at the hotel, exposing her neck.

Daniel can't stop the words from falling out of his mouth.

"I'm on the tenth floor. Would you like to check it out?"

Smiling, "I'd thought you would never ask. Let's go."

They ride up the elevator. Iris grabs Daniel's hand. He sees their reflection in the mirrored walls of the elevator. He doesn't like what's reflected. As the elevator climbs, the floor numbers illuminate to show a reverse countdown. He only has a few floors to tell the truth. He reaches into his pocket, feels the cold gold of the wedding band on his finger tips.

I'm only showing her the room. Nothing else will happen.

The chime of the elevator bell rings, the tenth floor. The doors open, they walk in silence to suite 1010.

He opens the door. In the back of the room she sees the floor to ceiling sliding glass doors with a view of the Riverwalk and the city skyline. She walks straight ahead. Pulls the doors apart, and steps out onto the balcony. The slight breeze pushes strands of her hair over her eyes. She takes her hand and puts her hair behind her ear. She gazes over at Daniel and waves for him to come over.

He approaches her. The city lights shine on her skin and sets a sparkle in her eyes. The breeze presses the shirt against her body, painting every curve. She has a beauty that would work in the rural towns of Texas or with a change in outfit, in any big city.

Daniel walks out onto the balcony. "Now this is a room with a view. You certainly have taste, Daniel." She leans back, elbows resting on the railing. Blouse opening widens. Under her green eyes, Daniel takes notice of light freckles.

"Come closer Daniel. Isn't this beautiful?"

"Yes you are. I mean, yes it is."

He stands in front of her. She grabs him by his shirt and pulls him closer and kisses him. An image of Lydia kissing him earlier flashes in front of his eyes. *This one tastes different, lips feel unfamiliar. There is more passion.* Excited, he brings her in closer. She pushes him into the room and backs him onto the bed. He falls over and lands on his back. He stares up at her, straddling him. She undresses. He drowns in her green eyes.

"Time to rise and shine." She whispers in his ear. She caresses his chest. Daniel hears an unfamiliar voice. He opens his eyes. It was not a dream. His heart sinks. He broke his marriage vow, cheated on Lydia. He committed adultery.

"What's wrong Daniel? Did I wear you out last night?"

Daniel sits up. "I have a lot of work back at the office and have to head out early this morning."

"So love me and leave me then?" She says coldly.

"I mean, I do have to finalize your contracts and I can't do them from here. I..."

"I'm messing with you. I have to get to work too. Wow, I can't believe I have to take the walk of shame. It's been years since anything like this has happened."

"Don't be silly. I will drive you home, give me time to shower."

"How about one more round before you go?" She lays down on her back and pulls him on top of her. He pushes himself up, looks at her and wants to be with her again, but the remorse from last night is so strong he cannot start something new.

"I wish I could, but I need to get moving."

She wraps her legs around his torso and draws him in, not letting him go.

"It will be worth it. Trust me." She pulls him down and kisses him.

Trying to clean her scent off of him, he washes his body and hair twice.

While combing his hair, he can't bring himself to look in the mirror. He wants to punch it, punch himself.

The car ride to her house is quiet, Iris taking a quick nap, Daniel wondering how he will manage two relationships. One with his wife and now his mistress.

CHAPTER TEN

Father Ephraim looks up from the altar while preparing for Sunday's Divine Liturgy. He sees a tall, imposing figure walking in the shadows of the church. He watches as it stops, turns, and heads to the rear of the church. As it passes by the candle stands, the flames flicker. The figure walks to the back wall and pauses at the icon of the Last Judgment. The sunlight from the church window shines a dim halo around the figure. It now turns and walks towards the altar.

As the figure comes closer, Father Ephraim makes the figure out. It is a man with jet black hair and beard. He has thick eyebrows that almost connect. It distracts from his coal-black eyes.

Father Ephraim recognizes the man from pictures.

"Father Lazarus, welcome to Christ The Savior." Father Ephraim greets the priest with a kiss of peace.

"I hope your drive here from Dallas was uneventful."

Father Lazarus looks around the modest church and smirks.

"It was. It took longer than expected. I was hoping to get here earlier to help you prepare."

Father Lazarus says as he looks past Father Ephraim.

"That is very thoughtful, but I have it under control. Reader George will be here soon to help. I was thinking, maybe you can be the lead priest today, and I will be your assistant."

The tall priest walks around the altar area. He tries to find something out of place.

"Are you sure? I don't have a sermon prepared."

"That is alright, just speak from your heart. There are times I have something prepared, then right when I am about to speak, a whole new thought lights up, and different words fall from my mouth. I speak of something different."

Father Lazarus stops at the edge of the solea, looks over the empty nave.

"Thank you Father Ephraim. It will be a blessing to lead today."

At 10 am the church bell rings and the congregation makes their way in. Last to enter are Jonah, Lydia and her children.

Father Lazarus moved Liturgy along at a quick pace. The choir increased their tempo to match the priest in his petitions. With a booming voice, the priest jumped in several times when he felt the choir was not keeping up with him. Father Ephraim gave the choir director a look of "it will be OK."

After the Epistle reading, Father Lazarus, peering from the gold covered bible, read the scripture for the day Luke 12:49-12:59:

"I came to send fire on the earth, and how I wish it were already kindled. But I have a baptism to be baptized with, and how distressed I am till it is accomplished. Do you suppose that I came to give peace on earth? I tell you, not at all, but rather division. For from now on, five in one house will be divided: three against two, and two against three. Father will be divided against son and son against father, mother against daughter, mother-in-law against her daughter-in-law and daughter-in-law against her mother-in-law.

Then he also said to the multitudes, "Whenever you see a cloud rising out of the west, immediately you say, 'A shower is coming;' and so it is. And when you see the south wind blow, you say, 'There will be hot weather': and there is. Hypocrites! You can discern the face of the sky and of the earth, but how is it you do not discern this time?"

"Yes, and why, even of yourselves, do you not judge what is right? When you go with your adversary to the magistrate, make every effort along the way to settle with him, lest he drag you to the judge, the judge deliver you to the officer, and the officer throws you into prison. I tell you, you shall not depart from there till you have paid the very last mite."

Father Lazarus closes the gold covered bible, holds it high in the air, then places it back on the altar. The congregation sits and Father Lazarus begins his sermon.

He looks around at the congregation and is comforted that they are like the congregation in Buffalo, Syracuse and Dallas. Made up of different nationalities: American, Russian, Ukrainian, Greek, Ethiopian, Egyptian, Mexican, and Asian. Young and old alike. He grabs hold of the large cross that hangs from around his neck.

"My brothers and sisters in Christ. Forgive me. I do not have a prepared sermon for today. But I still wish to speak of today's scripture, if you will allow. In today's scripture reading, Christ is speaking against a lack of discernment and warns of not having wisdom in this world. But what I wish to focus on today is Luke 12:57-12:59. Here, many have misinterpreted this scripture reading as a warning that our souls will be judged in the after life. That the adversary, demons, will take your soul in front of a judge. This is a fantastical way of looking at what happens to our soul after we pass, but that's what it is, fantasy. A fantasy used to scare early Christians, especially those who were pagans, into behaving. To teach something like this in today's world is heretical."

The congregation listens politely to Father Lazarus. But as the sermon progress, many shift and squirm in their seats. Some look at their watches, Sunday's bulletin or the various icons that are painted on the walls. A few who were uncomfortable with his sermon found this to be an opportune to use the restroom.

Father Lazarus continues while Father Ephraim, standing in the back of the altar, looks on, listening to the visiting priest use scripture to criticize his church and how he leads this mission.

"... My brothers and sisters, let's stay away from ancient fables and wrong teachings, and focus on how you live your life as the best Orthodox Christian you can for today. If you do that, then you will have no problems when and if your soul leaves your body. Christ is in our midst."

"He is and always shall be," the parishioners respond in unison.

A couple sitting in the rear of the church look to each other and whisper "Did he say if your soul leaves your body?"

Father Lazarus presses through the remainder of the Divine Liturgy. He administered communion and spoke the departing prayers. Once the service was completed, Father Ephraim addressed the congregation.

"Before we depart, I want to thank Father Lazarus for visiting us today, and leading us in prayer. We pray for his success at St. John the Baptist in Dallas. Father, would you like to say anything?"

Father Lazarus steps out in front of the congregation, crosses himself and clears his throat. "Thank you Father Ephraim. You have a beautiful church filled with beautiful people. When I read about the tremendous growth at Christ The Savior, I was skeptical. But being here today, I can see how. I leave you with this. When you depart from church today, make sure you read scripture throughout the week. Read scripture to learn and prepare. I will give you some homework. Read Matthew 7:15-20, Acts 20:29, 1 John 4:1 and 2 Peter 2:1. God Bless you and have a blessed week."

"Thank you again, Father Lazarus and yes, we all need to be watchful."

The parishioners form a line and proceed down the middle of the church, kiss the golden blessing cross that Father Lazarus is holding, take a piece of bread and exit. As the congregation flows out of the church, Father Ephraim and Father Lazarus are the only two that remain.

"Father Lazarus, why beat around the bush? Why hide your criticism of our church behind vagueness and citation of scripture? You should have come right out and said what you thought. We can handle it here. And you would not be the first."

Father Lazarus says nothing. And walks past the other priest. He takes off his robe and packs up his belongings.

"Father Ephraim, before I entered the church, I prayed for God to give me strength and to hold my tongue. Your parishioners don't know better, and I certainly would not embarrass you in front of them. I think you could be a good priest, but you are way off in your approach, boarding on heresy. You preach fantasy and fairy tales about the after life. We don't know what happens after we die. Even our Lord and Savior. Who died and returned. What did he say about the after life, our souls, when he returned? Nothing."

"Father Lazarus, you are wrong in John 14:30, "I will no longer talk much with you, for the ruler of this world is coming, and he has nothing in Me."

Luke 12:20 "But God said to him, "Fool! This night your soul will be required of you; then who will those things be which you have provided?",

Luke 12:58, Luke 16:22-23 "So it was that the beggar died, and was carried by the angels to Abraham's bosom. The rich man also died and was buried. And in being in torments in Hades, he lifted up his eyes and saw Abraham afar off, and Lazarus in his bosom."

Luke 18:1-8, the parable of the tenacious widow,

Ephesians 2:2 "in which you once walked according to the prince of the power of the air, the spirit who now works in the sons of disobedience and 6:12-13 "for we do not wrestle against flesh and blood, but against principalities, against powers, against the rulers of the darkness of this age, against spiritual hosts of wickedness in the heavenly places."

How about Colossians 2:15 "Having disarmed principalities and powers, He made a public spectacle of them, triumphing over them in it."

Hebrews 9:27 "And as it was appointed for men to die once, but after this the judgment,"

1 Peter 5:8 "Be sober, be vigilant; because your adversary the devil walks about like a roaring lion, seeking whom he may devour.."

Jude 1:9 "Yet Michael the Archangel, in contending with the devil, when he disputed about the body of Moses, dared not bring against himself a reviling accusation but said "The Lord rebuke you."

Should I continue, Father? Let's discuss the Old Testament:

Isiah 3:12 "O my people, your punishers gather you, and those who make demands of you rule over you." Psalm 7:1-2 "Save me from all who pursue me, and deliver me, Lest like a lion he snatch away my soul,"

Psalm 21:20-21, "But you, O Lord, do not remove Your help from me; Attend to my aid. Deliver my soul from the sword And my only begotten from the hand of the dog."

Psalm 118:80 "Let my heart be blameless in your ordinances, That I may not be disappointed, and

Psalm 123:4-5. "Do good, O Lord, to the good, and to the upright in heart; But those who turn aside to crooked ways, The Lord shall lead away with the workers of lawlessness."

Father Lazarus walks closer to Father Ephraim and stands toe to toe. "Father Ephraim, your idea of scaring your congregation to grow your church will fail. How are you going to compete with the new churches opening all around you? They preach of hope and how to live a purpose driven life. They have a message that helps people live for today. It's just a matter of time before your congregation tires of you and tries out the new church down the road."

"Father Lazarus, I'm getting tired of this conversation. But my job as priest is the prepare each parishioner for their eternal life. That is how I am judged. Not by how many in my congregation I had felt good about this life when they walked out the door on Sunday morning. If you want to be a part of that, then I would suggest you reconsider being an Orthodox priest. Now, I have to prepare to hear confessions. I would be happy to hear yours."

"Father Ephraim, be careful what you say to me and how you say it. I was hoping my visit today would have brought on a friendship amongst brothers, but sadly, it looks like we will be in disagreement. It is a good thing Texas is a huge state."

Father Ephraim watches as his brother priest gets into his car and heads out the parking lot. Jonah walks up from behind the church. "So, Father, what did you think?"

Father watches as the last of the car disappears from his view. "I think we are in for some trouble, Jonah."

CHAPTER ELEVEN

The drive home takes longer than usual. Daniel, lost in thought. How exciting his time with Iris over the weekend was, but now what will he tell Lydia? Will he tell Lydia?

This can't last forever. You can't carry on two relationships. You need to tell Iris right away that you can't sleep with her again. That this is strictly a working relationship.

He continues down the back roads. *I don't deserve this.* He says as he views God's treat; the beauty of the Texas Hill country.

Are you going to tell Lydia? If you do, you could lose her and your family. And even if she stays, it will eat at her and there is no way she will let you continue to work with Iris. You will be back to square one. The misery of trying to secure another account to make up for business lost. Back to the cold calling, wining and dining, and late nights competing against younger rookie agents.

He battles with himself for the remainder of the ride home. *Should I or shouldn't I?* He reaches the neighborhood, pulls around the corner and sees his house. Sitting at the top of the porch is Lydia reading the Children's bible to Paulina, their youngest. *I won't tell. I can't.* Lydia sees Daniel's car. Excited, she closes the bible, stands up with Paulina and descends from the porch steps and walks fast to the car.

Daniel gets out and receives a big hug from Lydia and he feels Paulina hug his legs. "Daddy's home."

Daniel looks at Lydia. He finds her more gorgeous than ever. *How could I have cheated on her? What was I thinking?*

"Hey sweetheart, we missed you. How did everything go? I tried to call you last night, but you never answered the phone."

"I'm sorry. The meeting ran late and by the time I got back to the hotel, I didn't want to call and wake you up."

"That's OK, I'm so happy you are home." They walk inside and Daniel heads to the bedroom to unpack. His stomach tightens. He salivates, and runs to the bathroom and, right in time, finds the toilet to throw up in. He wipes his face and the water from his eyes."

Lydia, hearing Daniel, runs into the bathroom to find him sitting by the toilet.

"Daniel, what happened?"

Unable to look into her eyes, "Must be a bug or something I ate. I'm fine now."

Lydia puts her arm out, Daniel grabs her hand and she pulls him off the floor. He walks over to the sink, gargles mouth wash and spits it out. He looks into the mirror and sees Lydia standing behind him.

"So tell me about your meeting? How is Iris? Are you sure you are her exclusive agent?"

"So far, but it was a productive meeting. The numbers are solid and this is going to be big for everyone involved."

"Did you tell your manager yet?"

"Not yet, I will. Soon as I go back into the office tomorrow." Daniel moves into the bedroom. He opens his suitcase the scent of Iris's perfume touches his nose. *It must be on the shirt I wore last night.* He immediately shuts the suitcase.

"Hey, I want to unpack and get our evening started. Iris gave me some great cutlery to try out. How about I make dinner tonight?"

Dinner is done, then the typical evening at the Roza house continues. A family walk around the neighborhood, a little TV watching, Bible reading and they put the kids to bed.

"Hey Daniel, the kids are in bed. You want to finish what we started before you left?"

At first, Daniel smiled, excited by the proposition. "Of course." They walk into the bedroom, close the door and kiss. Daniel's thoughts turn to Iris. About their night together. He's disgusted. W*hat if I got an STD from Iris, and if I sleep with Lydia, I could give it to her? She would find out it is from me, because she would never cheat on me.*

Lydia continues to kiss Daniel and tries to take off his shirt. Daniel stops her. "I'm sorry honey, I need to sit down. My head hurts."

"Are you giving me the 'I have a headache' excuse?" Lydia laughs.

"I want to be with you, but my head has been killing me the entire ride home. It did go away, but now it is back with a vengeance."

"We can just lay down together and talk. We can always be together another night." Lydia says.

They lay on the bed and stare at the ceiling. Lydia talks about the weekend.

"During this weekend, I got an uneasy feeling, Daniel. It was very strange."

Daniel took a deep breath. And waited for her next sentence.

"That new priest from Dallas came down. A Father Lazarus. I could sense there was tension between him and Father Ephraim."

"Really, how?"

"There were a couple of times Father Lazarus made inferences to Father Ephraim, not doing things right. That he was some sort of heretic."

Daniel sits up. "You are kidding me? He comes into our church and disrespects the head priest. I'm glad I wasn't there. I don't know if I would have kept my mouth shut. What did Jonah do?"

"Jonah kept quiet. It wasn't until after Father Lazarus left he realized something happened."

Daniel laid back down, Lydia rolled over and put her head on his chest. She could hear his heartbeat. She grabbed his hand and held it. "I love you Daniel."

Daniel, upset that his infidelity has ruined this moment. "I love you too." Daniel strokes her long hair. Everything he does with her or for her, from here on out, is tarnished.

"Daniel, is there anything else bothering you? Anything you need to tell me?" Lydia sensing that there is more than the headache.

This is your time to come clean. Let her know. Get it over with. She will find out one day.

He spies the family picture on the nightstand.

No, there is too much to lose.

"Daniel. Are you alright?" she says, looking up at him from his chest.

"Um, I'm just realizing that later this week I have to go to Houston with Ms. Iris. I mean Iris. I hate being away from my family."

"That's sweet. But, you have to do what's best for us. And I'm sure in a couple of years, you won't have to travel as often."

"I hope so. I'm OK with Texas, but I wouldn't want to travel out of state."

"Just take it one day at a time. It won't be the same a year from now."

"I guess you are right. Thanks for understanding." He gives her a kiss on the top of her head.

"Daniel, I am here for you... always."

They both drift off to sleep. Daniel has a terrible dream. Standing in a large banquet hall that looks to belong in a medieval castle, Daniel finds himself all alone. He knows he needs to escape, but can't find the door. He swivels his head, looking around the room, and he sees one wooden door that is two stories tall. As he walks towards it, he finds standing in front of it a pitch black being standing on all fours, with upright forearms similar to a gorilla. Its head has two points, and the creature's nose and mouth were protruded out like a muzzle. The creature turns to find Daniel. It spotted him, then gave Daniel a toothy grin and races towards him. Daniel frightened, tells himself to wake up.

"Wake up Daniel, you are going to be late."

Daniel opens his eyes to see Lydia hovering over him. Her deep brown eyes soothes him. But only for a moment. His happiness turns sour, remembering that he had cheated on her.

As his day wore on, Daniel couldn't help to wonder about the figure in his dream. *Was it just my imagination or was it a demon? Was it guilt that manifested itself into the figure? It was only a dream.*

On his way to the office, his phone rings. The caller ID shows "Iris".

"Hi Iris, how are you this morning?"

"I'm doing great Daniel. How are you feeling? You rested enough to get things moving for me? We have lots to get done."

"Yes, heading to the office now. I will put together a schedule for Houston. I know we have several locations that are just perfect for your stores."

"Here is my idea, Daniel. Our busiest days are Saturday. So from here on out, what I would like is for you to schedule long weekend trips for these site visits. I want to experience the foot traffic, the parking. Who the clientèle is in the day and night. I know you are workaholic like me, so I don't expect weekends will be a problem, do you?"

Daniel wants to say no, but remembers what Lydia said "Do what's best for the family."

"That makes sense, Iris. We will drive down Friday morning. Stay two nights and come back on Sunday."

"Did you say driving?"

"Yes. It's the same time between driving, then going to the airport, security, rental car, etc."

"That drive wears me out. Let's take the plane, we just have overnight bags, so we can don't have to get to the airport two hours prior. We will risk it and show up 45 minutes early."

"You are the boss."

"Yes, and if we miss the flight, there is one every hour on the hour. Kelly will email you the itinerary and flight information. I will meet you on Friday."

"Sounds great. Bye."

"Bye."

Daniel relieved, nothing about what happened over the weekend was mentioned. No innuendos, no nothing. Strictly business. "I guess I was just a one-night stand, and now we are back to a business only relationship." Daniel hopes.

Back in the office, Daniel researches five properties that will be perfect for Iris to review: The Galleria, The Woodlands, Rice Village, River Oaks, and City Center.

Daniel's phone rings

"Hi, honey. How is everything going at home?

"It's fine. The kids are off to school. So just myself here. It might be time for me to find a job."

"Don't you like helping at the church?"

"I do, but it would be nice to earn some money for us, the college fund. Maybe even a vacation."

"I'm fine with that. But you can afford to be picky. Don't take something you will hate, alright?"

"I won't. So how is your day going?"

"Good, and not so good. What do you want to hear first?

"I will take the good."

"I found some excellent properties in Houston to show Iris. It shouldn't take many trips there to find something."

"That's great. What's the not so good?"

"She wants to conduct site visits on the weekends. Starting this Friday. She says she wants to see the areas in person for herself, when they are the busiest."

"That makes sense, Daniel. I hate you will be gone and miss church again, but it's not every weekend. So, it's fine by me."

"You are wonderful. What's nice is that after I finalize these appointments I can come home early from work. No more long nights entertaining clients. I love you."

"I love you too, Daniel."

Daniel puts his phone down. He continues on with his research and builds the portfolio of properties along with their financials.

Daniel's phone rings again. "Jonah"

I don't want to speak with him. Daniel sends Jonah to voice mail. After a couple of seconds, the phone rings again. It's Jonah. Daniel continues to let it ring. The other agents in the cubicles next to him throw wadded up paper balls at him.

"Answer your phone, Daniel!" He hears from all sides.

"Alright! Hey Jonah, sorry I missed you the first time around. What are you up to?"

"Nothing. Missed you at church on Sunday."

"Yeah, I am sorry I had to miss it, too. I was down in San Antonio closing the Hill Country Kitchen and Cookware account."

"Nice job Daniel. It's still owned by that couple. The chef and his wife. She was pretty, from what I can remember."

"It's just owned by her, Iris. She and her husband divorced about a year ago."

"That's too bad. Awful thing about divorce. Hey, we haven't hung out in a while. You want to go out to lunch and catch up?"

"You know what, Jonah? That sounds like a good idea. Let's meet up at noon. Does that work?"

"Perfect, see you then."

* * *

Daniel enters the restaurant and sees Jonah waiting on the bench in the lobby.

"Hey Jonah, sorry I'm late. Just needed to finish something up before I left for the day."

"Did you say you are leaving for the day?"

"Yep. After lunch, heading back home and spending the rest of the day with Lydia and the kids."

"Good for you Daniel. You have been busting your, you know what, for ten years. It's time for a break."

A young, attractive hostess walks up to Jonah and Daniel. "Hi gentleman, are you ready? Booth or table?" She asked with a pleasant smile.

"Yes, we will take a booth." Daniel replies.

She turns and walks toward the booth. Daniel can't help to watch her while she walks. Jonah notices Daniel and lightly hits him on the shoulder.

They slide into the booth. "Daniel, she can't be more than eighteen years old. Twenty tops."

"Who, the hostess?"

"You shouldn't ogle women. It's not good for the soul. And that kind of temptation will bring most men, even church going men, down fast."

"Not a big deal, Jonah. I can't help it. If I see an attractive woman, I will look. That's all. I have a beautiful wife at home. And I need nothing else."

"Well, I hope not. There are sins, but committing adultery? It's a big one. It's a top ten."

"I know Jonah."

"I remember how you used to act on sales calls. You could get very flirty with the women. You would get right up to that line, just far enough to close the deal, then back down. A real master."

"I don't have a good sales game, so I have to use what

I God gave me. I guess."

"Do you still take your wedding ring off?"

Daniel disappointed by the question. Embarrassed that Jonah still remembers his trick.

"Sometimes, not as often. So what's going on with you?"

"I've been busy taking care of the church grounds, helping at the monastery, but I want to do more. Earn more money to give to the church, but also to buy some things."

"What are you considering?"

"I need to a newer car. With the amount of miles I am driving, I need something more reliable. The air conditioning stopped working last week, and in a couple of weeks, the heat will make it unbearable to be in the car. I also would like to save for a house. A little ranch home on some land. Nothing too fancy. I don't enjoy renting.

"Jonah, I am going to have my hands full with the Hill country account. It would be great if you came on board and were a part of the team. You could help with the contracts, which you know I hate. And of course, you can have time off to help at the church and monastery."

"That's a nice offer, but I really want nothing to do with that world. It brings the worst out of me."

"So, what are you going to do? I know you don't get paid that much from the church, and disability will not pay your mortgage."

"I have a couple of opportunities. First, I will work with the Monasteries in Greece in importing religious items like icons, prayer ropes, and books and selling them to church bookstores. And second, I am going to write a book."

"A book? What about?" Daniel takes a sip of coffee.

"My evolution from atheist to Orthodox Christian."

"Evolution? That will sure make the atheists upset."

"It's just a play on words. But, it's time to tell my story. I imagine there are thousands of atheists and agnostics that, deep down, are searching for God, but are afraid and don't know where to search. God is allowing me to use my accident not only to save my soul, but the souls of thousands."

"You do have a wonderful story. I can't wait to read it. But I have a question for you. You know we have never talked about happened to you when you died. But I hope there is enough distance between the accident and now for you to answer my question."

"I guess so. If not, I better figure it out. Because I am expecting questions about my death."

"Tell me about the demons, Jonah."

Jonah sits up from his seat. Takes a sip of his iced cola. His face tenses up. "Going straight for the juggler, Daniel."

"There is a reason I ask."

"Even after ten years, I am still frightened. They were horrible. I mean, I've seen scarier monsters at the movies, but it was their image mixed with the atmosphere they produced. I can only imagine it is the terror a person surrounded by sharks feels. They have their purpose and they want your soul. They snap at you from all directions, accusing of sins you have committed and they even make others up. All of it is believable. So believable that my Guardian Angel had a hard time defending me. And what I know for sure is that if they did not bring me back to life, my soul would be in Hell right now, with millions of other souls in constant sorrow." The intensity of Jonah's eyes leaves.

"Do you think it's possible to see demons while you are alive?" Daniel asks.

"Of course. They are all around us. Why?"

"I had this awful dream, and in the dream was a demon. And it seemed vicious. It looked right at me, showed me its disgusting mouth filled with fangs or razors. It seemed so real. I am thankful Lydia woke me up."

"Daniel." Jonah leans forward and brings his voice down to an almost whisper. "Daniel, demons are real. And you had one in your dream. Most of the time, no one ever sees them in this life. The devil has done a remarkable job of making people believe he doesn't exist, which makes it so much easier for demons to attack us. If you don't understand you have an enemy, why be on the watch for them?" He continues.

"You read the life of saints, in scripture and demons are everywhere, but today, no one mentions them. Why is that? Sure Father Ephraim does. But outside of our church. Other priests...and other church leaders are afraid to discuss them. I think they are spiritually weak and don't want to come across like some religious freak."

Daniel thinks for a moment. "But how? Where are they? Where do they live?" He asks.

"They are in the space, the air, between Heaven and Earth."

"Right above us?"

"Yes, above us, next to us. There are multitudes everywhere. We humans can't see them. But they are there."

"If that's true, it's scary. I know they exist, but I always imagined they occupied another space or dimension."

"You need to go back and read scripture: Ephesians 2:2 "in which you once walked according to the course of this world, according to the prince of the power of the air, the spirit who now works in the sons of disobedience" and Ephesians 6:12 "For we do not wrestle against flesh and blood, but against principalities, against powers, against the rulers of the darkness of this age, against spiritual hosts of wickedness in heavenly places."

"But if they are in the air, how or why did one show up in my dream?"

Jonah pondered about it for a moment.

"They can go anywhere. Remember in Mathew 8:28, the Gergesene demoniacs. When Jesus sent the demons from the man into the swine?"

"I do, but I have a hard time understanding. What does it mean?"

"I couldn't tell you. But it makes me recall Peter 5:8 "Be sober; be vigilant; because your adversary the devil walks about like a roaring lion seeking whom he may devour." If this demon shows up again don't talk to it. Don't engage it. Do not be frightened. But if you do speak with it, be firm."

At that moment a flash of him and Iris entered his mind. *Is the devil making me do it?*

"This is a lot to take in, Jonah. I should speak with Father Ephraim?"

"That would be a good idea."

Daniel stares past Jonah, remembering the sight of the demon. Then his sleeping with Iris.

"Hey Daniel, snap out of it. I want to tell you something. You will find this funny."

"What's that Jonah?"

"It's time I start dating. To find someone to marry."

"Jonah, that's not funny at all. That is wonderful news. Anyone special?"

"Yes. She works down at the monastery. Her name is Maria. She is beautiful. She is new to Orthodoxy. A convert from Catholicism. Her family, most still in Mexico, are very upset with her."

"I can understand. But that's great. So when will we get a chance to meet her?"

"Soon, I'm planning on bringing her to one of the services. But I'd like for both you and Lydia to meet her first. Will you be around this weekend?"

"No, I am in Houston with Iris for some site visits."

"Over the weekend? With Iris? Be careful Daniel."

"It's fine Jonah. She wants to see how the locations are during the weekend."

"If you say so. How does Lydia feel about it?"

"She wants me to do what I have to do, 'cause she knows in the long run it will be the best for the family. Like today, instead of grinding out a day of cold calls, I finished my work. Now I can meet up with my best friend for lunch and go home to spend time with Lydia and the kids."

"It sounds like you have it all worked out. But if you should run into temptation, pray. You can also excuse yourself from any tempting situation by calling me."

"Jonah, I am good. I love Lydia. Iris is attractive, but this is business."

"I will pray for you Daniel."

"You know Jonah. Maybe you should become a

priest."

Jonah bows his head. "Brother, nothing more than I would want to do. But, I'm not worthy."

"Think about it. No, pray. Ask God." Daniel checks his watch.

"I need to head home. I can't wait to meet Maria. Think about it. Let's plan for next weekend?"

For the first time in a while a smile break through Jonah's beard.

CHAPTER TWELVE

"What do you think, Iris?"

Iris and Daniel standing on the city sidewalk in front of the strip mall where her next store will open. "For a car centric city, there is a lot of foot traffic in this location. Most of the shoppers are young professionals and mid-career couples. Perfect demographic for high end cookware."

She walks ahead, Daniel follows behind.

"This is an excellent spot, Daniel. I can envision Hill Country at the end of the building. This might be one of the largest stores we open. Its so big we could build an in-store test kitchen, too?"

"That's a great idea. A test kitchen would be different, really setting your store apart from the competition."

Iris takes Daniel by the hand and walks him over to the empty space. "Daniel, you have the keys. Open the store. I want to show you what I am thinking."

Daniel fumbles for the keys. He opens the door and they walk in. Iris finds herself in the middle of the space. She closes her eyes and imagines the store setup like one large high end kitchen. Cookware on one end, silverware in another, cupware at the other end. She sees young and up-and-coming cooks as sales associates. Their expertise increases the likelihood of the sale. Over in the back is where the test kitchen is to be located. A commercial grade kitchen for customers to try cutting with high end knives, cook with pots and pans, and taste coffee from the latest coffee makers. She opens her green eyes.

"Daniel, this is going to be amazing. I don't care what you need to do. I want this space."

"It's yours. The paperwork is right here. All you need to do is sign the lease agreements."

Iris walks over to Daniel. "I don't see a table to sign the papers."

Daniel looks around, just drywall and a cement floor.

"I guess you are right. We can go to the coffee shop and finish the paperwork there."

"I don't do my business in coffee shops. That's for wannabe writers and entrepreneurs. This deserves something bigger. How about we sign the paperwork in my hotel room? I can order up some room service, steaks, and a bottle of red. How does that sound to you?" She gets close to Daniel, waiting for his answer.

Daniel, in his mind's eye, sees the demon from his dream prowling around the store staring at him. *Did it just smile at me?*

"It sounds like the perfect place to sign the papers. We still have two more properties to view before the day ends."

"Let's do those stores tomorrow. I'm ready for something to eat." She takes Daniel by the hand and leads him out the door.

He opens the door to Iris' hotel room, Daniel shivers. He knows what's coming his way.

"Daniel, let's get down to business." Iris walks ahead of him. Daniel moves to the desk in the hotel room and pulls out the paperwork for signing.

Iris continues on towards the bedroom. "Silly, that's not the business I'm thinking of."

Daniel remembered what Jonah said to him. Say a prayer or call him. He closes his eyes to say a prayer, but couldn't. He wants this.

"*You can do this. You are three hundred miles away from home. She will never find out. Enjoy yourself. Do you see her? She is amazing.*" He hears a voice tell him.

Daniel turns the corner and enters the bedroom. Iris stands at the large window, the Houston skyline behind her. "You ready for this?" She starts to undress.

"Yes." Daniel does the same.

"That's not what I expected, Daniel." Iris relaxing in her robe while drinking a glass of red wine. Feet coolly laid over the arm of the leather chair. Clean dinner plates except the t-bones from the steaks.

Daniel smiles. "What did you not expect?"

"The first time we did it, you were gentle, kind, almost respectful." She giggled.

"But tonight. A lot more passion. You took control. I had no idea where you were going to take me, but when we got there. Oh boy." She takes another sip.

"You are very sexy, and I just couldn't help myself. I really wanted you."

Iris takes the last sip from her glass of wine, stands up and reaches her hand out to pull Daniel up from his chair, but struggles to do so.

"C'mon. It's my turn to take control." She leads him back into the bedroom.

"*You forgot to call her.*" Daniel hears the voice say. His eyes opens wide.

What time is it? He fumbles for his watch on the nightstand. He squints his eyes to read the glowing dots and hands on his watch. "3:13 am"

"Shoot." He rolls over and hears the quiet breathing of Iris. He stares at her, trying to make her out. All he sees once his eyes adjust is the faint light of the city painting her shoulder. He reaches over, strokes her hair, and falls back asleep.

Daniel wakes up early, takes his shower before Iris awakes. He changes and prepares for the day ahead.

He gives Iris a kiss on the cheek. "Hey, time to wake up. I'm going to take a walk outside and get a good cup of coffee. You want something?"

She sits up, brushes her hair back. Even without makeup and uncombed hair, Daniel finds her sexy. "A coffee with a splash of cream and three sugars."

"You got it. Why don't you take a shower and we can get a head start looking at the other properties? We have time to make up."

"Of course." She pulls the sheets around her and heads to the bathroom.

Daniel rides the elevator down to the lobby. The doors open, he heads for the business center. Finds the phone, dials his number, Lydia answers.

"Hey sweetheart. So sorry I didn't call. By the time we finished everything up, it was late, and I didn't want to wake you up."

"I was worried. But, I'm happy that you are alright. Please don't let that happen again."

"I won't. Um, how was yesterday?"

"Pretty good. Guess what?"

"What?"

"I got a job."

"Wow. Just like that."

"Yep, I was in town and walked past the little travel

agency and they had a help wanted sign out front. I said, what the heck, ran in and spoke to the owner. We hit it off. She is going to train me on Monday."

"That's fantastic. You can find some great places we can vacation."

"I'm so excited, I can't wait to start. And get this. She is familiar with Christ the Savior and has been wanting to go to one of our services, but has been hesitant. I told her we are a very welcoming community and for her to come to church tomorrow, and I will introduce her to everyone and Father Ephraim."

"That's great Lydia." Daniel feeling that he is taking too long and Iris might wonder why, hurries Lydia off the phone.

"Well, Iris and I are starting early on the site visits. If I don't get a hold of you tonight, I will see you at home tomorrow. Proud of you in your new job. I love you."

"I love you too."

Daniel hears the click. He heads down the street, picks up his coffee order and returns to the hotel room. When he enters, he sees Iris just finishing getting ready. She is in her weekend Hill Country wardrobe. Jeans, t-shirt with casual vest, and hair pulled back in a pony tail. Just a touch of make up.

"You are truly pretty, Iris." Daniel puts the coffees on the table.

"Stop, you are going to make me blush. And you don't look bad yourself... a tad tired, though. I wonder what that's from?" She laughs.

"Are you ready? Grab the coffee and let's go."

The two visit the remaining sites, the last in the planned community of The Woodlands.

"It's been years since I've been in a mall. I wonder if

my store will work well here."

"This mall is a little different. Here, take a look at the directory. See the stores.? All high-end retail. And notice what is not in the directory?"

"A kitchenware store."

"Correct. And guess what? There is not one in the entire area. This is a growing community of well-to-do oil execs and stay at home moms."

Iris notices the people walking through the mall. It's mostly women with children. But by the clothes they were wearing or the purses they carried, she could tell without looking at the demographic profile this was the perfect location for her store.

"Daniel, is there any of my competition trying to get in here?"

"In speaking with the owner. No. Only the department stores sell the category. But, not the same brands."

"I'm interested. Where is the space located?"

"Follow me."

They walk through the mall, Daniel and Iris could easily be taken for any married couple shopping for the next best thing.

"There it is." Daniel points to the vacant store next to the entrance of the mall. "It has two entrances. From the inside of the mall or from the outside."

"This is a perfect spot. There is exposure to outside foot traffic as well as inside."

"It's a little smaller than the downtown location. But, I don't need the test kitchen here. This is great Daniel."

"So I am five for five? Not bad."

"You did good Daniel. What's next?"

"That's it. Sign the paperwork. Then your store

merchandising team can have access and begin planning the store."

"All right. Let's grab a bite to eat then head back to the hotel."

"This is the last one. Just sign here."

Iris, with a wide smile, signs the contract.

"Daniel, you are excellent at you job and know what you are doing."

"I understand you and your concept. That makes my job easy."

Iris hands the pen to Daniel. When Daniel tries to take it from her, she pulls it back.

"You have to kiss me first."

Daniel leans in for the kiss.

She grabs him by the shirt and pulls him forward. She wraps her arms around him. He does the same, bringing her in tight.

"Let's go to the bedroom." she whispers in his ear.

"*You didn't call her again.*" The voice says.

He opens his eyes. He's in the expansive room. Up against the large door is the demon. It turns to Daniel and snarls. It opens it's slobbering razor toothed mouth and in a gurgling voice mocks him. "You didn't call her Daniel. Didn't even think about your wife. Daniel. I understand you and your concept. That makes my job easy." The demon moves its long gorilla like arms and walks over to Daniel.

Remember what Jonah said. Don't talk to it. Don't engage it. Do not be frightened. But if you do speak to it. Be firm.

"Who are you? Where do you come from?" Daniel asks the demon.

The demon stops. Sneers at Daniel. And runs towards him.

"Wake up, wake up." Frightened. Daniel yells into the room.

"You are not asleep." Iris says to Daniel.

"What?"

"Daniel that was so weird. You were sleep walking Daniel. You stood over me and asked me who am I, and where do I come from?" Iris moves away from Daniel.

"I wasn't speaking to you, Iris."

"No, then who. I am the only one here."

"You wouldn't understand."

"Understand what?"

"Demons."

"The evil spirits. Of course I do."

"I have one that appears to me once in a while. It has always been around me, but for some reason, I saw it."

"Can you tell me more? When did you first see it?"

"The night after we first slept together. It was gloating. It won. And it beat me again this weekend."

"The demon won. By you sleeping with me? I know sex out of wedlock is a sin. But is it that serious?"

"Yes, having sex with someone who is not your wife is adultery, and that is pretty serious." Daniel looks at Iris.

"What are you talking about? Are you married, Daniel?"

Silence.

"Daniel, answer me, are you married?" Iris's green eyes fire up.

"Yes." Daniel whispers.

Iris jumps out of bed.

"How long have you been married? Do you have kids?

Answer me!"

"I've been married twelve years and we have three kids."

"Daniel, what did you do?" Iris' tone deepens.

"I got caught up in the moment. You are so beautiful, so fun to be with. I couldn't help myself."

"So you always cheat on your wife?"

"No, you are the first time. I've flirted, but I never even kissed another woman."

"Daniel, not only did you cheat on your wife, commit adultery, but you fooled me into sleeping with a married man. So now I have committed adultery too." Iris says a prayer under her breath.

"I didn't know you were very religious, Iris."

"When I was younger, I left the church when I met my ex. He was an agnostic. It was stupid. I felt I could change him. But he changed me. He cheated on me with the hostess at the restaurant." Iris looked around the room. At the unmade bed, empty wine glasses, clothes strewn about the floor. She feels sick to her stomach.

Daniel slides out of from the covers, puts his clothes on and sits back down on the edge of the bed.

"So now what, Iris?"

"I don't know Daniel. How could you cheat on your wife? I can't believe I am the other woman. Correct that, I was the other woman. You are lucky I did not develop any feelings for you, otherwise this conversation would be very different."

"So, you aren't pissed?"

"Of course I am. You brought me down into the muck and dirt. Your poor wife. Are you going to tell her?"

"No. I can't lose her or the kids."

"You should have thought about them before you

laid down with me."

"I know. But this is something I need to deal with. I'm the one who has to live with this. Every time I see her. Every time I see you."

"That's a laugh. You think we are ever going to see each other again?"

"Sorry. I understand if you want to end our business relationship."

"No. I told you at the start that our personal relationship would not affect our business relationship. You are still my agent."

"Serious. Thank you Iris."

"I'm keeping you on for many reasons. One, you are good at your job. Two, forgiveness is a virtue. Three, there is no reason I should punish your wife and kids for your sins. And last, you realize that even though you won't tell her, you will not get away with this."

"You are right."

"Now that we are just in a business relationship. You need to get all your belongings and go back to your hotel room. I will meet you down in the lobby at 10:00 am so we can head to the airport."

Daniel collects his clothes and heads out of the hotel room. He leans against the wall in the hallway. *You got lucky.*

The lock on his hotel room door clicks when it shuts. He stares at the empty hotel room. The bed in here is perfectly made, with sheets folded nicely over the comforter. *This is where I should have been last night. Why am I so weak?*

He walks over to the nightstand and pulls out the drawer and finds the Holy Bible. He opens the book, the spine cracking, and pages hard to turn. *I must be the first person to read this one.* He turns to Psalm 51, stands in the middle of the room and prays aloud:

"Have mercy on me. O' God, according to your steadfast love; according to Your abundant mercy blot out my transgressions. Wash me thoroughly from my iniquity, and cleanse me from my sin..."

He finishes the Psalm, closes the Bible and says his own prayer:

"Lord, you know all and have witnessed what I have done. I have only myself to blame. Please help me, give me strength. If my guardian angel has abandoned me please send him back to me and protect me. Lord Jesus Christ, Son of God, have mercy on me a sinner."

PART III

"For we wrestle not against flesh and blood, but against principalities, against powers, against the rulers of the darkness of this world, against spiritual hosts of evil in Heavenly places."

- EPHESIANS 2:2

CHAPTER THIRTEEN

10 Years Later...

"Daniel, Father Ephraim called, and would like for us to see him. He wants to ask us something." Lydia says.

"Sure, do you know when?"

"Today."

"Alright, but I still need to hang the Christmas lights and put the tree up."

"Ask one of the boys. They are big enough to help you out now."

"Yeah, you're right."

Lydia and Daniel walk into the church office and see Father Ephraim behind his desk.

"Hi Father, sorry to disturb you. I know we are a little early."

Father Ephraim looks up from his paperwork.

"No, no. Please come in. I was just working on Sunday's sermon. Please sit down."

"So what can we do for you Father?" Daniel asks

"Have you ever heard of the monks of Mt. Skete?"

They look at each other.

"No, not really. Do they need help?" Lydia asks.

"That is kind of you Lydia. A while back, you had mentioned that now that the kids are older it would be a perfect time to get a dog. Well, the monks raise German Shepherd dogs. And several of the puppies are up for adoption."

Father Ephraim slides pictures of the puppies over to Lydia and Daniel. They are black and tan six week old puppies. Fur balls with big ears and huge paws. Some with no ears up, some with one up and one down, and one with both ears standing up straight up , like perfect triangles.

"They are so cute, Daniel. The kids would be so excited. Father, do you think we could have one here before Christmas? A puppy would make a wonderful present."

"Yes, the monks could handle that. So.."

"Daniel, look at this one here, it is so cute." Lydia points to the black puppy with tan markings, with one ear up and one ear flopped over.

"What do you think, Father?"

Father Ephraim flips the picture over and sees the note F3 6 weeks.

"The notions indicate your puppy is a female, the third of the pack and, at the time of the photo, six weeks. She is yours if you want her."

"Yes Father. Thank you for thinking of our family."

"Lydia, I'm glad I remembered. This puppy is going to be a great addition to your family. And German Shepherds are wonderful family dogs. So smart and protective. I will contact the monks right away."

Daniel looks at the strewn about paperwork on Father Ephraim's desk and sees a note written in his journal. "Lazarus, 2000 diocese."

"Father, is something going on with Father Lazarus?" He points to the note.

"Yes, he is to be elevated to the head of the diocese next year."

"Are you serious? He has been battling you since he arrived in Texas ten years ago. Few people like him. How did this happen?" Daniel asked.

"Daniel, I'm sure it will be alright. Father Ephraim knows how to deal with him." Lydia tries to calm Daniel down.

"I pray with his elevation that it brings him to where he expects he needs to be and takes his focus off of our work here and helps Orthodoxy grow within the diocese."

"Yes, Father. But growth at what cost? To encourage the churches into sugar coating God's message of salvation, redemption, sin and judgment?" Daniel upset.

"Let's pray that is not the case. But don't worry. We will continue our work, and what ever happens is in God's hands. So for now, let's enjoy this time of year. The Nativity season, and prepare for Christ's glorious birth."

"Agreed Father." Lydia and Daniel respond in unison.

"I will let you get on with your day. And I will contact the monks and we expect to receive your new puppy right before Christmas."

"Thank you Father."

* * *

Lydia, Daniel, and the kids finish unwrapping all of their presents. The three children sit around the tree trying out each present, figuring which toy, game, music instrument they will use first.

"Are you ready?" Daniel whispers to Lydia. She nods.

"Hey, kids. I forgot, there is one more present. It's in the garage."

They all look over Daniel with excitement.

He returns carrying a large box. He set it down by the kids.

"It's not wrapped. Come and look see what's inside."

They all drop what they are doing and circle around the box. Liev opens the box and inside, they all look down on a black and tan fur ball, with one ear up, and a red ribbon tied around her neck. The little puppy sees its new family and jumps up the side of the box, trying to get out to meet them.

Daniel reaches inside, pulls the puppy out and sets her on the floor. Immediately, the puppy wiggles and runs to each child, then to Lydia. It runs through the crumpled up balls of wrapping paper, then back to Daniel. The house fills with laughter watching the little puppy run around. It sees a tennis ball, one of Paulina's presents, lying on the floor and tries to put its tiny mouth around it. But fails. After several minutes, the puppy stops, pants. Everyone surrounds the puppy, wanting to pet it. She rolls onto her back.

"It's a girl." Simeon exclaims.

They pet her belly and she runs again. She settles down at the feet of Daniel. He picks her up and puts her on his lap. She places her head in his lap and closes her eyes.

"Daniel, put her back down. You do not want her to turn into a ninety pound lap dog."

"What should we name her?" The kids ask.

"She is German. So maybe a German name." Lydia says.

"And it has to be short, so she understands." She adds.

"How about Heidi?" Their daughter suggests.

"I finished reading a book about a girl named Heidi. She lives in Germany."

"What does everyone think? Should we name her Heidi?"

They all agree and start saying the name Heidi to the little puppy.

RING RING RING

"Hi Lydia, Merry Christmas, Christ is Born!" Father Ephraim says on the other end of the phone.

"Glorify Him. How are you Father?"

"I did not see you or the family at church today and was checking in. I'm guessing it had something to do with the recent addition to the family?"

"Yes, the kids adore her. We just couldn't stand leaving her alone. I hope we had enough people in the choir."

"We did. The church was full. It was a beautiful morning. I am so happy about the new puppy. What is her name?"

"We named her Heidi."

"Wonderful name. I pray that you and the family enjoy one of God's creations. What are the plans for the rest of the day?"

"Jonah and Maria are stopping by for dinner. You are more than welcome to join us."

"I might. Me and Matushka Helen don't have plans. Thank you."

* * *

Dinner is complete, and the adults are eating dessert and washing it down with coffee. All the kids are spending their night away from toys and games, and paying all attention to Heidi.

"She's going to be worn out." Jonah says.

"Not only her, but the kids, too." Lydia adds.

They continue conversations about Christmas and what it means to each of them. They tell of their favorite Christmas' and Maria becomes silent.

"Maria, are you alright?" Father Ephraim asks.

"I don't know. I am troubled, Father."

"What is it?"

"During Christmas and Pascha, I become very homesick. I miss my family so much. But this year is worse. Several days ago, my mother told me that when she dies, she wants to be cremated."

"Don't the Catholics forbid cremation?" Daniel asks.

"The Catholic church still frowns upon the practice, but they've allowed it since the early 1960s." Father Ephraim mentions.

"So why don't we cremate?" Jonah asks.

"For several reasons. We our made in the image of God, therefore we need to treat our bodies with respect. Not just while we are alive, but when we pass. Our bodies are our gifts, that house our souls. We also believe that at the resurrection, God reunites our souls with our perfected bodies. And last, cremation is what pagans do. We've separated ourselves from the pagans since the beginning of Christianity. Although we don't use the term "Pagan" today, our society has grown to embrace paganism, with one symptom being the more and more occurrences of cremation."

Father Ephraim turns to Maria

"Maria, there is still time to speak with your mother and tell her why she should forgo cremation. If you need my help, please let me know."

"Thank you Father."

The night comes to a close and all the guests depart from Daniel and Lydia's home. They come back inside to see the kids laying asleep next to a sleeping puppy.

"Should we wake them?" Daniels whispers.

"No, for tonight, let them be together like this."

* * *

The new year has come, and Father Ephraim is blessing the waters for Theophany. Daniel, Lydia, Jonah, and Maria huddled together, trying to stay warm. Now, Daniel and Lydia's boys serve in the altar, their daughter sings with the choir.

"Jonah, do you remember twenty-seven years ago when we were standing here?" Daniel asks.

"I do, and I am embarrassed by my words."

"What did you say?" Maria asked.

"I was saying hateful things about God. That's when I was an atheist."

"That was the day I saw my wife." Daniel says.

"What are you talking about?" Lydia asks

"Jonah and I were talking. He was asking me if I wanted to leave with him. I was about to say yes, then I saw you running up the stairs into the church. I had to meet you. So I declined Jonah's invitation."

Lydia smiles and gives Daniel a kiss on the cheek. "You are so sweet."

Father Ephraim throws the cross into the river, the boys, dressed in swimsuits, run, jump into the frigid waters, and swim to the cross. One boy who is on the high school swim team reaches the cross first. He swims with it back to shore and gives it to a boy sitting in a wheel chair.

Father Ephraim and the procession walk past the four friends and they follow inside. The parishioners pack the church with many unable to enter. Father Ephraim's message of repentance has grown the church year after year. And this is the year they agreed to expand the size of the church building.

Once the faithful return to church, Father Ephraim begins his message.

"My brothers and sisters in Christ. Christianity and Orthodoxy in particular, has always been said to be upside down in the modern world. Where we hold steadfast in our faith, this world is changing. And for many, it is changing for the worse. And it is not just in society, but Christian churches, and some Orthodox churches too. Where they have thrown out their Christian Dogma, altered it, to suit today's modern Christianity.

We feel the pressure of the outside world, the neo-pagans, to become more accepting of people's sins. To treat their sins as normal. We should relax and let people be people. This, my brothers and sisters, is wrong. As I have stressed for over a decade, the choices we make today not only affect us now, but in our eternal life. Don't fall for the lies that everyone is going to heaven. To live your life, as for repentance at the end and all will be fine. It won't. You need to repent daily and to confess your sins. You need to give alms to the poor. It's necessary that you try. As we all know, we never know when God will call us home. So be prepared. Christ is in our midst."

"He is and always shall be." responds the congregation.

Before Father Ephraim turns and heads back into the altar, he sees Father Lazarus looming in the back of the church.

"Father Lazarus. What a pleasant surprise. Please come forward and join me in the altar.

Father Lazarus nods, and walks in between the people, like a parting of the red sea. He enters the altar.

"Father Ephraim, you need to be careful about what you say. You are expressing some very dangerous ideas."

"Thank you for your concern, but it needs to be said. Now please pray with me and help me with the blessing of the water."

The two priests continue to pray.

The service concludes, with the parishioners filling up their empty bottles with holy water.

"Father Lazarus, what brings you here? Today is Theophany. I am surprised you are not in Dallas."

"There are changes taking place, and I thought it would be a good time for the junior priest to lead a major feast day."

"He is doing it all by himself?"

"Yes. It's not like here, where even on weekdays, attendance is large. In fact, compared to Christ the Savior, our attendance has been gradually declining over the years."

"To be honest, Father. If you did not try to turn your church into some sort of feel-good, everything will be fine, Orthodox church, you would not have lost so many. It's not like attendance dropped for all Orthodox churches. Only yours."

Father Lazarus' cheeks and forehead reddens. "It is temporary. We cannot grow as a church if we continue with messages like yours. Sadly, many other churches copied what you did and are applying it to their messaging."

"And has it helped?"

"Their attendance has increased, but does it matter how many people they have attending, if they are all hearing the wrong message?"

"The wrong message? How to prepare for and care for your soul? That is the correct message."

"Father Ephraim, I am asking you to stop what you are preaching."

"Father Lazarus, you are not Metropolitan yet. And even when you are, you will not have authority over how I run my church or God's message of salvation. Now, unless you wish to help clean up, it is best for you to return to Dallas."

"I will leave you with this. You are leading people astray. And I will not let this continue." Father Lazarus grabs his bag and rushes out of the church.

"Father Ephraim. Everything alright?" Lydia asks as she approaches.

Father Ephraim leaves the altar and approaches Lydia. "Yes, everything is fine. The tornado known as Father Lazarus is still trying to make things difficult."

"When is he being promoted to Metropolitan?"

"There is no firm date. But he acts like he is the

Metropolitan now. I pray for wisdom in this decision."

"We were standing in the back and we noticed several new people today. But they didn't stick around to visit with us."

"That's OK. At least they came today." Father patted Lydia on the shoulder.

"Father, Maria's mother isn't doing well. She hasn't come right out and said anything, but from what Jonah has said, it's just a matter of time. He expects Maria to head down to Mexico at the end of the week to spend time with her."

"Lord have mercy. We will pray for her and her mother."

"It's difficult because our views on what happens after we pass differ from that of the Catholic. Is there any way for her mom to be ready for what comes next?"

"Without confusing her too much. It's important for Maria to contact a priest to come over and hear her confession and administer communion."

"I will see. Thank you, Father." Lydia gives Father Ephraim a hug.

As he walks out, Father Ephraim notices a man standing in the back of the church.

"May I help you?"

The man stares at he priest, smirks, turns around and exits the church.

CHAPTER FOURTEEN

"Ephraim, phone call for you. It's someone from the Metropolitan's office."

Father Ephraim leaves his study and picks up the phone.

"Father Ephraim. This is Steve from the Metropolitan's office. He hoped that you could come up to the diocese office tomorrow."

"That is short notice, but alright. And this isn't something that we can't discuss over the phone?"

"No, he needs to see you in-person."

"I will be there as fast as I can. Have a blessed night."

Father Ephraim puts down the phone.

"Who was that?" Matushka Helen asks.

"The Metropolitan wants to see me tomorrow. In-person?"

"That is strange. Do you think it has something to do with Father Lazarus's elevation?"

"It's possible, but that is something I am not a part of."

"Well, if you are driving up in the morning, you need to go to bed early."

* * *

Father Ephraim travels north on interstate 35 to Dallas. He pushes his late model sedan as fast as he can to keep with the flow of Texas traffic. He watches the speedometer to make he is keeping it under 10 miles over the speed limit. *The last thing I need is another ticket.*

Passing by the town of Waco, he continues to ask himself what this meeting could be about. *The church is growing by leaps and bounds, stewardship continues to increase. We average two new converts per month. Everything is going well at Christ the King.*

He finally reaches the Metropolitan's office, a separate building in back of Father Lazarus's church property.

Walking in, he sees Steve, the Metropolitan's assistant at the desk. Steve stands up once he sees Father Ephraim enter.

"Hi Steve, I see I am a little early. Traffic was moving pretty fast."

"I believe the Metropolitan is ready for you. Please step into his office."

Once he stepped in and surveyed the room, he felt he was about to be ambushed. At his desk was the Metropolitan. In one chair was Father Lazarus, in the other three chairs were two men he hasn't seen before and one he recognized from the back of the church several weeks ago.

"Metropolitan. I am here. Now, what can we discuss that we weren't able to over the phone?"

"Hi Father Ephraim. Thank you for coming on such

short notice. Please take a seat."

Father Ephraim sits down and looks at the men and Father Lazarus.

"Father Ephraim. I'm very troubled. Yesterday, I learned of some very serious accusations regarding your behavior, and I felt it was best to hear your side of the story before I move any further. With all the negative press priests receive, I think it is best to keep this between the six of us here."

Father Ephraim takes a deep breath. Says a prayer under his breath before responding.

"Negative press? What are you accusing me of? And why are Father Lazarus and these other gentlemen here?"

"Father Lazarus, of his own accord, has been utilizing these men, all police officers and detectives from his parish, to monitor you. They recorded some of your sermons and cataloged other activities at Christ the Savior."

"Are you serious? So what did they find?"

"Well, they are accusing you of heresy, incorporating your teachings from books outside of Orthodoxy. And, worse of all, they are also accusing you of inappropriately touching women."

"What? That is a very dangerous accusation. Who did I touch? Was there a complaint?"

"My friend here saw you touching a woman at the end of liturgy several weeks ago." Father Lazarus says.

Father Ephraim looks over at the man. "That's right. I saw you standing in the back of the church. I don't know what you think you saw. But that was not inappropriate. In fact, you can call Mrs. Lydia Roza and ask her yourself."

The man walks over to Father Lazarus and stands beside him. "Lazarus, I saw this priest put his arm around the lady, then place his hand on her rear end. The woman had a frightful look on her face, but did nothing."

Father Ephraim, glanced at the Metropolitan then over to the accuser and at Father Lazarus. He clinched his teeth, balled his hands, quickly stands up and comes face to face with Father Lazarus.

"Sir, that is a lie. Father Lazarus, I do not understand what your issue is with me. But what you are accusing me of is slanderous. Worse, it is evil. I've never been inappropriate with anyone at Christ the Savior. Men, women, boys, girls, no one. Everything I teach and preach to my parish is straight from scriptures and the church fathers. Father Lazarus, although I am a priest, I am still a man. A God created man that, unfortunately for you, given the emotion of anger."

At that moment, Father Ephraim opened his fist and slapped Father Lazarus across the face. The men stand up and grab Father Ephraim. Father Lazarus staggers back, holding his cheek with one hand, and searches for a chair with the other. Two of the men help Father Lazarus sit down. He continues to rub his face and wipe the tears from his eyes.

"Father Ephraim, you just struck another priest!" Metropolitan exclaimed.

"This is unacceptable behavior."

"Metropolitan, you've known me since I graduated Seminary and you are seriously considering these accusations ? Until Father Lazarus shown up, has anyone from my congregation ever accused me of any moral wrong doings? What I have done, which Father

Lazarus seems to be envious of, is building our parish by staying true to Orthodoxy. The only difference between what I preach and others is that I am helping people prepare for their next life. I don't sugar coat the fact we will all die. And when we die, we will be judged. And the church fathers, through their wisdom and experience, gave us the instructions on how to be with God after death, and not with the evil one. If anyone is a heretic, it is Father Lazarus." Father Ephraim points to the chair.

Father Lazarus stands up and walks behind the Metropolitan. Hiding like a child.

"Father Ephraim, the only thing I can do now is investigate these claims. So in the meantime, I forbid you to celebrate the Divine Liturgy or teach to your congregation."

"You are kidding me? So, who is going to be the acting priest during this?"

"Father Lazarus, will fill in for you?"

Father Lazarus, with a reddened cheek, smiles.

"Lord have mercy?" Father Ephraim says under his breath.

"Is there anything else, Metropolitan?"

"That is all. I will notify you of the outcome of the investigation as soon as possible."

Father Ephraim walks out of the office and past Steve.

"Father, what is wrong? What happened?"

"Steve, why didn't you warn me?"

"About what?"

"Forget it. You have a blessed day."

As he drives home, Father Ephraim's cell phone rings. He flips it open, he sees his wife is calling him.

"So Ephraim, how was the meeting?"

"I can't believe what happened. They are going to investigate me, and in the meantime, I am not allowed to serve at the church."

"Oh my, why?"

"Father Lazarus has convinced the Metropolitan I am a heretic, and that I was inappropriate to women of the congregation."

"I don't know if I should laugh or cry at that last accusation. But calm down. Once they investigate, you will be vindicated."

"Although the Metropolitan said this was all behind closed doors, I do not trust Father Lazarus. He will leak the accusations and it will make it much harder for people to believe my innocence. I need to tell everyone as soon as possible. Will you get a hold of Daniel, Jonah, Lydia and the rest of the parish council? Tell them important meeting late tonight."

"I will. Please focus on the road. I love you."

"I love you too." He closes his phone.

* * *

All seated around a long wooden table in the fellowship hall, which is sometimes used as a conference room, are members of the parish council. After the opening prayer, Father Ephraim at the end of the table stands and addresses the room. "Thank you for meeting with me tonight. There is some terrible news, and I thought I would get ahead of it."

"The Metropolitan has accused me, brought on by Father Lazarus, being a heretic. Teaching against the churches teaching on salvation, and touching women.

In particular you Lydia. For that, they are investigating the claims and during that time, I cannot serve. Father Lazarus will replace me."

Lydia gasps. "Father, let me talk to them. I will tell them, never ever, did you do anything inappropriate, or that made me feel uncomfortable."

"This is almost comical, Father. Can't you protest and not allow Father Lazarus to serve at the church?" Daniel asks.

"It's not that easy. If I went against the Metropolitan's directives, then they can remove me and it's possible they could close down the church."

"Father, there is no way I can work here if you are not here." Jonah adds.

"Jonah, the church is most important. Do not lose sight of this. Everyone needs to continue as normal. The investigation will prove my innocence and I will be back in the altar in a short matter of time. Now, if you will excuse me, I must head home, spend time with my wife, and work on my sermons for when I return. You have a blessed evening and most of all, pray for me."

As Father Ephraim leaves the church, the members of the parish council remain.

"That is why he is a priest and I am a repentant sinner." Daniel says.

"What do you mean?"

"He is putting all of this in the hands of God, where I don't think I could do that. I would raise holy... you know what."

"Remember what Father says. We need to think about the church and not about who the priest is. We will do our best, and hope that..."

"It's not going to happen." Jonah jumps into the

conversation.

"What's not going to happen?" Lydia asks.

"I am not coming anywhere near Christ the Savior while Father Lazarus is here. And I can guarantee you that once the parishioners find out, they will be gone, too."

"Jonah, please just wait. Let's see what happens on Sunday and we can go from there." Lydia pleads with him.

"I will give him one chance. If this is going to go the way I think it does, we will need a different plan." Jonah exits the church, with the others not far behind.

* * *

The congregation enters the church all unaware in the change of priests, except for the parish council. The people in the church standing and praying while the Deacon sings the morning prayers, others continue to file in the church. Daniel, Lydia, Jonah and Maria stand in the back. The church bell rings and the people watch as the tall, slender raven haired priest holds the gold plated Gospel in the air singing, "Blessed is the Kingdom of the Father and of the Son and of the Holy Spirit now and forever until the ages of ages." His voice is deep. Some in the congregation recognize him as Father Lazarus, others whisper to each other, "where is Father Ephraim?"

Several members of the congregation turn around, making eye contact with Lydia or Daniel as if asking what is going on?

Father Lazarus continues through the petitions,

with the choir answering each with "Lord have mercy." Towards the middle of service one of the high school students reads the epistle lesson of the day, once she finishes Father Lazarus sings "Stand upright, and hear the Gospel according to Saint Matthew." Father Lazarus reads Matthew 24:3-13. After which, he closes the Gospel, returns it to the altar and comes back out to speak to people.

"Christ is in our midst." He proclaims.

"He is and ever shall be." The congregation says in unison.

"In the Gospel reading, Christ's last week on earth is approaching. In Mathew chapter 23, Christ charges the scribes, Pharisees and other leaders in the community inverting God's values of being mean-spirited, judgmental, greedy, ambitious, absorbed in externals and blindly self-righteous. Then as we read this morning, Christ warns the disciples, of what occurs in the beginning of birth pangs, and says, "And then many will be offended, will betray one another, and will hate one another. Then many false prophets will rise up and deceive many." Father Lazarus stops, clears his throat for attention. Now all eyes are on him.

"This is a warning to watch out for, not only the first century but all centuries, up to today. Now, in today's world, it might not be false prophets who are seen a mile away, but some are more subtle. And some can be in our clergy."

The congregation looks at each other. Lydia, Daniel and Jonah stand straight. Daniel looks sharply at Father Lazarus.

"And let us not mistake popularity with being right. And I am not talking about the TV preachers. They are found in churches of all sizes and all locations. As much as I wish Seminary could weed poor priests out, sadly, some make it through."

At that moment, Jonah took Maria by her hand, shook his head at Daniel, and left the church. Others noticed Jonah leaving and followed him out.

"You cannot give people false hope. We cannot say what happens to our soul after we pass away. And to preach things like the Last Judgment, it is false. It's a perversion of our faith. Now, there are some saints who tell of what they experienced in visions, but none died and came back. My Saint, Lazarus, never said what happened to him while he was gone for four days. And because we don't know, we must focus on today. Not some time in the future. Enjoy the gift of life that God has given to you."

Some within the congregation nodded in agreement with Father Lazarus.

"Now, I plan to be with you for the foreseeable future while Father Ephraim tends to personal matters." Father Lazarus returns to the altar.

Many more in the congregation file out of the church, leaving only a handful. Daniel sees an older woman, by the name of Anya, walking towards him. With tears in her eyes, she asks Daniel and Lydia. "Where is Father Ephraim? My husband, he could go at anytime. He promised he would be there to give him Communion, to hear his confession and to pray for him as he passes from this life to the next." Tears appear and stream down her face.

"He can't do it alone and is scared. And without Father's help, he will be so frightened. Please find Father Ephraim."

"Anya, call me when it is time and I will make sure Father Ephraim meets you."

"Oh thank you Daniel. I will, I will." She hugs him and Lydia. And walks out of the church.

"How can you promise that? Father is not allowed to perform any priestly tasks while he is under investigation." Lydia asks.

"What was I supposed to say? Sorry, he is on his own? We will find Father."

Father Lazarus, peering out from the back of the altar, took notice that the church now has seventy percent fewer people than the start of service. With fewer people, he has a clear view to the back of the church where he sees Daniel and Lydia arguing.

Father Lazarus continues with prayers of the service, administers Communion to the faithful and gives the departing prayers. At the end of service, he says."To those of you that stayed, thank you. Not for me, because even if there is just one person, I will perform the Divine Liturgy. But for yourself. It should not matter who the priest is. We are all here to worship God. And we cannot pick who we are worshiping with. Father Ephraim has personal business he is attending to and could be back at a later date. Please don't speculate or start rumors. Have a blessed week."

Father Lazarus, holding his cross, stands while the remaining congregation approaches him and kisses the cross. The last two people to approach are Daniel and Lydia.

"Daniel, Lydia, I need to speak with both of you."

"Yes, Father, how can we help you?" Daniel asks.

"I saw the two of you arguing during liturgy. Is there anything I can help you with?"

"No Father, I think we can handle this on our own." Daniel replies

"Are you sure?" Father looks over at Lydia

"Is there a way for us to get in touch with Father Ephraim? It is very important that we speak to him." Lydia asks.

"No. You realize why Father Ephraim is not here, right? That is why I cannot allow especially you Lydia, to speak with him."

"What? You have no authority over who I may speak with." Lydia fires back.

"Fine, he cannot speak to any parishioner during the investigation. If he does, we could automatically expel him from the church. Now, what can I do to help?"

Lydia looks over at Daniel. He shakes his head and looks down.

"One of the parishioner's, her name is Anya. Her husband Constantine has been battling heart disease for ten years now. He was doing fine until this month, where the medication stopped working. There are no more options for him and his time is short." Lydia tears up.

"Father Ephraim was working with Constantine, getting him, I mean, his soul, ready for eternal life. He's scared, and is expecting Father Ephraim to be there at his side when the time comes." Daniel adds.

"I see." Father Lazarus strokes his long black beard.

"So, can you give us Father Ephraim's number or his whereabouts?" Lydia asks with a crack in her voice.

"No I can't. But what I can do is meet with Constantine tonight. And take over for Father Ephraim."

"I don't think that is a good idea. It will shock

Constantine if there is someone new."

"Well, I am his only option. Don't worry, I've been with the dying before. Tell Anya I will be there after six tonight. And I will speak with Constantine, give him Communion and hear his confessions.

Father Lazarus arrives at the Hospice home with Lydia and Daniel waiting by the front door.

"Hi Father, I hope there was no trouble finding the place," Daniel asks.

"Not really. It's not too far from the church."

"Anya is inside. Constantine is bed ridden, so don't expect him to get up when he sees you."

"Of course."

Anya walks out to the front door and greets Lydia and Daniel.

"You brought Father Lazarus? Where is Father Ephraim?"

"I'm sorry, I could not locate him." Daniel lied.

"Oh no. Constantine will be so upset." Anya weeps.

Father Lazarus walks over and interrupts the conversation.

"Dear Anya. I appreciate Constantine has a relationship with Father Ephraim, but he is unavailable. However, I am here for your husband. Please, take me to him."

Anya turns and walks back towards the bedroom. Father, Lydia and Daniel enter the room. The room is not like a room found in a hospital. It resembles one you would find in someone's house. A very nice guest room with an on suite.

Father Lazarus looks around and sees Icons of Christ, The Theotokos, St. Constantine and one of Constantine's guardian angel.

He looks down into the bed and sees a very frail, and skinny man. He is laying flat in bed, his head sunk into the pillow. The priest stares down at him and can't believe the man he is looking at is only fifty-one years old.

Father Lazarus walks towards the bed and takes a seat next to him. The sheets and comforter too heavy for Constantine to sit up, and tries to roll his head to the side to see the priest. Expecting to see Father Ephraim, his face shows disappointment.

"Who are you?" Constantine whispers.

"I am Father Lazarus. I am the acting priest at Christ the Savior until Father Ephraim returns."

"But he was going to help. Can you help me, Father?" Constantine speaks slowly.

"I am here for you. I brought the sacraments of Communion and Holy Unction. Let's get started."

Father Ephraim opens up a small black rectangular box. The inside is covered with red crushed velvet. Father pulls out a small bottle of oil with a tiny paint brush. He recites several prayers while dipping the small brush in the bottle of oil. He continues to recite prayers while administering the oil to Constantine's face in the shape of a cross. Forehead, chin to the right cheek, then left cheek.

"For the servant of God, Constantine."

Father takes out another small bottle, this one holding the sacraments of Communion. He uses a small silver spoon and takes Communion, the body and blood of Christ, and administers it to Constantine.

Constantine struggles to sit up. He has enough strength to lift his head. Not all the sacrament makes it into his mouth.

Father dabs Constantine's chin.

"Constantine, are you good with God? Did you confess your sins?"

"Yes...Father, I fear what is happening next."

"Don't be afraid Constantine. Your sins are absolved, and you are baptized."

Struggling to speak, Constantine asks, "But the demons. How will I get past them? There are sins I don't remember. I forgot after so long, and I did not confess."

"Constantine, everything is going to be fine. There are no demons on the other side. On the other side, we don't know. There could be demons. It could be a long tunnel where your family will meet you, or you can go for a very long sleep in darkness. We don't know. But if you have followed the faith, you will receive an incorruptible body. And you will rise with the second coming of Christ."

Constantine reaches out his hand, trying to touch Father Lazarus. Father Lazarus pulls back and stands up. He walks back to Daniel.

"I think he is leaving us. While I am speaking to him. He is dying. Where is Anya?"

Anya comes forward and takes the empty seat. She grabs Constantine's hand and kisses it.

"Constantine, my beautiful Constantine. I love you so much. Thank you for the life you've given me. The beautiful children we raised. Oh, how much I love you." She brings his frail hand to her chest. Tears stream down her face.

Constantine's breath labors. He tries to speak, but she can't hear him.

"Closer."

She puts her ear next to his mouth.

"I love you Anya. I want to speak with the priest."

Anya looks over her shoulder. With tear-filled eyes, she calls for Father Lazarus.

Father Lazarus sits back down. He chooses not to take Constantine's hand.

"Father, I'm scared. I don't want to die. I am not ready."

"Constantine. You have no choice. It's God's doing."

"Prayers, say prayers for me." He pleads

"They are unnecessary, and won't help you."

Tears fall from Constantine's eyes. He feels his weak heart beat faster.

Anya, Daniel and Lydia take notice and walk closer.

"What did you say to him, Father?" Daniel asks

Father Lazarus ignores him

"Constantine, I can't help you. No one in here can help you. You are on your own. God has decided. You will be with him or sent into blackness."

Horrified by what they heard, Daniel pulls Father Lazarus from the chair.

"What are you telling him, Father? You are scaring him. He is dying. Where is your compassion?"

"Father Ephraim has lied to this poor man. He needs to understand that no one knows what happens when we die."

"Now is not the time or place, Father. Constantine only has a matter of minutes and you are torturing his soul."

Father Lazarus and Daniel continue to argue, their voices becoming louder, raise and carry out of the room and down the hall. Father Ephraim hears the voices and speeds up his pace. He enters the room and sees a broken down Constantine with Anya stroking his hair telling him everything will be alright. In the corner are Father Lazarus and Daniel arguing. Father Lazarus sees Father Ephraim and heads over to meet him.

"What are you doing here Ephraim? We suspended you from duties."

"Father Lazarus, get out of my way. He is my patient, my friend. I promised I would be here and do all I could do to help him be with God."

"Father Ephraim, if you come anywhere near to him. I will report you. And you will no longer be a priest." Father Lazarus threatens.

"Do what you have to do. Now, move out of my way." Father Ephraim rushes past, knocking into Father Lazarus' shoulder.

"Constantine, Constantine. I am here." He wipes the tears from Constantine's eyes.

"Is that you Father? Oh, thank God you are here."

"I am not going anywhere."

"Prayers?" He whispers

"Not yet. It's not time. Let me read from the Bible." He reaches into his bag and pulls out his worn leather Bible.

"In the beginning God made Heaven and earth..." He continued to read Genesis from 1:1 through 4:1 and when he ended.

"Constantine, and when Christ died for us, he went down to Hades and trampled death by His death. He beat the devil. Do not be afraid of death."

Constantine's face relaxed and a slight smile returned.

"Constantine, you prepared well for this day. You have confessed, taken Communion, given alms. We will pray for you."

"And the demons?"

"The demons have nothing on you. The scales are tipped in your favor. "

"I need to rest." Constantine closes his eyes. Anya changes places with Father Ephraim and takes her husband's hand.

"Father Lazarus, here is your choice. You can stay and assist me in reading prayers when the time comes or leave. All of us in here believe in what the Holy Fathers say about what happens at the hour of the departure of the soul. If you truly believe it to be heresy, then leave. Now."

"Ephraim, you are cursing this man's soul to hell." Father Lazarus storms out of the room.

The afternoon turned into night. Constantine's breathing labored, then continued to become weaker. Father Ephraim, with the help of Daniel and Lydia, read prayers for several hours until Constantine took his last breath.

CHAPTER FIFTEEN

Through the cracked lens, the crooked hands of his old analog watch shows 9:55 am. He turns from the altar table to the back of the church. The choir area is empty, the reader has not shown, and not one parishioner is in the church. He continues to prepare for Sunday morning liturgy. He hears the door open. It's a woman, dressed in black, with her head covered. She's a widow and is there to light a candle for her husband long time passed. She places the candle in front of the icon of Christ, lights it, crosses herself. Turns and walks out of the church.

"Sigh." Father Lazarus holds the Gospel high and begins liturgy. "Blessed is the Kingdom..."

Within forty-five minutes, he finishes liturgy to an empty church. He blows out the one candle, locks the church and heads outside. The parking lot is empty. He wonders what happened. *Where are the people?*

The week passes by. It's another Sunday at 9:55 am, the church empty inside. The widow from last week does not even show. At 10:00 am he holds the Gospel, this time with half stretched arms. He says quietly, "Blessed is the Kingdom..." He completes the liturgy in thirty minutes, puts his robes in the closet and heads out the door. As with last Sunday, the parking lot is empty except for his car. He unlocks the door, sits inside and wonders what has happened. Finishing early, he drives to one of the parishioners' homes. He pulls up to the house and sees thirty cars parked in and around the house. Father Lazarus leaves his car and marches towards the door, but stops. He hears heavenly singing emanating from the back of the house. He walks to the backyard and witnesses over fifty people standing in a semicircle with the five choir members in the middle leading hymns.

Those who are there are smiling and full of joy. This isn't liturgy or a Bible study, nothing that would get them in trouble with the church. He steps forward to speak with those who are there, but stops, realizing he is not welcome. He slinks away, returns to his car, and heads back to his temporary home.

The third Sunday arrives, Father Lazarus prepares again for liturgy and just as before, no one arrives. Besides the people not returning to church, the tithing has stopped. Worried about the church's financial health, he contacts the Metropolitan.

"Father Lazarus, how is everything at Christ The Savior?"

"To be honest, not well. Attendance is down and so is tithing."

"How far off are you?"

"There's been no one at church for three weeks, and no one has contributed in that time period as well."

"Are you kidding me, Father? What happened?"

"Honestly, I don't know. The people just stopped coming. They get together at one of the parishioner's homes, Daniel's I believe, and sing songs and read the Gospel."

"Father Lazarus, this is not good. Christ the Savior

was one of the most active and vibrant churches in the diocese. Now, it is a dead church? You need to come to Dallas as soon as possible."

Father Lazarus returns to Dallas. He walks into the Metropolitans' office and this time it is he who feels ambushed. In the room are Daniel, Jonah, Lydia and standing next to the Metropolitan is Father Ephraim."

"Father, please sit down." The metropolitan motions towards the chair in front of his desk.

"Metropolitan, why is Father Ephraim and these other people here? I thought this was to be a private meeting.

"It will be Father, but first we need to speak with Father Ephraim and his guests. Father Ephraim, please speak."

"Thank you Metropolitan. In a matter of three weeks, Father Lazarus has destroyed all we were doing at Christ the Savior. He has insulted the congregation, the choir, and the clergy. He has talked down to them, challenged their beliefs and worse yet. Tried to confuse, humiliate and scare a man on his death bed."

"And Daniel, why is the church empty?"

"When word got out about how Father Lazarus acted with newly departed Constantine, everyone decided they cannot attend Christ the Savior. He is going against everything we learned from Father Ephraim. Now, we still gather at our house for song and fellowship, but some others are trying to find the closest Orthodox church near us or even looking at other denominations like the Lutherans and Catholics."

"And what do you think we can do to bring everyone back to church, Lydia?"

"Father Ephraim needs to be reinstated today. And

Father Lazarus needs to be removed from the diocese."

"From the Diocese?"

"Yes, you are going to see that wherever you put this man, the people will stay away." Lydia says.

"Father Lazarus, what do you say?"

"Father Ephraim has turned Christ the Savior into a cult. He is teaching doctrine that goes against the church. It is becoming a death cult. Everything is about dying, and what happens after we die? And all of our time needs to be spent on assuring a place in Heaven. How does Father Ephraim know such things? And he is keeping people from enjoying their lives today."

"As for Constantine, he was so worried about being met by demons before he died. That's all he could talk about on his death bed. Instead of that, he could have spent his remaining moments speaking to his wife. Father Ephraim is doing a disservice to the church. Just give me time. I will weed out his followers and start a new church. And first thing, these three should never be allowed to step foot in the church again." Father Lazarus points at Daniel, Lydia, and Jonah.

"Father Ephraim?" The Metropolitan asks.

"The church, the people, need to be shaken. To be woken up from the day-to-day complacency. The devil has tricked them into living for the day. If the people live like that, the devil will win in the end. There is a pathway to Heaven. You know it as well as I do. And there are instructions given to us by the Holy Fathers on how to get there. We need to be straight forward. And if we are mocked and threatened, so be it. Christ warned us this was going to happen, but to forge ahead. Metropolitan let us at Christ the Savior lead the way."

A creak from the Metropolitan's chair is heard as he

leans back and ponders.

"Typically, I would pray on this type of decision. But this one does not require the guidance of God, because he has already guided me. Father Lazarus, I am relieving you of your duties at Christ the Savior and any church within the diocese until further notice. Father Ephraim. I need you to return to Christ the Savior and continue with your work. Please forgive me for my accusations and putting you through all the trouble. If there is anything I can do to help you, please ask."

Daniel and Lydia hug. Jonah hugs Father Ephraim and kisses his hand. Father Lazarus stays silent and storms out of the office in anger.

* * *

A new Sunday has arrived, it's 9:30 am. Father Ephraim listens as the reader recites the morning prayers. In the background, he hears the choir outside practicing the hymns for the day. With a quick peek over his shoulder, he sees the people file into the church. By 10:00 am at the start of liturgy, the church is full, with people standing outside. The crowd size rivaling that of an Easter service.

In a loud and booming voice, Father Ephraim sings, "Blessed is the Kingdom..."

His voice strong and full of energy, he flows through the liturgy. The choir keeps pace and mimics his strength. The parishioners feel the energy. Smiles are on everyone's faces, knowing that Father Ephraim is back and Christ the Savior is alive. At the point in the service where Father Ephraim has his sermon, he continues on, saving it for the end of the liturgy. The line for communion extends to outside of the door. Daniel, Lydia, and Jonah do their best to keep people in line. Father Ephraim smiles as he says each person's baptismal name before administering communion.

At the end of liturgy, Father Ephraim walks out from the altar. The altar boys exit through the doors and they, along with the choir, find a place to stand and listen.

"Christ is in our midst!"

"He is and always shall be," the people respond.

Father Ephraim gives a smile.

"Wow, it is a blessing to see a packed church. Thank you for returning to Christ the Savior. This is not my church. But God's house. If you expect me to use this time to disparage the hierarchy or the former priest. I will not. Because, in the end, God has made it work out. And when we say "He works in mysterious ways," this is true. Because the outcome of all of this is a stronger church and a parish that has increased their faith. But I will tell you, there will be changes. As of today. I will be upfront as possible. When people ask about Christ the Savior, and what we are about. The response is, this is the church you go to if you want to go to Heaven. That is it. If you want a church to make you feel good about today. This is not the place. If you want a place to grow your business and network, this is not the place. If you want a church that tries to keep secrets, this is not the place. The outside world can not lead us astray. We are not our own gods. We are not eternal, all of us will die. The Orthodox church's main purpose is to heal the soul of the faithful through your struggle to attain illumination and Theosis, and thus acquire the Holy Spirit while in this world. We want all members to be saints. And once you receive the Holy Spirit and persevere in God's love to the end, the mission of the church is fulfilled (in them). And now the passage to Heaven through the tollhouses is assured, because you already gained the Kingdom of God within yourself.

Most in the congregation nod in agreement with Father, but he sees some whisper to others "tollhouses?"

"Yes, I said tollhouses. The aerial tollhouses, where the demons will torment me and you. At each tollhouse, the demons will accuse us of sins. some true and some false, in their attempt to wrestle your soul away from God, and you enter with them in Hades. But the work we are doing here is to help you bypass the tollhouses. And to do that, you need a spiritual father who knows the way, and who you entrusted your spiritual lives in unhesitating obedience. Something that not found at the large churches.

I am your guide to prepare you for your new journey to a new world. And the first step to do this is for you to understand the devil has been working the long game. A slow and big lie that has fooled many into, unwittingly, turn away from God. He has deceived Christians to give up their dogma to be aligned with "universal Christianity." So today's Christians are putting aside their beliefs to be acceptable to the secularists. What they once thought was evil, they now call good. If you do not think the devil is hiding in wait for your souls, you are fooling yourself. But I won't let that happen to you. As Saint Luke is the physician of your soul, I want to be the trainer of your soul, to help strengthen your spiritual life so your soul will bypass the tollhouses and go straight to Heaven. And it might seem difficult, but this again is a lie of the devil. It is very simple to prepare your soul: repentance, confession, prayer, alms giving, and frequent communion. Use the lives of saints as examples. Read scripture for wisdom. All of this around you is all you need to prepare.

And as you have your earthly duty, mine is not only for today, but when it is time for you to depart from this life. This cannot wait until Monday or next month. This must start today, with the confession of all your sins. From as far back as you can remember to this very moment. Why? Because of the sins you are forgiven for today, you won't need to account for when going through the tollhouses. And I will leave you with this. It is something that we tend to forget. It is something that priests fail to tell. And it will stick with you the moment you hear it."

Father Ephraim pauses for a moment. He scans the nave, making as much eye contact as possible.

"Once you have passed, you do not get an opportunity, ever again, to confess your sins. No longer is the opportunity to give alms. You are left with what you have done and your remaining sins and there will be an accounting for it. I will stay as late as needed today for some or all of you to confess your sins. Lord have mercy and save us."

Father Ephraim ends the service. The altar boys gathered to his side, one holding the basket of the blessed bread to be distributed amongst the faithful after they approach the priest and kissed the golden cross he held in his hand.

At the end of the line is Jonah. He approaches and kisses the cross. "Father, it is a blessing that you are back. But, there is some troubling news. A former colleague of mine contacted me. She said her husband is at the hospital and would like an Orthodox priest to visit him. His name is Alexios. Father, would you please visit him?"

* * *

"Hello, Alexios, it's Father Ephraim. Your wife asked me to stop by and pay you a visit." Father Ephraim, standing in the doorway, wearing his black cassock with a large golden cross necklace that hangs midway over his chest.

The man in the bed looks over at the priest. Finds his remote control and turns off the TV.

"My name is Alex. Come in if you want. There is a chair by the window if you would like a place to sit." Alexios watches as Father Ephraim moves by him and sits in the burnt orange seat.

"So, which church are you from, Father?"

"Christ the Savior. We are an American Orthodox church here in the hill country."

"I see, so there are no Greek Orthodox churches close by?"

"No, the furthest one is at least an hour's drive from here."

Alex looks Father Ephraim over, he sighs and disappointment sets upon his face.

"I was hoping for a Greek priest. Not that it matters."

"How do you mean Alexios?"

"I've run out of time to make everything right and I am going to hell."

"When was the last time you confessed your sins?"

"Over ten years ago. We are not very religious, Father.

We go to church on Good Friday and Easter. Sometimes Christmas. I know I am a Christian, but not one that is practicing the religion. And Father my name is Alex." He diverts his eyes away from Father, and looks at the scenery through the large pane window.

"Your baptismal name is Alexios, that is your God given name, and that is what I will call you. Now Alexios, with eyes open, and you breathing, there is still time. We can begin with confession."

"I don't think so, Father. You will be here for days. And I don't know if I am comfortable telling you my sins." Alexios adjusts his body and winces in pain.

"It's not me you are telling your sins to. I am just here to guide you. You are confessing your sins to God. We can begin now, and you can talk as long as you feel like. And if you want me to come back, I will. Are you ready to start?"

"I guess."

Father takes out a Bible and an icon of Christ. He gives the Bible to Alexios and has him place his hands on top of it. He then places the icon of Christ on his bedside table.

"Where do I begin, Father?"

"Start from wherever you want. Your most recent sins or sins from your youth."

Alexios takes a moment. "Father, I have committed almost every sin. I lied, committed adultery, been disrespectful to my parents, placed idols before God, and, as a drone pilot, I killed hundreds of our country's enemies. I am not a good man, and I don't believe anyone can save me. You should go and help those who have time."

"No, God in His infinite love and goodness will do

everything possible to save a soul."

"Then, he will bless me with more time? Father, I'm a stage four colon cancer patient. My time is near. I was so stupid. I never saw a doctor to get a physical or a colonoscopy. Always too busy with some stupid business deal. All I had to do was take a day off and they would have found the polyps." Tears well up in his eyes.

"My four children. I won't be able to see them married, or hold my grandchildren and worse yet, grow old with my wife. My soul does not deserve to be saved.

"Don't let the devil fool you Alexios." Father sternly says.

"The demons are always with us, whispering something in our ear to keep us from doing what is right in God's eye. And for those that are close to death, the fiercer they become, because they want your soul. So stop listening to them. You need to fight. And I am here to help."

"Alright Father, I will start. When I was a little kid. I stole cookies from the grocery store. It is forty-five years later and I still feel guilty. When I was in high school, I used to bully several girls. I did drugs and got drunk and I lied to everyone, even my parents, teachers and priests. In high school, I had sex with girls; I can't tell you how many women I have been with from high school until I got married. I know it was a lot. I got several pregnant, and they had abortions. Even though I am married, I still sought pornography to get me off. I have been in bar fights where I broke noses and almost killed people. Let's see, during college, I was an atheist and disparaged God. And I sin every day. There are so many to account for. Especially the lying. I lie to my wife, kids, customers. I might even be lying to you."

Alexios continued on for several hours, recounting his sins, telling of his life, and how he carried the burdens of his sins until today. "I wish I confessed more often. I am feeling at peace." His eyelids becoming heavier.

"Father, I need to sleep. I am exhausted. There is still more I need to say. Will you return?" He speaks as his eyes close.

"Of course Alexios, I will be here tomorrow. God bless you."

Father Ephraim anointed him with the Holy oil and administered the sacrament of communion. He looked down at him and watched as he rested.

"Until tomorrow."

PART IV

"Be sober, be vigilant; because your adversary the devil, as a roaring lion, walketh about, seeking whom he may devour."

- 1 PETER 5:8

CHAPTER SIXTEEN

Midnight, and darkness fills the space. A voice in the distance breaks the silence.

"I hear Him. But I can't see Him," she cries.

"It's pitch black out here." Another woman's voice cries.

"It is so cold." Another says.

"Did you hear that? It is time."

"Wake up. Is everyone awake?" Says the fifth.

"Over here. We are awake."

"Where are you?" She cries out.

The ten young women feel around in the sand, trying to find their lamps. One by one, the lamps light up for the first five.

"I hear Him. He is close, let's go meet Him." The first says, and the other four follow.

"Wait, what about us? Don't leave us here. Our fear is great. We can't see you. Give us some oil from your lamps." She begs.

The five continue to run. "Behold, the Bridegroom is coming." One yells in jubilation.

Their cries of anguish are heard in the night air.

"How could they leave us?" One asks.

"I want to be with Him." A voice cries

"Does anyone have any oil in their lamps?" Another

yells.

They each try to light their lamps, but it's an exercise in futility.

One rises and walks, "I hear them, they are this way."

The other four follow. The sounds of the wedding celebration becoming louder as they drew near.

"We are getting close. Let's hold each other's hands so we don't get lost."

They walk in small steps. Their bare feet stepping into the cold sand, careful not to step on thorns or rocks. The sound grows louder and they feel themselves walking up a hill. Down below, they see a mansion that has lit up the night sky. They release their hands and run down the hill. Laughing with excitement, they made it to the wedding.

They approach the door of the mansion. One knocks and yells, "Lord, Lord, open the door to us! We are here!" They step back and wait in anticipation.

The Lord opens the door, looks at them and says, "I do not recognize you." And closes the door.

The women, devastated, cry out. "Why?" and walk back into the cold, pitch black night.

"What shall we do?" One whispers.

"You are now with me." They hear the moaning of an old voice.

"Look up, and you can see them, but you can never be with them." They tilt their heads and see the bosom of Abraham.

"No!" one virgin cries out. "I still have time. Let me go back."

The women look beyond the rich man and see the light from above trickle in, illuminating the faces of hundreds, then thousands of people. Faces full of sorrow and pain.

"You, why are we with you and them? You didn't feed the poor man. And these people behind you are terrible. Why are we with you? This is a mistake." She cries.

The rich man slowly moves towards her. "You should know that you used up all your oil before you fell asleep. You sinned and did not repent. Showed no mercy to the poor and you wasted your life in that world. And it is now too late for you as well."

"What about them?" She points to a small crowd of people. They all belong to Christ the Savior. The rich man looks over at the gathering.

"Hey priest, what are you doing here?" Father Ephraim turns around, looks at the faces and they all melt away except for one.

"Daniel?"

"Daniel!" Father Ephraim wakes up.

* * *

"It's not how I want to die. Not like that."

"I'm sorry. What did you say, Daniel?"

"Cancer. I would hate to die of cancer. You are diagnosed and spend the remaining part of your life being poisoned and radiated. Then the weight loss, hair loss, the throwing up, the tiredness. And if diagnosed as terminal, why fight it? But you feel you need to for your family's sake. So your choice is fooling yourself thinking you are going to be one of the five out of the one thousand to beat it or not fight it and spend your remaining months managing pain, saying your goodbyes and if healthy enough, take that vacation you always dreamed of."

"Daniel, every year you come in here worried about dying. Last year, it was about a massive heart attack. The year before that an aneurysm, the year before that Ebola. You need to not worry so much." His doctor flips through Daniel's record.

"I guess as I get older I feel my mortality. Why do we try to tell ourselves fifty is middle aged? Few people live to one hundred. Middle age is thirty five to forty years old." Daniel thinking out loud.

"Daniel, looking at your records, you stopped smoking fifteen years ago, you hardly drink, you could stand to lose ten pounds. Blood work is normal. You don't have a lot to worry about. And with advances in medicine, more and more people are living well into their nineties. A good ninety, not bed ridden or an invalid. But still active and doing things. So continue to exercise and watch what you eat."

"Thanks doc." Daniel leaps up off the physician's table, finds his pants and puts them on.

"You know, there isn't a good way to die. Except for passing away in your sleep. But most are rather painful and drawn out: emphysema, heart disease, diabetes, kidney failure. You and I might escape a cancer diagnosis, but something is going to get us. And not to sound like a cliche, but live today like it's the last day of your life." His doctor says.

"If that was the case, doc, I would be on a beach, next to my wife, drinking some tropical frozen cocktail watching the sunset. Not here."

"You and me both. Well, we will see you next year." His doctor walks out of the exam room.

Daniel puts on his shirt. His eye catches the sales

brochures on the exam room counter touting the latest life saving drug. *Life saving or life extending?*

* * *

He pulls into the driveway. Daniel sees Lydia in the kitchen window. *Dinner must be ready.*

Out the car door, he opens the gate to the back patio. He hears the squeals and bark of Heidi. She is excited to greet him from his long day of slaying dragons, or in this case, finding more locations for the Hill Country Kitchen Shop.

He opens the door, Heidi runs out of the house, jumps up on Daniel with her front paws.

"Hey girl, off, this is my good suit."

Heidi continues to squeal and runs circles around his legs. Then bounds to the back of the yard to retrieve her tennis ball.

"Not now girl, it's time for supper."

Heidi drops the ball and runs past him into the house.

"That was quite a greeting." Lydia says as he puts the last dish on the table.

"You should be so happy to see me." Daniel jokes.

"I will show you how happy in a different way." She walks past and pats him on his rear.

"So, tonight is chicken enchilada night." She brings over a large casserole dish holding eight cheese and enchilada sauce covered enchiladas.

"Wow, that looks great, but you know there are only two of us now."

"It's hard cooking for only us. I guess it's enchiladas

for dinner tomorrow night, too."

They sit at the table. Three of the five chairs are empty. He grabs his knife and fork and cuts into his dinner.

"Wait, we should say grace first." Lydia says.

"Is that necessary? The kids are gone now. And I'm starving."

"Of course it's necessary. We should thank God for all of our blessings. Do you want to lead us in prayer or should I?"

"You go ahead." He closes his eyes and bows his head. She does the same, but reaches over to him to grab his hand.

"Lord Jesus Christ our God. You blessed the five loaves in the wilderness and fed the multitudes of men, women, and children. Bless also these Your gifts and increase them for the hungry people in the world. You are the One who blesses and sanctifies all things and to You, we give glory forever. Amen."

"That was nice." He goes to grab his fork.

"And don't forget to cross yourself."

"Right." With his thumb, index finger, and ring finger touching, he crosses himself. Head (Father), stomach (Son), right shoulder (Holy spirit), left shoulder (Amen).

"Anything else before we eat?" With his stomach growling, he finds himself a little bothered.

"We did not use our faith just for show. Something used to keep the kids turning out bad by making the wrong decisions."

"I know. Sorry for getting snappy. Just hungry."

"It's alright. But remember how important prayer is and to be thankful. So, how was your physical?"

"Doc says I'm pretty healthy for a fifty-five-year-old man. Just keep doing the usual: eat right, don't drink, don't smoke, exercise and try to find time to relax."

"Did you talk to him about your cancer fear?"

"I did. He gave me some good advice. So I will not worry about it. He suggested I live each day like my last. Do you want to get on a jet plane and fly to Anguilla and enjoy a frozen cocktail with me?"

With a wide smile and a sparkle in her eye. "No, but we need to get away and spend time together and reconnect. Now, with Paulina at graduate school, we are officially empty-nesters. Let's take advantage of this time."

"Alright, use your travel agent skills and find us a place to go for next summer."

"Next summer? It's just me and you now. We can go whenever we want. How about next month? October is a great time to avoid the crowds."

"Do it. Just find a place that looks like one of those beaches you see in the magazines. Crystal blue water, white sandy beach, palm trees, and lounge chairs. Oh, and see if there are tuxedo clad waiters that bring out drinks."

"Tuxedo clad. In the Caribbean? You think that would make them sweaty?"

"You're right, but chair side service would be great."

* * *

She leans her head into his office. "What are you working on?"

He stops typing, saves and closes the file.

"Nothing, some work stuff. What's going on?"

"I found the perfect place for our impromptu vacation."

"Where is that?"

"It's not a place, but a sailboat cruise of the Caribbean. Look at this."

She hands him a brochure of the sailing cruise. The picture is of a three mast 200 foot long sail boat. On board is a restaurant, bar, and deck. Pictures show smiling vacationers drinking, eating, and spending time at seven of the Caribbean's most secluded beaches. He can see them on the ship and beach.

"Go head. Book it."

"Are you serious? Just like that. You don't want me to look at other options, different destinations. You are going to make this that easy?"

"How can we go wrong picking this vacation? Beautiful boat, exotic locations, cabins with kings size beds. This is an easy decision."

"I love you." She takes the papers back from his hands, turns and runs down the hall to the kitchen to book their vacation.

He moves his mouse over the file and opens the document he was working on. He continues to type for several hours into the evening. Tired, he finishes for the night, reads over what he has written, saves and heads for bed.

"Hey, sleepy head, it's time to get up and get ready for church."

"Honey, I'm exhausted. Do we have to go today?" He rolls over and pulls the comforter over his shoulders.

"You sound like one of the kids... when they were ten. Of course we need to go. It will be good for your soul."

"I know. I went to bed late"

"I woke up in the middle of the night and heard you typing away in the office last. Is it that new project you are working on?"

"Something like that."

* * *

"In today's Gospel reading, it is important to reflect on the meaning. I recognize that to some, the Gospel readings don't seem to apply to them. They are boring, they are hard to understand and to some a time to reflect on the big game later in the day."

A quiet laugh is heard among the congregation.

Daniel looks down at his watch. He wonders how long this will take.

"Stop looking at your watch. Pay attention." She whispers to him.

"Alright." He folds his arm over his chest and does his best to listen to the sermon.

"Of the three readings we had earlier, I wanted to highlight several lines. First Luke 7:41: "There was a certain creditor who had two debtors. One owed five hundred denarii, and the other fifty."

Then from Matthew 18:23-18:24, "Therefore the kingdom of Heaven is like a certain king who wanted to settle accounts with his servant. And when he had settled accounts, they brought one to him who owed him ten thousand talents."

He watches Father Ephraim take a moment to adjust his robe. "What do these parables have in common? They are about debt. Not just a monetary debt, but according to Christ, these are debts that are accrued through sin. Some will have more and some, in the case of ten thousand talents. A lot more. These are debts that we ourselves accrue throughout our lives. But here is the thing. Now pay attention."

Daniel looks up from the floor, eyes widened, back straight, prepared to listen.

"We accrue debt through sin, and your reckoning is before the Lord. But, with humble repentance and the mystery of confession to your spiritual father, the debts of sins are stricken before the Judge. So now you ask what if I did not confess my sins, and I die what then happens? Then you will answer for those, or pay your debts from 1 talent to 10,000 talents. To those who think we have time, we don't. As no one ever knows the time they are called home."

* * *

The road winds. Daniel in deep thought. *Everything comes to an end. This road, my life. It's time for me to...*

"Honey, are you alright? You haven't been the same since we left church." Lydia speaking in her easy southern accent. She places her hand on top of his, he continues to drive home.

"Something about what Father said in his sermon. About paying our debts. And our debts being sin. It's been a while since I went to confession. I mean to go, but I always run out of time and it doesn't happen. When was the last time you confessed?"

"Daniel, I go every month, you know that."

"It's surprising. I mean, you have that much to

confess?"

"I sin daily, Daniel. Lies, judging my neighbor, focused on the wrong things in life. There are some churches where the priest requires you to go to confession every week. If not, you do not take part in communion."

"It is time I go to confession more often. I am getting older. I don't think I can go every week, but at least once a month."

"So, is there much to confess? Hope whatever sins you need to confess occurred before were married." She said, half smiling.

"Of course. I mean, there is nothing big. It would be nice to get absolved of all my sins."

"Daniel, it is wonderful for you to speak like this again. When we were younger, you were a strong Orthodox Christian. You took part in church life, attended most of the services. You volunteered at the church functions and you did a year as a Sunday school teacher. We worked together to bring the children up in their faith. Then, once you got wrapped up in the Hill Country account, you kind of fell away. It's a blessing that you care about your soul again."

* * *

Stepping into the church, Daniel finds it to look much different from Sunday morning services. The church is dim, with several candles lit, creating a warm and comforting atmosphere. Daniel walks between two icons as he enters the church. The icon of Christ on the right and the icon for the most Holy Virgin Mary on the left. He sees Father Ephraim standing in the nave's front, waiting for him. Once he sees Daniel, he waves at him to come over. Father Ephraim hugs Daniel and thanks him for coming.

"Thank you Father. It is long past due. I should come more often."

"The important thing is that you are here. Do you want to take a moment to talk? Then we will go over to the icon of Christ, speak what is in your heart and confess your sins."

"Father, what you are doing at the church for those that are close to dying? People like my father. You prepared them for their next life. So was it only a matter of confessing their sins and they were good with God? Their slate is clean?"

"Yes, the one's they confess are forgiven. So Daniel, are you ready?"

"Yes, and I hope you weren't planning on going anywhere, Father. I have a lot to confess."

"That's why I am here. If it takes all night, it takes all night."

They take a step up onto the solea and stand next to each other. They face the icon of Christ. Daniel turns around to make sure no one else is in the church. They both stand in silence. Daniel focuses in on the eyes of Christ and says.

"Father, I am a sinner. I have not been a dutiful husband, father, and son. I passed up opportunities to help those in need. I use the Lord's name in vain and raised my voice in anger at those I love. I have not kept the fast, I avoided going to church. I lie and curse. I look at other woman."

"Daniel, don't speak in generalities. Be more specific.

You need to account for each individual sin."

Daniel closes his eyes and thinks back to as far as he can remember.

"I stole candy from the little grocery store in our town. It was one summer, and I was with some friends. We all dared each other to steal something. I wanted to take a giant pixie stick, but that was too big, so I stole baseball cards. I can't mention all the dates and times I lied. But I lied to my parents, teachers, priests, friends. I was full of lust once I hit puberty. All I did was imagine girls from school naked and having sex with them. In college, I drank a lot, got drunk and experimented with drugs."

Daniel takes a break from listing his sinful acts.

"Continue." Father speaks

"I put myself above others. And I found myself worshiping money. When my children were younger, I raised my voice to them."

Silence. Father waits.

"That is all, Father."

"Are you sure?"

Daniel thinks. He wants to confess several other sins, especially his affair with Iris. But he isn't ready to tell.

"I am good for now."

Father Ephraim motions for Daniel to kneel in front of the icon. The priest puts the stole over him. He feels him tap the sign of the cross on his head, reads a prayer of absolution, and tells him to rise.

"Thank you Father."

"Of course. You understand you don't need to wait months to confess. You can come every day if you want to."

Daniel smiles. "I promise it won't be months."

"Daniel, you are not the first Christian to go wander off the path. There are thousands that choose to do that every day. The important thing is to recognize it and ask for forgiveness. Remember how peaceful your father was when he passed from this life? We should all be that prepared before it is our time to come home."

He opens the door of his car, he slides inside and sits, puts the key in the ignition, starts it up and stares at the church. At first he thought he got away with something, but then sighs as he cheated himself. Before he realizes what it was, he hears a tap on his window. It is Father Ephraim. He rolls down his window.

"Yes, Father."

"Is everything alright?"

With all seriousness, Daniel looks at the priest.

"No. There was more I had to say, more to confess to, but I was fearful of what you might think of me."

"Daniel, I do not judge. And I listen to so many confessions I don't remember who confessed which sin. Please come back inside? I can open up the church."

"That's alright. I will come back next week. By then, I can work up my courage."

"Well, you don't need to worry or work up courage to the all knowing and all forgiving Lord. Please come back inside."

Still not ready. "No, I would like to wait 'til next week. I do trust you. I'm just scared."

"It's your choice. If not today, I will be happy to see you tomorrow, next week, whenever you are ready. Just don't wait too long."

"Yes, I don't want to be like one of the five virgins who didn't make it to the wedding in time."

Father Ephraim is taken aback. "No, you don't want

to be like one of them."

"You have a good night, Daniel. And pray for me."

"I will, and thank you."

CHAPTER SEVENTEEN

A beautiful fall day, made up of blue skies and sunshine covering all of central Texas. The summer heat and humidity have dissipated, and Texans feel comfortable to leave their air conditioned homes and enjoy one of God's many gifts.

"Hey girl, come here." Heidi barrels towards him from the back of the fence. She stops, picks up her tennis ball, runs to him, drops the ball at his feet.

"Good girl." Daniel says with his voice one octave higher. He leans down, pats her head, picks up the ball, and throws it to the back fence.

In a matter of moments, she has the ball in her mouth and brings it back.

Sitting and looking at him with a ball in her mouth, tail wagging, wanting to play more.

"Not now, girl. Long day today and ready for dinner."

He enters his house, before he allows the dog in, he commands her, "Drop it." She releases the ball, and it rolls around on the patio to wait for another day.

"Will you take the garbage out?" Lydia asks Daniel.

"No problem." He grabs the kitchen garbage bag, passes by his wife, stops and gives her a kiss. She continues to wash the dishes. Stepping onto the patio, his first step out of the door lands on the tennis ball. He briefly twists his ankle and stumbles forward.

He looks back at the ball. *She needs to be careful where she drops that.*

Lydia following from behind "Are you alright?

"Yeah, just a little twist of the ankle, nothing to worry about." He says while rubbing out the pain.

"You are still a tough guy. That's why you are such a turn-on."

"Now, with talk like that, maybe we should both stop what we are doing and head back into the house." Daniel limps forward and waves her over.

"That's pretty sexy. On second thought. I think I will let you rest up and I will head over to the store. Do you need anything?" She puts her sunglasses down from the top of her head.

"Nope. I'm good. See you soon."

They exchange "I love you's" and Lydia steps into the old mini van and heads down the driveway. She opens the window and waves at Daniel one more time.

* * *

Daniel alone on this typical fall Saturday. Now, with the kids away at school, there is only yard work to fill the hours. No more running from one side of town to the other, dropping the kids off at their sporting events. Fifteen years have come and gone in this part of his suburban life. This time is about adjusting and catching up with neglected maintenance on the house and marriage.

The monotony of raking leaves allows him to think. Think about today and tomorrow. About the past. He's generated innovated ideas with this time alone with nature. Air powered automobiles, the solution to bring about world peace, replacing the gray squirrel with flying squirrels. With each scrape against the ground brings him closer to the next million dollar idea.

Daniel's mind wanders from business ideas to his brief affair with Iris. It was difficult to keep the business relationship up without being intimate, especially on their nights out of town. He is thankful that her faith was stronger than his. Even though a decade later he can still see every curve of her body, feel it in his hands as he caressed her, and fascinated by her emerald eyes.

Revisiting that time with her, and playing it back in his mind's eye, he didn't even realize he raked up the last pile of leaves and bagged it. While heading across the patio to drop the bag in the garbage, he thought about the last time he was with Iris. Laying in the hotel bed, watching her sleep. Daniel closed his eyes, reliving the night one more time.

The memory is short lived as a loud yelp from Heidi shattered his thought. Daniel turns and sees that she was scratched by the neighbor cat she cornered by the fence. "That will teach ya, girl." Daniel chuckles.

Daniel grabs the bag, turns and his next step lands on Heidi's tennis ball. This time, his foot kicks out in front of him. The weight of the yard debris bag makes him top heavy, flipping his legs above his head. The movement is fast. In a moment he is alive, the next he feels the back of his head crack against the brick porch. Eyes wide, pupils dilating, his last vision on earth are of birds flying against a bright blue sky.

Heidi runs up to him, circles him and whimpers. She licks his face, then his hands. She knows something is wrong with the leader of her pack. She yelps.

Lydia returns from the store. She pulls into the driveway, parks the car in the garage, and grabs the bags of groceries. As she walks out of the garage carrying the bags of food, she sees Daniel lying on the patio. Heidi sitting by him, protecting her injured master.

"Daniel!" she yells to him. Lydia moves closer and sees a crimson halo behind his head. She drops her groceries and purse and rushes towards him. She falls to her knees, puts her head to his chest. Silent. She tries to scream "No!", but the word doesn't come out. Just air. She looks into his eyes. *He's gone*. She puts her hand over his face and closes his eyelids. She leans over and lies on him, crying. Heidi now has two to guard.

From across the way, Lydia's neighbor sees both of them laying on the patio. She drops her dishes in the sink and yells to her husband. "Ray, call 911."

She runs out the door to help. As she realized there was nothing she could do, she slows down, covers her mouth, tears stream down her face.

Ray comes out of the house. "I called 911. Help is coming."

She whispers "It's too late."

CHAPTER EIGHTEEN

"Help me. I can't see anything. It's all a blur."

"What are those sounds? Why can't I move? I should be in a tunnel of light. Where are my relatives?

I think I see them. They are getting closer. No, that isn't them. Who are you? Oh, God, they are hideous. They are surrounding me. Demons!

Get away from me. Stop laughing at me!"

The demons surrounding Daniel, laughing, barking, snorting, making the most awful sound he has ever heard.

"Why do I feel this pain? My soul wants to be free."

The demons stand over Daniel, contorting their faces, mocking him, making false accusations against him.

"I never did that. That is disgusting. I would never sexually abuse a child. Or beat an old woman. And never did I participate in an orgy."

The demons kept on telling lies and half truths, confusing Daniel. He sees one, and it looks like it is holding documents. He's passing it around to the other demons and they laugh, shriek and yell out the sins of Daniel's life.

"They are not true." Daniel is paralyzed.

"Daniel. Stop looking at them." A voice from the darkness.

The voice, strong like thunder.

"You pests, you shameless savages. Cowards always running ahead of the angels. Do not be so joyful. There is nothing here for you."

The demons run to the voice. Holding papers in front of his face.

"Look, see what he has done. He's a liar. He lies to everyone. His parents, his children, his friends, his boss, his wife and even his priest." A demon hisses.

"Oh, and look here. He stole money from the blind man. He took the money right out of his can. And worse, he walked by him the next day and pushed the blind man over. And then kicked him in the head."

"Get away from him. He is not worth your time. Go save someone else. We will take his soul right now." Another growled.

The area Daniel is in is silent again. Faint clanging and heavy foot steps approach. Daniel panics. At first, he sees a beast. Lion, bear, yak. No, it's an enormous man, carrying various medieval weapons. Dull and rusted. Hatchets, axes, knives, blades of all sizes.

Daniel trembles.

"Get away from Daniel. He is not full of sin." The angel pleads for him.

The gruesome being snorts. He stands over Daniel and starts to pull him apart. Joint by joint, bone by bone, nail by nail. There is no escape from this horror. He sees the giant grab a long blade. And feels it slice across his neck. Then, the fingers of his large hands dig up under his skin, grabbing onto his lower jaw and yanking his head off. Daniel's soul thrusts itself away from his body with all the fright in the world.

The vision from the soul of Daniel's eyes are clear. He scans the area. Demons are gone. He looks again. He peels back the darkness. From above, he sees himself lying on the ground. Police, fire, and EMS surrounding him. His wife is in the arms of her neighbor, his dog barking at those that are standing above his lifeless body. "Good girl Heidi, Good girl."

And off to the side, he spots his killer. A $.25 yellow tennis ball.

"Not a real heroic way to go, is it?" He asks himself.

He watches as Lydia removes herself from the arms of her neighbor. She takes her phone and with jittering fingers, tries to press the numbers. Frustrated, She throws the phone on the ground, runs into the house. When she returns, she is carrying a book. She opens it and reads prayers over his body. The prayers for the departed. He can faintly hear them as they pass him by.

"It's not what you thought was it, not how you thought you were going to die?" The deep thundering voice, now softened, asks.

"No. I thought I was going to die an old man." Daniel trying to move around and answer the voice.

"That's what all the souls believed. They were going to live to one-hundred, then die peacefully in their sleep. Death is not peaceful; It is painful. When your soul is leaving your body, it's as painful as birth. But remember, this is how your death is planned from the beginning."

"What, who are you? Are you my angel?" Daniel asks

into the realm he now finds himself in.

"Yes."

"I can't see you, I can't see me. I can't see anything. The darkness is scary."

"Wait." The angel replies

Daniel hears crackle, a shock of thunder, not in the distance, but near him and his angel.

His new world is now unfolding in front of him. A world filled with darkness with flashes of reds and what appear to be souls above and below him.

He looks at his angel. It is what he imagined. A genderless being. Clothed in robes with large white wings. Young in looks, but eyes full of wisdom of the universe.

"Scared, you can see now."

"Now that I see you, I am not scared."

"Not now. Soon you will."

"You are my guardian angel."

"Yes."

"You have been with me since I was born?"

"No, I arrived at your baptism, the time when Christians receive their guardian angel. We arrive to fight off the demons."

"Demons?"

"Demons are everywhere. But you can find they like being around churches. They wait, and wait, then become active, especially around baptisms, weddings, and funerals. They are vultures and feed off the souls of infants, attack the bride and groom, and sit and wait for lost souls at funerals."

"Wait for what?"

"To take them, to torment them. If you don't have your guardian angel, you have no chance against them.

You will lose, and they will win."

"What do they win?"

"They get you, your soul."

"Thank you for being here."

"I am here because you are baptized in Christ. I am here because you prayed to me. I am here because you believe, you believe in me, believe in God. In Christ."

Daniel looks for the world he just left. He feels prayers from Lydia, and now Father Ephraim. The Angel feels it too.

"Daniel, that life is over. You are now in your new life. You can't see it again."

"Do you have a name Angel?" Daniel's voice saddened.

"You can call me Leo."

"Leo, you are to be my guide now. To take me through the tollhouses?"

"Maybe." Leo rushes to Daniel, inspects his soul.

"What are you doing, Leo?"

"If you know about the tollhouses, then you know I have to defend you against those horrible demons. I can only defend you if you have done good works and have lived a Christian life."

"I've tried to do all that is right. Please stay with me through this."

"Daniel, I will. But from here on, be brave. Don't be scared. Say your Jesus Prayer. I am warning you, this is going to be terrible." Leo lifts Daniel up and swiftly moves through the realm.

The blackness opens up and they reach the first aerial tollhouse Daniel sees it is not an area with a structure, like that depicted in the icon of the last judgment. It's just a cave like area where you can't proceed any further. Leo and Daniel stop and wait. One by one, the ghouls and demons come from the realm. As they approach, Daniel hears them accusing him of the slander he committed in his life. Some of them were truthful, many accusations were lies.

The closer they got, he could see the demons. He found them awful to look at. Some spindly, with bulbous heads, sharpened teeth, long curved fingers, scaly skin, and no eyes. Others are larger standing over top, looking down onto the Leo and Daniel.

"Oh, fantastic. We have another one of Ephraim's. Father Ephraim missed this one. His soul is tarnished. Leo, give up this soul. You are wasting time." One of the large slathering demons commanded of Leo.

"You accuse him, now show me." Leo demands

The smaller demons with excitement, jump in recounting the many times Daniel lied about others to get what he wanted: money, sex, or for jest.

"And see what he did to his friend. He lied to his girlfriend about him. He told her he was cheating on her, just so he could bed her."

"I did not do that Leo."

They encircled the two and spinning around them and yelling accusations again. Time, place, who he hurt, what he did to them.

"Enough!" Leo commanded.

"You giving him up?" The larger demon asked.

"No. You know, he has confessed to most of these accusations. And he would have confessed to the others, but they occurred in his youth. He has used his words to eulogize, praise and buildup others. Later in his life."

"Yes, but that is not enough to get past us. Do you have anything else?" The demons surround Leo, looking him over.

"Take this and let us move on." Leo hands over what looks to be gold coins to the demons. They move out of the way. The cave opens and allows the two to continue.

"What did you give the demons?" Daniel asks.

"Spiritual gold. It's not gold coins, but it looks like it to them. The gold is the good works you did in your earthly life, prayers from loved ones, the times you went to church, Divine Liturgy, received communion. When I can't defend each accusation, I pay them spiritual gold. I pray we have enough to make it through all the tollhouses, as it looks like you did not confess all your sins."

Daniel's soul draws back. *Does Leo know? If he does, then I must be safe because he is still by my side.*

"Leo, you have been with me during all of my days? Why did you not intervene to stop me from sinning?"

Leo turning to Daniel, "Sometimes, we angels will leave the people they assign us to."

"Why would you do that?"

"Because as much as we try to stop it, our people will become so evil we cannot bear to know anymore. We give up and move on. Now, if that same person repents, confesses their sins, renews their lives and prays for us, we will return."

"What about me?" Daniel asks.

"Daniel, there are some things you did where I had to leave you, you were living a sinful life. But I returned when you prayed for me."

They reach the next aerial tollhouse. In the distance is a bright red cave. The two see the demons surrounding a soul that has no angel to defend it. They close in tight, then yell at it in a variety of languages, and bark at it.

"What is this place we are coming to?" Daniel asks.

"This is the tollhouse of Verbal Abuse. That soul in front of us has no chance against the demons."

The demons continue their assault on the weak soul with accusations of the person. They tell how he verbally abused all those that cared for him. His wife, his parents, and his children. The demons gave examples of him intimidating his child, demeaning her by calling her ugly and stupid. He used his words to beat down on his wife. First, by bringing her up with a compliment, and once her guard was down, he would tell her she was an awful wife. How she was a whore because she had sex with other men before they were married. That she cannot please him. The demons showed the consequences of his abuse. Things he did not know. His words turned his daughter into an alcoholic. She would use drink to numb the pain she felt when she looked into a mirror. "Daddy was right. I'm disgusting."

His wife, trying hard to please him, went on afternoon dates to sleep with strange men to learn how to become a better lover.

The soul whimpered, then the demons engulfed the soul and took it away. And as those demons left, a new set of demons took their place.

Leo and Daniel arrived. The new demons study the two, then confer amongst themselves. One of the slug like demons without eyes sniffed around Daniel's soul, then returned to the other demons.

Leo goes near the demons and says, "This man has abused no one through his voice and words. Let us continue." Leo takes Daniel. As they move closer to the demons, the cave opens up and they move on through.

Leo and Daniel continue to move in an upward trajectory. In the distance is a cave made up of emeralds and gold. As they move closer, it wasn't demons milling about and waiting, but humans. All well dressed and fitted with jewelry. From crowns to ruby shoes.

"What is this Leo?"

"The tollhouse of envy Daniel."

Now in the cave, the demons approach Leo and recount all the days, times, and places Daniel was envious of others.

"Leo, I confessed those sins."

"Daniel, it does not seem as if you confessed all."

A finely dressed demon comes up to Leo and began his accusations. "As you can hear, Leo, this wretched soul did not confess all the times he was envious of others. Worse of all, he was envious of evil doers. How they got away with their sins and were rewarded."

Another demon approached. This one looked female, scantily dressed, with long golden hair covering one part of her face. "And his poor wife. Daniel, would stare at the wives and girlfriends of his friends and be envious that they get to lie with them, and he has to sleep with her."

"That is not true. My wife is beautiful. I never was envious of another man because of his wife!"

A demon clothed in what looks like a three piece suit shows Leo a scene of Daniel sitting in his car after meeting with a client that was his own age, but much wealthier. He showed Leo, Daniel staring out the windshield, tearing up because he has not achieved the same level of success as his client."

Leo pulls out gold coins and gives it to the demon.

The demon rushes to meet up with the others, then cackles. When they pass by the demons, the emerald, gold, clothing, the good looks all melt away into a brown cave of half bodied demons.

"What is the problem with envy, Leo? That is how the world goes round. It is the motivation for many that ends up doing good for the world."

"Because we do not envy sinners, but be in fear of the Lord all day long." Leo shot back.

As they continue on their ascent, Daniel senses worry in the angel.

"What's wrong Leo?" Daniel asks.

"The next tollhouse is one that we lose many souls. It's a sin that people commit so often they could not confess them all."

As they come near, the tollhouse cave is large. There are many souls. Too many to count, that are being dragged out and back past Leo and Daniel. When coming closer, it sounds like a party. Chatter of the demons in foreign languages, music without rhythm or tone playing throughout the cave. The demons are here, because they are lazy and the souls are easy to pick off.

"What is the sin?"

"Daniel, this is the tollhouse of falsehoods. For liars."

CHAPTER NINETEEN

Father Ephraim walks into the chapel and sees Lydia in front of the icon of Christ, holding a long black prayer rope, slowly moving each woolen knot between her fingers. Candle light flickering, lighting the new widow in an amber glow.

Father Ephraim tries to walk quietly, so not to disturb Lydia, but a creek from the old church floor caused her to break from her prayers.

"Father, is that you?" Lydia whispers into the dark.

"Yes Lydia, my apologies for interrupting your prayers." He walks closer to her.

"It's fine Father, I am glad you are here. I have questions about the memorial service and what I need to do to help Daniel while he is on his journey." Her eyes swollen from crying night and day since his passing.

"Let's take a seat in the back."

Lydia follows Father Ephraim to the rear of the church, where there are several wooden benches for those who need to sit during church services. Father Ephraim invites Lydia to take a seat next to him.

"Father, everything is moving so fast. It's been two days since he passed, but I feel like he is still in my arms.

And that I just left the bedroom, where I washed his body before the funeral home came and picked him up. And..." Lydia weeps.

"Yes Lydia." Father Ephraim asks her to continue.

"We were just standing together here. Now, we will never go to church together again." Tears stream down her face.

"Lydia, you will have one last service together at his memorial tomorrow, then you will be together again one day in your magnificent resurrected bodies."

"Father, I am trying to do everything right. The way you instructed us. I am praying ceaselessly for his soul. But how do I know if it is helping?"

"Your prayers, your children's prayers, prayers from the faithful all help Daniel on his journey. Come over here." Father Ephraim gets up from the bench and walks over to the icon of the Last Judgment. He looks at the bottom of the icon, showing the start of the soul's journey.

"Lydia, remember? We discussed this many times. When a person dies, their guardian angel meets them. Some have one, others have many. The angel will take the soul on their journey upward, but they must pass through the tollhouses where the angel will defend the soul."

Lydia, for the first time, noticed the detail of the icon. Creepy dark figures with torn wings holding scales at each stop along the path. Souls of people falling off the path into pits of fire, others moving through. In the upper middle of the icon is Christ, sitting on the throne.

"You see, Lydia, there are many stops along the route. Stops to account for your sins. Some souls go past because they did not commit that type of sin or they confessed for it to their spiritual father. But, if they did not confess, their guardian angel will pay off the demons with spiritual gold. Made up of good deeds, church attendance, partaking of communion. But most importantly, prayers from family, friends, those at church, nuns, and monks at the various monasteries."

"Father, I understand if you can't tell me. But did Daniel confess his sins? Do you think he confessed enough to get him past these horrible demons?"

"I cannot tell you what he confessed, Lydia, but he confessed his sins. For a period of time, he was not diligent with his confessions, but prior to his passing, he confessed more often."

"Did he confess enough?"

"I don't know Lydia. That is why we continue to pray for those that departed. To give spiritual gold to their guardian angel. As you can see, some of these tollhouses are very difficult to account for, as some sins are more numerous than others."

"Where do you think he is right now, Father?" Lydia trying to imagine what Daniel was experiencing at that moment.

"He is possibly through the tollhouses of slander and verbal abuse, maybe envy. Tomorrow he will approach the tollhouse of falsehood or lying."

Lydia trying to read the tollhouses that continue after, but the script is in Greek.

"Lydia, you must go home. We have the Trisagion prayer service tonight, then the memorial service tomorrow morning. You have your children and your church family ready to help you. You can reach out to them or, as always, to me. Now please go home and get some rest."

"Thank you Father. I will."

Lydia kisses the priest's right hand and exits the church. Father Ephraim goes to blow out the candle, but before he does so, he crosses himself and venerates the icon of Christ.

* * *

A small gathering returns to Christ the Savior for the Trisagion service. The prayer for the soul. Lydia is the first to walk in, and in the front of the church is Daniel's casket. A simple one made of pine with an Orthodox cross carved into the top and the words "Holy God, Holy Mighty, Have Mercy on us" written on each side. Lydia approaches, crosses herself three times, then kisses the casket. She steps aside as each person behind her does the same. In a moment, her grown children; Liev, Simeon, and Paulina stand on each side of her. There for a shoulder to cry on, arms to wrap around and comfort or to catch her if she falls.

Father Ephraim enters the church from the altar. He censes the church with incense and continues on with the service, while the choir sings the songs for the reposed. Lydia closes her eyes. Some might mistake her for praying, but she does not. Her imagination gets the best of her. She thinks of Daniel lying still in the box. *How alone he must be.*

She imagines him on the other side, watching as the angel tries to defend him at each tollhouse. Then, for a quick moment, she conjures up the most hideous image possible of what the demons must look like. Hideous with charred skin, the smell of rotten flesh, razor-sharp teeth to eat the souls, long talon-like fingers to rip the soul out of the body or the clutches of the guardian angel. The terrible face looks directly at Lydia. She opens her eyes in fright. She feels the arm of Liev wrap around her.

The service comes to a close. Those in attendance exit the church, leaving Lydia and her children. Father Ephraim calls the family to the casket. The two altar boys, the oldest of the group, remove the flowers that were sitting atop of the casket. Then Father instructs them to remove the lid.

Lydia opens her eyes and sees Daniel lying there in peace, dressed in his best suit. Lydia looks down at him. As long as she stares at him, he still does not move, which troubles her. She puts her hand on top of his head to stroke his hair. His skin is cold. She can't help but notice his lips and eyelids are glued shut and they combed his hair straight back instead of parted. Disturbed by the sight, she takes her hand and moves his hair to the side.

"I love you Daniel Roza. We will be together again some day."

Lydia turns and walks away. The children together stand at the casket and give their last words of love, thanks, and apologies to their father. They each cross themselves and walk to their mother. Then turn and watch as the altar boys put the lid back on the casket.

"Mom, I am going to stay behind and read prayers over dad, then Simeon and Paulina are going to take my place so I can return home, sleep and be ready for the memorial tomorrow." Said Liev.

Lydia nods her head, then gives him a hug. She watches as he opens up a prayer book and reads over the casket.

* * *

The image in the mirror looking back at her is that of a stranger. Covered in black dress, pale skin, reddened eyes and swollen lips. And alone. Lydia brushes her hair one last time. She glances at the picture of her and Daniel on the night stand. Then walks past their encased wedding crowns hanging on their bedroom wall.

"Mom, do you need help?" Liev asks, standing at the bottom of the stairs.

Lydia, looking down upon him, sees Daniel as a young man.

"I'm fine. I think it is time to head over to church."

Lydia and her sons arrive at church. They are one of the first to show up. Father Ephraim, Reader George, Jonah, and the choir arrived earlier preparing for the memorial service.

Father Ephraim comes out of the church to greet the family. They each approach and kiss his right hand.

"Lydia, may the Lord give you strength on this day. Paulina has been here all night reading prayers over Daniel. She is changing in the bathroom and will meet you inside the church."

Father Ephraim, followed by Lydia and her sons, walk up the stairs and into the church. If they could see what angels see, the gathering of demons surrounding the outside of the church would have frightened them.

The grieving family stand near Daniel's casket, which is placed in the middle of the church. The candle stands are arranged at the head and feet of the casket. When loved ones and friends enter, they surround the coffin. In a matter of minutes, the church is so full of people, many are standing outside.

Father Ephraim enters the nave from the altar. He walks around the coffin three times, censing it each time he does. He continues and censes the interior of the church and all those that are in it, leaving the church full of the sweet smell of incense. To those who never witnessed an Orthodox memorial service, it will seem foreign. It is a last church service for the departed instead of a "celebration of life."

Father Ephraim begins the memorial service with petitions, prayers, backed up by the singing from the youthful choir. Lydia's thoughts are no more on the coldness of the coffin, but sadness mixed with joy. She is sad that her husband is gone, but joy knowing that today he will receive spiritual gold to help him on his journey, and that one day they will be together again.

Lydia feels the love of the congregation that surrounds her, Daniel, and family. The service becomes a blur. Some things come into focus as others remain blurry. She looks at the icons of Christ, the Theotokos, and the resurrection. The details of each icon become so real, they almost look three dimensional, as she could step inside. In contrast, the people's faces have lost all definition. The coffin, though feet away, seems small and distant. Lydia can hear the hymns of the choir, but has difficulty deciphering the words. Words she sang many times as a member.

Several people standing outside, listening to the choir, start to hear other things. Words and thoughts that surprised them:

"You see, look how young he was and God takes him from his wife and family just like that, in an instant. What kind of God would do that?" One hears.

"He and his wife come to church every week. They fast, pray, take communion, confess, and this is their reward. Dead at 55 and a widow at 54. Why even bother?" Spoken into another.

"You are right. You need to live for the moment. Enjoy life while you can, because God can call you home anytime." Heard by another.

"There is nothing after this life. We are all worm meat. There is no judgment. Do what you want. They call it sin. I call it pleasure." Is spoken to several.

The demons roaming about those outside seeding doubt into their hearts. They pass back and forth between each person. Introducing new thoughts and ideas about death and the after life. Each thought to prevent the person from hearing the words of the beautiful memorial service and to keep those from doing what is necessary to escape the tollhouses, making it easier for the demons to take each soul to hell.

Inside the church, hundreds of prayers are thought, spoken, chanted and sung by priest and congregation. All moving upward.

The memorial service ends with everyone within the church singing "May His memory be eternal."

At that point, Father Ephraim has the lid of the coffin opened for those to say their last goodbyes.

Lydia is the last to approach Daniel. She smiles, looking down at him. "This is not you. This is just your body, but your soul lives on." And with today's service, his soul is bursting with energy.

Lydia and her family ride in the limo to the cemetery

for a graveside service.

"Don't worry, this is a small service with close family and friends. But it is important to have him blessed one last time before..."

Lydia stops herself, as she can't bear to say, Daniel will be put in the ground.

"Mom, I overheard some people asking why you weren't crying at the service." Paulina asked.

"I've done my crying. I don't have anymore tears to give." She whispers while looking out the window.

They reach the cemetery, Daniel's coffin is already at the grave. Next to the coffin is Jonah reading prayers over him.

The small congregation makes their way to the graveside. Chairs are placed by the coffin, but everyone chooses to stand.

Father Ephraim begins the graveside service, more prayers for Daniel.

"If anyone wishes to say something about Daniel, please come forward." Father Ephraim asks after the service.

At first no one comes forward, then with some hesitation Jonah steps up, walking away from Maria. He stares at the coffin, takes a moment, then begins.

"Everyone here knows I am a man of few words, and a man who likes to get right to the point. So here it goes." Tears fall from Jonah's eyes.

"Daniel, you are my brother. We shared so much together, from altar boys to each others best men and God parents for our children. You had patience with me as I found my way back to the Lord. You believed me when I told you about the horrible demons I saw when I died. Daniel, you were taken from us too soon. Way too soon. But we, our church, will take care of your family. I love you Daniel. See you soon, brother." Jonah steps away from the coffin, takes off his boutonnière and places it on top of the casket.

His three children try to come forward, but the moment they do, they each break down into tears, so neither spoke for their father.

Father Ephraim returns and tells the people. "I have a few words, and I pray that what I say here spreads to not only the rest of the congregation, but to your friends and family. Even if they are not Orthodox. What you need to tell them, what people need to understand, is do your priest a favor. Do me a favor. Get to know your spiritual father. Your parish priest. Why? Because I have performed hundreds of funerals, and the worst ones are those that I can't say anything about the departed? I can't say anything because I don't know them. They never come to church, go to confession, and take part in church life. They come to church for weddings, baptisms, funerals. Maybe Christmas and Pascha. And if I do not know you, if your priest does not know you, then how will Christ know you? Now, without revealing too much, I have known Daniel for years. He came to church, he repented during his life, not waiting to do it on his death bed, and he gave his talents. Let Daniel be an example. Don't be a stranger. God bless you all."

The grave diggers return and remove the flowers from the coffin and lower Daniel into the ground. Lydia, her family, Jonah, and his family stay and watch. While they put the coffin into the ground, a man standing thirty feet away, dressed in Scottish garb, raises the horn of the bagpipe to his lips and plays "Amazing Grace."

* * *

"I can't believe you put all of this together in three days." Maria tells Lydia between bites of the traditional fish dinner served after funerals.

"I had a lot of help. And we had all of this planned after Daniel's father passed away. We bought the plot and headstone. And as creepy as this sounds. Daniel purchased a custom made coffin for Orthodox Christians. It has been under wraps for a decade now in storage. It is beautiful."

Maria finishes her plate and takes Lydia by the hand. "Lydia, Jonah and I are here for you. Anything you need. If you need to get out of the house, our door is always open to you." She pats Lydia's hand.

"Thank you Maria. I'm afraid all of this is going to hit later. In the quiet of the night when my mind races. For now, say a pray for me for strength."

"Of course Lydia." She releases Lydia's hand, sits up and pushes a shot of Greek whiskey towards her.

"One shot Lydia, it's tradition."

"I'm not a drinker Maria, and this stuff tastes horrible."

"Just one shot." Maria pushes it closer.

"For tradition." Lydia takes the small shot glass filled to the top with the caramel colored drink and swallows the whole shot. She puts the glass on the table. Shakes a little and says, "that's all the tradition I can stomach."

CHAPTER TWENTY

A pack of demons breaks off from the larger gathering and head over to Daniel and Leo. Leo moves in between the demons and Daniel to stop their frenzied attacks. Their voices mingled accusations of lying against Daniel. Although the voices were deep, the speed of their words were quick.

"Angel, this one lies to everyone. Big lies. Minor lies. To their faces and behind their backs. Give him to us. He's not worthy to continue on." The demon snarls.

Another one approaches "Look here, May 28th, 1991. He lied to the street beggar, saying he had no money, But his wallet was full of dollar bills." The demon laughed after he finished with evidence against Daniel.

Demon after demon swarmed yelling accusations of the lies told by Daniel. They gave names, dates and the results of the lies. Some accusations were true, others the evil demons made up.

"Leo, I confessed the sins of lying, but I cannot account for each individual one. They are right. They are too numerous. How can anyone get past this tollhouse? We are all liars."

Leo pushed past the demons in search of the chief demon in charge of this tollhouse. Crouching in the corner, with its black bat-like wings wrapped around his skeleton like body, is the chief.

"Get up you!" Leo wakes the demon.

The demon raises its head from its wing wrapping and opens its red eyes. It's grin showing a mouth full of razor like teeth.

"Go away angel and leave the soul in the room behind me with the others. We will burn the trash later." The demon puts its head back into the folds of its wings.

"This soul is a sympathetic soul. He confessed to being a liar."

"And yet he continued to lie after he confessed. He can't go through."

Leo bends down and comes face to face with the demon.

"Demon, if I was allowed to rip the wings off of you and crush your skull, I would."

"Why? We are doing God's work as well. Do you honestly want all the souls in Heaven? Especially these filthy ones?" The demon points one of its bony fingers towards the room behind it.

"God is the judge, not you. Now here, take these coins. That is enough to cover his lies."

The demon unwraps itself and reaches towards the coins. It takes the small bag and folds it into its wings.

"You may proceed. For every one soul that gets past, thousands more thrown into the room of liars. Now, move on." The demon tucks its head back into its wings.

A space behind him opens up for Leo and Daniel to continue on.

* * *

"Angel, there were so many souls in that room. I could feel them and see how miserable they were. The pain and regret gush out of the door. Why so many?"

"Daniel, as time goes by and the world below grows older, people move further away from God. More and more people are caught up in vain pursuits. They have become self indulgent, only caring about money, luxury and deceit. They waste all of their time living for the now that they find no time to attend church and read scriptures. All of which clearly teach about the grave harm these vices are on the soul."

The multitude of souls stuck at this tollhouse troubles Daniel's soul, and he can only imagine how much worse it will be.

"It is so simple. Read scripture. And you can foresee all the temptations that will lead you to sin. You can fight off the demons of the world pulling you towards those sins. So if you read scripture, you understand and you are prepared to fight. Fight with prayer, ask for strength."

"You mean the Jesus prayer? It has that much power?" Daniel asks.

"Yes, a simple prayer with only nine words, "Lord Jesus Christ have mercy on me, a sinner" has enormous power. It keeps you from sinning and helps you instantly repent."

Daniel feels them moving upward, and he tries to recall the icon of the Last Judgment for an idea of the next tollhouse. He tries, but he can't remember.

In the air, Daniel hears the barking, growling,

howling, whimpers, roars and yelling. The sounds cause fear in his soul.

Out of the darkness, several demons appear. Some not saying a word, yet opening closing their mouths, others are biting at each other, ripping their spiritual flesh from each other's bones. Leo pushes the demons aside as they try to attack him. As they move forward, new demons appear. This group is made up of fewer demons, but they are larger and fierce.

"This one is mean. So much wrath and anger." One says to the other demon.

"Yes, so angry. Angel, he can't move forward. He was terrible to his children. Back in November 2001, his children brought him so much anger he swore at them."

"And he raised his fist. He almost hit the girl." Cried out another.

"Oh, and he hit his wife. On June the 10th, 2010. They were arguing about finances. He raised his fist and punched her on the right side of her face. She fell to the floor. Cold."

"That is not true!" Daniel, for the first time, defended himself against the demons.

"I would never hit my wife or my children. Liars, go away."

The demons laughed.

"All that anger and fury. You have struck people in fights. Thousands of times, you rose your voice in anger. To your wife, children. To perfect strangers."

The demons continued with their accusations.

"And worse, you would yell at them, and when they would talk back, you mocked them."

"And if you couldn't yell at them or strike them, you would throw savage glances at them."

The demons snarled and pushed up against the two, firing out more evidence against Daniel. Daniel started to defend himself, but Leo stopped him.

"Do not engage the demons. It is what they want." Leo whispered.

"This soul has confessed to these sins. And it has been many years since he has raised a fist to anyone. His fights were in his youth. Let us proceed."

The demons disappeared from the air, and Daniel and Leo moved on.

"Leo, I have a question. How do these demons know all of my sins? All the details; when, where, and to whom they occurred?"

"Because they are with you. The demons are assigned to people and they spend their days with you writing down all your sins. Then, they deliver the sins to each of the corresponding tollhouse."

"No one ever told me about the demons. I knew they would attack me, tempt me, and put thoughts in my head. But I thought it was occasionally. I had no idea they were following me around all of my days."

"Yes, the moment you receive a guardian angel at your baptism, you receive a wicked angel. And unlike us, when the human continues sinning, chasing us away, the wicked angel stays to document all the evil and sins committed."

"Everything?" Daniel worries.

"Yes, everything."

"Where to now?" Daniel asks

"It used to be a tollhouse that had little activity. Most souls passed right by, but as times went by and people moved away from God, and more toward man, then to themselves, this tollhouse is much more crowded taking more souls to Hades than before."

"What is it?"

"The tollhouse of pride." Leo responds.

They approach the tollhouse and several demons come to greet the two. The demons are not as hideous as the previous ones. They point to the rear of the dim cave, instructing Leo and Daniel to move right through. "This soul has shown no pride in putting himself before God."

"That happens?" Daniel asks.

"If they cannot find anything on you to accuse you of, they will let you pass."

They continue upward. Daniel, full of memories of his life, still feels connected to the world he left. He misses his wife.

"Leo, when I was on earth, people would say they saw ghosts or their loved ones came back to see them. Is that possible? Will I have a chance to see Lydia or my children?"

"Can a baby go back into the womb?" Leo asked.

"No."

"Then your soul cannot go back to earth until Christ's second coming, when your soul is joined with your perfect resurrected body. That is, if we can get you through the tollhouses. We must continue on."

The journey through the tollhouses continues and they come to another cave. This one is empty of demons.

"What is this, Leo?" Daniel rotates back and forth to find the demons.

"Just wait for it. They always try to make a big deal of this."

A door from the side of the cave opens and several

large demons charge after Leo and Daniel. They grab Daniel, but keep away from the angel, and they pull Daniel back into the room.

They enter the room, with Leo following behind.

The chief of this tollhouse, in a loud blustering voice, yells towards Daniel.

"You are guilty of idle chatter. Your mouth is full of obscenities, useless words. Here angel, this is a list of all of his offenses." The demons pass a scroll to Leo.

Another demon comes up from behind Daniel, tries to peek into his soul, and quickly moves away.

"We have noted all your offenses from the moment you could say a word. At six years old, you used swear words. Cursing at your parents for not letting you be with your friends. You called your mother a bitch. And when you were with your friends, you joined them in idle chatter. You insulted the girls from down the street by calling them ugly, flat chested. And when you were older, and learned more words, you talked about the girls behind their backs saying how you would lay them. And how they would do dirty things to you."

Daniel feeling ashamed as the demons stirred these memories up.

"And he would sing songs full of foul words. In his car, traveling from place to place. He even had his friends join in singing the songs."

Daniel looked over to Leo for help as the attacks were relentless.

"Angel, isn't it pathetic? He had the Bible with him on his desk, but instead of reading it. He read books with dirty words. Daniel, all you had to do was open the Good Book to 2 Timothy:16 and read "avoid godless chatter, because those who indulge in it will become more and more ungodly." And you would not be here in this tollhouse."

An increasing number of demons attack Daniel with more examples of his sins.

"Leo, I can only confess what I could remember. Make it stop."

"You can stop now. You are aware this poor soul confessed to using idle chatter. And not only did he confess, as he got older, he refused to say those words, and instead used his words to spread the message of the Lord and Savior Jesus Christ."

"That is not enough."

"That is not enough," another demon repeats.

"That is not enough," another adds on

"Give us the gold, give us the gold." A demon with a smashed face and broken neck says.

Leo takes a small bag and throws it at the feet of the bent over and broken demon, making it difficult for him to pick it up.

"We are finished here. Let's go Daniel." Leo moves past the demon, still struggling to grab the gold, while Daniel follows.

The two find themselves back on the celestial path on their continued journey upward.

"Leo, how much spiritual gold do I have? I don't think I will be worthy enough to make all the way." Daniel asks.

"The gold is still heavy, but it all depends on what you confessed to and how you confessed."

"And there is no chance for me to confess to you my sins now. I wrote all my sins down. I was working with my spiritual father and my confessions. They were so many sins that I did not confess everything before my untimely death. So can I confess to you?

"No, only God can forgive sins. He has bestowed upon your spiritual father to hear your confession, and God forgives through your priest."

"I see. I thought I had more time." Daniel says.

"A good priest will always be available to hear confessions. A good priest will push people to confess, not physically, but to teach how important confession and repentance are for eternal life. Those that don't, will have to answer for it. God has entrusted them with souls who need their guidance."

"I have a good priest. Father Ephraim understands."

"We realize that. And what is awesome is when a Christian confesses a sin, the sin disappears from the ledgers the demons keep on people. So when the soul approaches the tollhouse, they rush out, open the ledger, then see... there is nothing. I wish more Christians learned that confession is an easy and quick way to save their soul."

"Maybe a lot people are afraid, ashamed."

"That is the sin of pride keeping them from confessing. Do you want to know a secret? The priest hears so many confessions, he forgets. It is very important to have one spiritual father to confess. Some people try to be tricky by splitting their sins between priests or find a strange priest, confess and never confess to their spiritual father. It does not work that way."

Daniel felt silence fall upon the two as they traveled higher. Out of the darkness, the next tollhouse appeared. The fierce demons of this place came at Leo and Daniel. The first ones accused Daniel of Usury; giving money to the poor and charging interest. Daniel laughed at the allegation. "Leo, I had no opportunity to make loans to people. I gave temporary loans to friends and family, never asking for interest. And I gave freely to the poor." The demon, upon hearing Daniel, disappeared.

They tried to move on, but more demons approached. The group surrounded Leo and Daniel and stared at the two. After a moment, a huge demon approached, stepped on several demons, tossed others to the side.

"Genesis 3:1 Now the serpent was more crafty than any beast of the field which the Lord God had made. And he said to the woman, "Indeed, has God said, 'You shall not eat from any tree of the garden'?" The head demon said to Daniel.

"What?" Daniel asked Leo

"Genesis 3:4-5 The serpent said to the woman, "You surely will not die! For God knows that in the day you eat from it your eyes will be opened, and you will be like God, knowing good and evil."

"Wretch. What are accusing this soul of?" Leo asks.

"This soul is deceitful. Just like the serpent when it deceived Eve, this soul deceived many to get what he wanted."

"Never. Have him prove it." Daniel asked of Leo.

"Demon, are you trying to deceive us to take this soul?" Leo shot back.

The demon shrunk back and waved Leo and Daniel on.

Back on the spiritual journey upward, Leo interrupts the still of the air.

"Satan works in this world and the world you came from. Deception is one of his most powerful tools. Look at what he did to Paradise; deceiving Eve into biting into the fruit, then convincing her husband to do the same. If he isn't directly deceiving, he is using the spiritually weak to do his deceiving. One deception that is common is that you can save yourself by only repenting and praying, not confessing. This will not benefit the soul at all."

They come upon the next cave. Plastered to the back is one demon on top of the other. Some try to peel themselves off, but fail and fall and disappear into the abyss. Underneath each demon, Daniel sees a multitude of souls, most not active, just lying in a state of sleep. Several of the horrible spirits come off the wall and grab a soul and hold it in the grasp of their bony talon like hands.

The larger demon of the group leads the pack that approaches Leo and Daniel.

"Welcome to the tollhouse of slothfulness and vanity. I see you have made it this far Leo, you have done well guarding this soul. He must have been very good on earth."

"If you have nothing on this soul, we need to pass." Leo demanded.

The demon shoves his talons into the soul next to him and pulls out a ledger.

"I wonder if your soul here knows he needed to confess to these sins." The demon moves his grotesque fingers down and around the ledger.

"So many are lazy these days, making it easy to whisper temptations into their ears, suggest that they take it easy, let other people do..."

"Do what?" Daniel asks Leo.

"Help the poor and the needy!" The demon shouted

at Daniel.

"I see nothing here on that, but look here. Ah yes, "Vanity of vanities! All that is done without God's guidance is vanity. Futile, meaningless--a wisp of smoke, a vapor that vanishes, merely chasing the wind. It seems your soul here thought that his word was more important than God's word. He was so self absorbed. He made decisions without God. Never in the fear of God. And not remembering God is his creator."

"Demon, you speak in generalities. Stop lying. As if I would easily give up this soul. Prove his guilt or let me pass."

The demon flustered, moved the ledger backward and forward, turned it upside down and right side up. He hissed, took the ledger, and shoved it back into the soul.

"The next one you bring here, Leo, won't get by. We are winning down below." The demon put his arms to the side, still holding onto the soul and pointed for the Leo and Daniel to move on.

The two gliders of the aerial plane continue upward.

"Was that demon right? Are they winning?" Daniel asks of Leo.

"You know the answer, Daniel."

"I've noticed changes since my youth. I didn't realize it is worse all around."

Leo, becoming more agitated by the success of the demons responds. "Daniel, not only in the visible realm, but in this realm, we all see it. I have had to abandon thousands of humans I had the task to guard. The sinful life they chose became so disgusting, I could not avert my eyes anymore. If they repent, confess and stop their sinful behavior, then God will send me back and I will guard them again."

"What has happened?"

"The technology is another tool that Satan uses to deceive the masses. There is so much confusion below between what is man's law and God's law."

"But isn't this the way it has always been? Falling away from God, realizing your errors, repentance and back in the good graces of our Lord." Daniel asks.

"It's different this time around. Back then, people believed. His presence shook the foundations and people would change. Now, because they lack belief, it will take the Lord bending the Heavens for the second coming for the people to understand. By then, it will be too late."

As Leo finishes the sentence, Daniel sees a wide expanse filled with souls and demons. The demons are yelling, cackling, howling, and barking. The souls seem as if they are crying. In teams of two, the demons rush up to a soul, read the ledger, and take it. Only a few of the souls escape punishment. They push the remaining souls into a shaft at the end of the room and dropped below into the void.

Several demons come towards Daniel and Leo.

"Nothing" One demon says.

"Nothing, are you sure? Impossible." His partner says.

"I looked everywhere, nothing."

"Everyone loves money. This tollhouse is filled with greedy souls. I don't believe it."

Demon #1 hands the ledger over to his partner.

"You have a special soul, Leo. Unlike the thousands that try to pass through the house of avarice and fail, the soul you are protecting has nothing for us to hold him back. Proceed on." The demon leaves and attacks new, arriving souls.

"I guess they have so much business he doesn't need to falsely accuse me of sinning." Daniel says.

"That is good. You tried to live by the word of God. I only have so much spiritual gold and some of the tollhouses coming up are difficult to pass."

CHAPTER TWENTY-ONE

Lydia looks into Daniel's home office. Papers spread over the desk. Folders on the floor strewn about and his bible opened up to Ephesians Chapter five. *Alright Lydia, it's been almost forty days since Daniel left. Time to be brave and clean this place up.*

She walks into the office and sits down at Daniel's desk. She reviews all the paperwork. Most are documents relating to Hill Country Kitchens' real estate dealings. She grabs one folder laying on the floor, opens it and inserts the documents. She goes through the rest of papers and tosses out items that have no use. At the end of the desk are unopened envelopes containing bank statements and junk mail. She throws the junk mail into the trash and puts the rest of the envelopes to the side for reading later.

Lydia recalls the nights Daniel would stay up late and could hear him typing away. He was always secretive about what he was writing. *Maybe he was writing a book, a blog or an online diary?*

She moved the mouse, and the screen lit up, a screen saver of the two of them on top of Enchanted Rock with bursting orange and red sky behind them. Her eyes welled up looking at him. She clicked through the picture and opened the file directory to find the folder of his masterpiece. She reads aloud the name of the files "family, photos, vacation ideas. Oh, vacation ideas, where was he planning for us to go?" She opens the folder. There were seven pdf files: Cancun resort, Virgin Island Resorts, Tahiti Resorts, Baja vacation, Green Islands getaway, Mediterranean cruise, Holy Land tours.

"Oh Daniel, why did we wait? We should have gone when we had the chance. I don't want to go anywhere without you." She says into the empty office. As she continues on reviewing file names: *workout routines, life after 50, personal and confidential,* she clicks the last one.

In the files are sub files: insurance, bank account information, investment information, birth certificates, passports and the final sub folder "ASAP". She opens the folder, and it is a document with the name "x". She opens it and utters "oh."

The headline reads "My confessions." Lydia closes the file. "I can't read that. He meant it for God, not me."

Lydia hears clicking in the hallway. The sound comes closer. Sticking her head in the doorway is Heidi. With ears at full attention, she tilts her head. "Everything's fine girl. Come here." Heidi walks into the office. She hasn't been in the room since Daniel died. Since then she has slept outside of the office, waiting for him to return.

Heidi sits next to Lydia. She puts her hand on top of Heidi's head and pets her. She closes her eyes and tries to rest, but her mind's eye shows her the document she closed out. *Did I really read that? It's not possible.* She continues to pet Heidi. After a minute of silence, she says "Lord forgive me." She moved the mouse, opening the screen. She found her way back to the document, opens it, and reads.

Daniel wrote out all of his confessions in chronological order, from as far back as he could remember. He started his document with a brief introduction. Something scripted for him to say before his confession. To keep him from losing his nerve.

"Dear Lord, now I know, and because I know, I want to confess all my sins, so I am not held accountable when I pass from this life. I have many sins, and I cannot remember them all. But I will try my best to confess what I can. My sinning is from periods of time where I was weak in faith, allowing the temptations of the devil to be strong, leading me off the path to you. Please Lord, forgive me for the sins I have committed."

Lydia looks at the bottom of the document where it says she is on page 1 of 5.

"Goodness." She scrolls down the first page, which documents his sins as a boy:

Age 6: I lied to my parents about being ill so I could skip school

Age 6: Shoplifted soda from the grocery store.

Age 6: Bullied the neighbor kid.

Age 7: I cannot remember anything at this age.

Age 9: More lying and disrespecting of my parents.

Age 9: Fighting with the boy next door.

Age 9: Swearing and cursing when with my friends

Age 9: Using the Lord's name in vain

Age 10: Shoplifting from the convenience store. I took some bubble gum.

Age 10: disrespectful to my teachers

Age 10: Found dad's nudie magazine, first time looked at pornography.

Age 11: I can't recall anything at this age

Age 12: continues swearing and cursing

Age 12: Began questioning God's existence

Age 12: Said lewd things to the girl in the neighborhood.

Age 12: Began masturbation

"Heidi, he sure remembers a lot." Lydia continues to read about his boyhood sins. Most of which revolve around shop lifting, disrespecting his parents and lust. She moves on to the next page in his teen years.

"Age 16: Continued to look at pornography

Age 16: Parents got cable. Watched R-rated movies

Age 16: Lied to parents, teachers, friends. Too many to name and account for.

Age 16: Got drunk with friends for the first time. Continued to drink for several years after.

Age 16: Stole cigarettes, started smoking

Age 16: First kiss with the girl from the neighborhood

Age 17: Did everything sexually with a girl down the street except intercourse. Continued on for several years.

Age 17: Doubted the existence of God. Entertained the atheist view point. But still cursed at God.

Dear Lord, I began to lose my way when I turned eighteen. I was easy prey for the demons. There are too many sinful acts to detail, but at eighteen to twenty two I:

1. Had sex with many women (is that adultery?)

2. Intoxication. I drank a lot once in college. To the point I could not remember where I was, who I was

with.

3. Missing church months at a time. Not confessing or taking the sacraments.

4. Lying, swearing, cursing

5. Viewing pornography

I don't know if this is a sin, but I regret the way I treated Lydia in the beginning. I was aroused the first time I saw her. I was rude to her at the party and several times after. I wish I asked her out the first time I met her and not wasted so much time with other women. Lydia is a blessing, and I love her so much."

Lydia started to tear up. "Daniel, I love you too. You were just a stupid boy."

She continued to read on, thankful most of the sins he committed when he was single did not occur in his twenties.

"And as a new husband, father, and starting my career, I did sin, but nothing particular sticks in my mind. I told many lies, deceived, a love for money, did not give alms or help with charity. My faith could not match the intensity of Lydia's."

Lydia smiled, then scrolled to the next page. Her smile disappeared.

"I was deceitful because I hid my marriage. My boss told me not to wear my wedding ring when calling on female accounts. He said that because I was good looking, the women would want to give me a chance. He also suggested I flirt with them. Take it to a point where they believed something would happen, then pull back. I did this several times to land some large accounts. I thought it was the best thing to support my family. And I admit I enjoyed flirting with those women."

Lydia pushed herself away from the computer. Stood

up and walked out of the office and headed towards the kitchen. Heidi following close behind. She opened the refrigerator and stared into it. She notices how bare the shelves are. *When you are cooking for one, what do you expect?* She grabs a bottle of water and closes the door. She takes a sip and tries to rationalize Daniel's sin.

He was just doing what every sales person does and what he felt was best for our family and his career. What was he going to do, tell his new boss no? She put the lid back on the bottle and headed back to the office. She sits back in the chair. Still warm. Heidi sat next to her. Lydia patted her. "You're a good girl."

Lydia woke the computer, and the document once again appeared. She scrolled down to the last page.

"Father, guess I should have started with this sin first. I understood God sees all sins as equal, but I wonder if this sin is worse than lies of a six-year-old. I will avoid trying to make excuses for this sin. Because there is no excuse for this sin."

"Daniel, what did you do?" Lydia continued to read. Tears welled up, tears dropped onto the desk.

"Lord, I committed adultery. I cheated on Lydia with a woman who I worked with. Not only did I commit adultery, I made her an adulterer because I did not tell her I was married. What's worse is that I would have kept on with the affair, but it was her who ended it when she found out I was married. Over time, I realize what a terrible sin I committed. I have lived with the guilt and it is torture, especially when I look at Lydia and see nothing but good. I would tell her, but I don't want to get a divorce. I love Lydia with everything I have, with all of my heart. I know I will burn for this if I do not confess to this and get absolution."

Lydia hit with a flood of sadness and anger.

"Daniel, how could you!" She yelled at their picture on his desk. Heidi, sensing her sadness, put her head in Lydia's lap.

"Not now girl, go lay down." Lydia said, while sobbing.

Heidi adjusted her position, looked up at Lydia, and did not budge. Lydia petted her and after each stroke, felt some calm.

"Daniel, this is so unfair. How am I supposed to deal with this? Now I have to live with your admission. I guess I should have never looked at your confessions." She walks out of the office, turned off the lights and headed to her bedroom, closing the door behind her. She crashed on the bed and stared into the darkness. Silence except for the slight whimpering of Heidi on the other side of the door.

Who was she? Lydia tried to remember all the women that were in his life. She first thought of women at church. *That's stupid Lydia.* Then moved on to family friends. *No, impossible. What about his customers?* Lydia sits up. "I am so dumb. It had to be Iris." She has visions of Daniel and Iris walking hand in hand down different streets in various cities across Texas. Dining out together as a couple. Then she imagined the two of them stripping down naked, and having sex. Lydia struggled with these images all night long. And if one's eyes were open and could see all, they would be terrified of all the demons surrounding Lydia's bed, putting all these visions in her head and whispering to her all what Daniel and Iris did in the hotel rooms.

* * *

She pulls up to Christ the Savior. Lydia looks into her vanity mirror. Eyes puffy from last night's events. Never falling asleep as she went back into the office and read his last sin over and over. She had a question and only Father Ephraim could answer.

TAP TAP TAP. Lydia startled by Jonah knocking on her window.

"Hi Lydia." Jonah waves.

Stepping out of her car, Lydia greets Jonah with a hug.

"Hi Jonah, how are you? How is Maria?"

"Blessed. I pray you are getting some sleep and peace." Jonah said.

"I have my good days and bad. I pray to God for strength to help me through this. I still can't believe he is gone." Lydia looks off to the side. She desperately wants to ask Jonah about Iris. And if so, why didn't he tell her?

"You always have us to talk to, and of course Father Ephraim, who I take it you are meeting today?" Jonah points to the office.

She sees the kindness in Jonah's eyes. *Jonah never knew.*

"Yes, I don't have an appointment. I have a question for him. The answer might help me sleep. It was nice seeing you, Jonah." She gives him a kiss on the cheek and walks past him and heads over to the church office.

Even with the size of Christ the Savior, Father Ephraim never hired an assistant. He considered it was a luxury and they could better use the money for the church or one of the charities. Plus, the volunteers did a fantastic job of helping him when needed.

At his desk, writing in his journal, Father Ephraim

hears someone walk in.

"Hello?"

"Hi Father, it's me Lydia." She enters his office.

"Hi Lydia, what brings you here today? Is there a choir rehearsal?"

"No father, I came here because I have a question and I hope you can answer it."

"I will try. Please sit down." He extends his hand to the seat in front of his desk.

"I don't know if what I am about to tell you is a confession or just a question for guidance. It could be a little of both." She reaches into her purse and takes out a precisely folded piece of paper.

"I was missing Daniel last night, so I went into his office and snooped on his computer. He was spending late nights in there typing away, and I imagined he was secretly writing a book or a journal. Whichever, he never let me see what he was working on."

"Yes."

"Well, I found a file that was interesting and when I opened it, it brought up another file and in that file was this document." Lydia holds up the folded piece of paper.

"What is it Lydia?" Father Ephraim straightens up in his chair.

"He wrote a document containing all his sins. Or at least the one's he remembers. I hope that these are the sins he was confessing to you." She handed him the papers.

"Lydia, I can't tell you what he confessed. It's between him and God."

"I understand, but this is different. I am not asking what he confessed to, just if this is what he confessed.

It's very important."

Father Ephraim reads through the first page and nods. The second and continues to nod. "Yes, he confessed to these sins." Father Ephraim read on. Page three, he nodded, page four he nodded, then he turned to page five and stopped. He brought the page closer to his eyes, then placed it flat on his desk.

"Lydia, Daniel, and I were working on a confessional plan. He said he could only do so much. And that he wanted to break it up over several weekends."

"Yes, go on Father."

"Well, he is right. He should have started with that sin first. But he never did. We were planning on meeting for one final round. I guess this is what he wanted to confess."

Lydia wept.

"I imagine learning about his sin this way is shocking. I'm troubled by this too. He never let it show. He hid it well."

Lydia stood up from her chair and ran out of the office.

"Lydia, what's the matter?" Father Ephraim rose from his seat and followed her into the church. She ran through the narthex into the nave, to the back wall, and stopped at the icon of the Last Judgment. She traced her finger up the snake. "Slander, verbal abuse, envy, falsehood, wrath and anger, pride, idle chatter, usury and deceit, slothfulness and vainglory..." she said under breath.

"Lydia, what is it?" Father Ephraim is out of breath.

Her finger running past the other listings of the tollhouse and stopped.

"Adultery. Father, if he is still on his journey, how

will he make it past this tollhouse?" Lydia turned to the priest.

"You still care about what happens to him?" Father asks.

Lydia pursed her lips and nodded. "Yes, he is my husband. I want to be with him again." She whispered.

"It all depends what happened before he gets here. Did he do enough in this last confession to counter the demons? Did he come to church, partake in the holy mystery, and, of course, confession? How much spiritual gold does his angel have to get him past the tollhouses? The demons will do anything they can to take a soul."

"What if he ran out? Is there anything we can do? I can do?"

Father Ephraim pondered for a moment.

"Father, could I confess for him?"

"No."

"What if I forgive him right here, right now?" Lydia searching for something to help.

"That would help your soul, not his. There is only one thing that can get him past." Father Ephraim says, while looking at the icon.

"Prayers." He says.

"Prayers? Alright, can we pray for him now?"

"Not just you and me, he is going to need lots of prayers from many people. You will need to find a way to gather enough people to pray for him. The best time is in the next couple of days as we approach his forty day memorial."

"How many people?"

"As many as possible. The church will have the special memorial service and we will invite all to attend and pray." Lydia understands what needs to be done. "I will have enough people here to pray him into Heaven."

CHAPTER TWENTY-TWO

Leo and Daniel continue their ascent. It's quiet in this realm. Leo seems focused on what lies ahead for Daniel. Daniel, taking everything in wonders about the non-believers and those of other faiths.

"Leo, what of the atheists, agnostics, Muslims, Buddhist, Jews, and others? What happens to their souls when they die?"

"Do you know your Bible, Daniel?" Leo asks

"Not word for word, and I can't quote scripture, but I know it."

"Mathew 11:20-24. This reading is when our Lord rebukes all the cities that saw his miracles, his mighty works, but still didn't repent. So it is a far greater sin to have seen Christ's works and rejected Him than to never known Him at all."

They continue on and what feels like coming around a bend, they run into two demons, barring razor teeth, swiping at Daniel. Leo pulls him away.

The two ghastly ghouls, wretched and foul smelling, try to accuse Daniel, but their words are garbled and are not understood. Then one demon puked.

"Ah, now I feel better. Looks like we have another drunkard here. How much wine did he drink?" The demon asks his partner, who turned and puked towards Leo and Daniel.

"Too much to count." He turns his ledger for all to see. It's scratchings of dates, places and hatch marks. "But he is a drunk. A drunk that made a lot of poor decisions."

The demons point over to a bar behind them. On top of the bar sits all the glasses of alcohol he consumed his whole life. The glasses were stacked so high they could not see the bartender.

"Angel, would your little soul like a drink? Maybe we could take it and dunk it in a bottle for you. I am sure he would like that." The demon growled.

The other one looking at the ledger.

"He drank on feast days, he drank during lent, tsk, tsk, tsk,"

"Leo, yes, I drank a lot, but that was when I was younger. I can't remember the last time I was drunk."

"But did you confess to this behavior?" Leo asked.

"I did, but not every single occasion."

"You two, this soul did some good on earth. The times he was sober, he took care of his drunk friends. He drove them home, keeping them from killing themselves and others. He refused drugs, that were worse than alcohol and kept others from going down that road too. And he helped lead a job recruiting effort for recovering alcoholics."

The demons chatter quietly with each other. As one demon bit at the other, their arguing became louder, turning into shouts, the terrible voices turned into screeching, hurting Leo and Daniel's ear. Then they calmed down.

"We need the gold." The head demon demanded.

"Even with all of his works, he did not confess to everything. We need some gold." The other demon added.

Leo reached under his wings and grabbed another bag of gold and tossed it to the demons. Once they caught it, the view of the bar disappeared, replaced by a door for the two to exit.

* * *

They enter a new area of the aerial realm of the tollhouses setting a warning for Daniel.

"At one time, in the earlier days, the demons fixed the tollhouses in such a way to capture the souls. They placed the sins where temptation ensnares most, at the end. They laugh at the poor soul that believes they made it, only to be ensnared at one of the final tollhouses. So what you will encounter is not the same as you see on the icon of the Last Judgment. As some sins become more prevalent than others. For instance, the next tollhouse used to be barren, no activity now..."

The angel wipes the darkness away and Daniel sees an area made up of pink and white crystals. There, souls packed from one side to the other. Each yelling at the other while the demons laugh at them. The demon spies Leo and Daniel and marches over with a ledger in hand.

Leo taking his usual stance between the evil spirit and Daniel. "Why bother with us, ghoul? You look busy enough."

"Shut up angel. I'm trying to find this one's record.

But there is nothing. Impossible."

"There are still some that aren't like those." Leo pointed to the crowd of angry souls.

The demon closed the ledger as another demon approached. This one was ghastly, without eyes, just two large holes in its bulbous head. It went around Daniel as if it was searching for something, sniffing something out.

"He will find it." The demon snorted.

"Find what Leo?"

"Malice. If you were malicious."

"No, never." Daniel said as he was trying to pull back from the faceless spirit.

"Get out of here, angel." The demon said while the other one howled in pain.

"That place is packed with souls. What has happened?" Daniel asks as they travel upward.

"The technology that has come into existence has made the devil's work so much easier. There is so much malice towards others. Because of their beliefs. It gets worse as the days go by. First, people would disagree, then when that was satisfying, they grew malice in their hearts and tried to destroy the other person. Deliberately lying to hurt the other one. Many, many lives destroyed. And even after death, the malice stays with the soul, and that is why they seem to hate each other."

They continue on and reach the next tollhouse. Unclean spirits in the shapes of snakes, serpents, and horned asps fill the area. The creatures that eat the dirt and crawl on their bellies encircle Daniel.

"Where are we?" Daniel whispered

"The tollhouse of the occult, magic, divination."

"I would never."

"They are just checking. They can smell it with their tongues." Leo grabbed a serpent, looked into it's evil eyes, and threw it as far as he could into the abyss.

After a few moments, the serpents uncoiled from Daniel and slithered away.

"Time to move on?" Daniel asks.

"Yes."

Moving away from the tollhouse on and upward to the next. The realm they were in shouldn't smell, but it did. It reeked of feces and rotting flesh. The putrid odor grew more intense as they reached the area. The evil spirits in this tollhouse resemble pigs, boars and hogs. Some walking upright, others with four hooves on the ground. Some bodies were skeletons, other blobs of skin with heads attached that gasped for air.

"It's the house of gluttony Daniel." The angel pointed.

The pig like spirits turn from their mush as a herd chase each other towards the two travelers.

"Hold still. They will stop." The angel reassuring Daniel.

"Welcome pig, you are now home." The pig reared up and stood on two legs.

"Are you ready to join your fellow pigs?" Another one snorted.

Daniel looked over and saw souls being eaten and defecated out of the boars repeatedly.

"You are disgusting." Leo says to the pig.

"Not as disgusting as these pigs over there. They stuff their faces with food, all day and night. This one with you is no different from those."

"Tell them what he did. Tell him." The other pig said.

"Angel, this one ate snacks throughout his youth, and when he was older and knew better, would sneak out and eat meat during the great lent. And so scared of what people would think before he ate, he would not thank God for His blessings. He just ate, ate, ate."

"Pigs, he confessed to this sin. Now back away."

"He confessed to eating, but not to eating during all the fasting days." One snorted.

"Yes, but during lent, the money he would normally use on meats and sweets he instead gave to poor so they could eat." The angel fired back.

"It is still not enough. Give us the gold." The pig fell back on all fours.

Leo searched deep into his wing and found another bag of spiritual gold and put it into the slobbering mouth of the beast and journeyed on.

"Leo, I hear stories of people dying and returning. All of their accounts sound the same. They die, see a bright light, then walk into the tunnel of light where departed loved ones greet them. This is nothing like what they say."

"Remember when I greeted you when you passed? And the demons were there too? Others, the ones who passed, do not have guardian angels, making it very easy for the demons to deceive them. Yes, some will attack the poor soul at the time of death. But on occasion, the demons will deceive a few humans with the "tunnel."

"Why would they do that?" Daniel asks

"Those that enter the tunnel lead sinful lives. Then when they return, they tell others through some sort of mass communications that they were on their way to Heaven, but got called back. That is the deception.

Now all the sinners believe they can continue sinning. No one will hold them accountable and still "get into Heaven", when in fact their souls end up in the place of pain and misery."

"Now be thankful you are an Orthodox Christian as the next tollhouse has been a snare for so many."

As they approach the next tollhouse they hear screams and cries of "I thought I was right, I thought I knew better. I'm sorry." And other cries of "but I am a Christian, let me go?"

"What is this Leo?"

"The tollhouse for heretics, apostates, idol worshipers, and schismatics. Their leaders instructed them that you can be a Christian but reject some of Christ's teachings or turn away from church's authority. And others like those poor fools that replaced God with their fellow man. Be it politicians, celebrities, or athletes. Humans are created with God written in their heart, but the devil fools many believing there is no God. But the heart yearns for something, so it fills the void with other sinful humans."

Daniel and Leo look on as the souls plead their cases with demons who look like they walked out of a medieval drawing. Small, burnt in color, carrying pitch forks and poking the souls. Others carrying about scales showing the souls they failed.

"Why aren't the demons coming after me?" Daniel asks

"Because, as an adult, you stopped questioning God or the church and are a faithful servant. Those demons know it and will not waste their time."

Proceeding upward, Daniel was glad that they did not need to use more spiritual gold, as he was sure there were tougher tollhouses to get through.

At the next tollhouse, a gang of demons stops the two sojourners. All different and hideous. Some were without faces, others were missing jaws, and many standing crooked.

"Another thief is here." The demon with no face announces.

"He has stolen so much: cookies from the store, candy, coins from his parents."

"I confessed those sins, Leo."

The demons continued with their accusations. "Here it says he stole from the poor man laying on the street. Took his wallet. And it is written that he took money from the church basket."

"They lie Leo. I am not a thief." Daniel defending himself from words of the demons.

"But look at all the items he stole from work and brought home. Pens, pencils, papers, even a computer."

"I did not steal those."

"If they did not belong to you, you stole them." It sneered at him.

The demons continued on, digging up every time Daniel took an item or borrowed money without repayment.

Leo storms ahead over to the demon. "Shut up, demon, here is some gold. Take it and let us pass."

The demons giggle and move away from the celestial path where Leo and Daniel proceed.

"Those demons are viscous and persistent. They don't stop." Daniel mentions to Leo.

"Yes, they are trying to deceive me so I will let them take you. But don't worry, I know what you have done, what you confessed to." Leo mentions.

Onward, they arrive at a place that is filled with terror. The souls of the worst people on earth are here. They are being tortured, raped, scourged and beaten. Over and over again, relentlessly.

One of the blood covered demons, with a soul hanging on the side of his gaping mouth, approach Leo and Daniel.

"Hmm. He has never murdered or tortured anyone. You should go from here." The demon says while chewing on the soul.

Daniel, mortified by what he is witnessing, cannot move.

"Daniel, we must go."

"How long will they torture these souls?" Daniel asks.

"Forever until the end of times." The demon cackled.

"Daniel, we must move on, right now." Leo scooped Daniel with one of his wings and moves on to the next tollhouse.

Further upward, Leo and Daniel come upon the next tollhouse.

"This one surprises many." Leo says with much concern.

"What are you talking about Leo?"

"Since Adam and Eve, humans always thought they knew better than God, and invented their own rules in what is wrong or right. The idols from your world has set the rules, and the godless are believing it to be true. That right is wrong, upside down is right side up, men are women and women are men. This is the tollhouse of homosexuality, pedophilia, and perversion."

Two scrunched up gargoyle looking dogs rush towards the two. Each one salivating and snapping, trying to take a piece of Daniel. They get closer to the tollhouse, manned by evil spirits resembling serpents, rats, and pigs. All filled with evil and bitterness. The serpent with horns piercing out of the side of its head slithered over to Leo. "I don't see that your soul here ever laid with a man or child. But let me ask it. Puny soul, did you ever fantasize about being with a man? Maybe when you were younger at school or college."

"Never."

"I see. But you did defend that lifestyle? Did you once say, "Sex between consenting adults is acceptable? Who cares if it is of the same sex? And didn't you attend a gay wedding?"

"I did. The pressure of society forces you to say things you don't believe. If you don't follow along, they severely punish you."

"Poor baby. I guess you missed the Gospel reading where He says that if you follow Him, people will hate you."

"I read it, but I was weak."

"Snake, as he said, he was weak. However, this soul gave money and time to charities that fought against pedophilia and sex trafficking. He also led a group of parents protecting the school from enacting policies in favor of transsexuals over boys and girls. If they put these rules in place, it would harm the children."

"That is not enough."

The serpent slid around Daniel's soul, fluttering its forked tongue, trying to detect anything foul. Nothing.

"Give me some gold and you can pass."

Leo digging further down into his wing, found a bag of gold and mocking the serpent. "Here you go. Where do you want me to put it?" Then dropped it. The serpent put the bag in its mouth and gulped it down.

As they travel through the winding path, Daniel asks: "So, if one is attracted to someone of the same sex, they don't pass that tollhouse?"

"No, it's in the persisting of those activities that prevent them from inheriting God's kingdom."

"Leo, I meant what I said. It is very difficult to be righteous in the world I left. You can lose your whole career, livelihood, friends, family members, everything you have worked on if you say you are against same sex behavior."

"Yours is not the first generation, and it will not be the last to go through this. We have more work to do Daniel."

CHAPTER TWENTY-THREE

A candle lit, she prayed ceaselessly in front of her icon corner. She's praying for the strength, bravery, and wisdom to set her pain aside and do what she could to save Daniel's soul.

Forgiveness is all she prayed about. *Please Lord, give me strength to forgive Daniel. And Lord, please have mercy on Daniel's soul and forgive him, too.* With only two days until his fortieth day memorial service, Lydia needs to use all the time she has in preparing for the service such as making the koliva; The boiled wheat served at the end of service.

Her biggest problem, how to get as many people possible into the church to pray for his soul. She hears the name "Jonah" and picks up the phone and calls him.

"Hi Lydia, are you alright?" Jonah always a concern for others.

"Hi Jonah, I think so. Listen, would you and Maria come over? I need some help with the memorial service on Saturday night. I can't do this alone."

"Of course. We will be over as soon as we can. See you soon." Jonah ends the call with Lydia and calls for Maria.

"Yes, Jonah?"

"Maria, we need to see Lydia right now. It is very important."

The two make their way over to Lydia's. On their way up the steps of the front porch, Lydia opens the door prior to them knocking. She greets each with a hug and a kiss on the cheek.

"Thank you for coming." Lydia walks the two into the dining room to sit and talk. On the table in front of the couch is a glass of red wine for Maria and a cold bottle of cola for Jonah. They each take a sip.

"How are you Lydia? How can we help?" Maria asks.

"Your call sounded urgent." Jonah added

"It is. Daniel's forty day memorial service is in two days and I need as many people at church as possible to pray for Daniel's soul."

"Pray for his soul?" Maria asks.

"Yes. His soul is going to need help to get into Heaven." Lydia speaking with firm conviction.

"But he should be fine, Lydia. He will get past the evil spirits."

"He won't Jonah."

"How do you know Lydia? Did something happen?" Maria asks.

"Yes, but I would rather not talk about it. All I can say is that Daniel didn't finish his confessions with Father Ephraim. And I'm afraid he lacks enough spiritual gold to get through all the tollhouses. I want to see him again." Lydia said with a quivering voice.

"I'll reach out to the parish and have as many there as possible." Jonah said.

"I don't know if that is enough."

"Why don't we see if any of the monks from the Monastery can come over? And also invite people from the other Orthodox churches that are nearby. The Ethiopian, Russian and the Greek ones." Maria suggested.

"We will fill the church, Lydia. Let us handle the heavy lifting on this." Jonah said.

"Is there anything else we can do for you Lydia, do you need any of us to stay over?"

"No thank you, the kids will be here tomorrow."

"Lydia, before we leave, let us all pray together."

"Follow me over to my prayer corner." Lydia says.

They enter her bedroom and in the corner is a small table with a half burnt candle in a candle stand with a mound of beeswax below. On the wall above the table are icons of Christ, the Theotokos, St. John the Baptist, her guardian angel, the Nativity, the Resurrection, Saint Theodora, Saint Katherine, Saint Lydia and the elevation of the cross.

Lydia strikes a match, the small flame erupts on the wood stick, she lights the candle's blackened wick. The prayer corner now dimly lit with flickering amber, the three stand before the icon. Jonah, pulling his small blue prayer book out from his back pocket, turns to the prayer for the dead, and leads:

"In the name of the Father, Son and Holy Spirit. Amen. Glory to you, our God, glory to You." They each make the sign of the cross.

"Christ our Lord, grant rest to Your servant Daniel among your saints, where there is no pain, sorrow, or suffering, but everlasting life. With the righteous who have reposed in Your peace, grant rest. Savior, to the soul of Your servant Daniel, and bestow upon him the blessed life which is from You, mercifully Lord.

Lord, remember Your servant Daniel, who has fallen

asleep in the hope of the resurrection. Forgive him every transgression he has committed in thought, word or deed. Grant him peace and refreshment in a place of light where Your glory delights all the saints. For you are the resurrection, the repose, and the life of Your departed servant Daniel, and to you I give glory now and forever. Amen."

The three remain silent. The only sound comes from Lydia. She clears her throat and starts to pray,

"Lord, remember all Daniel has done in this life. He was a good man, a wonderful husband, father and, most importantly, a steadfast follower and defender of Christ. Please protect him on his journey through the tollhouses and allow him to pass all the evil spirits who look in their ledgers and try to find any sin, regardless of how significant, to keep him from ascending to Heaven. Lord have mercy and save us. Amen."

The three end their prayers, hugging each other. Lydia whispers "Thank you" to Jonah. Lydia leans over the table and blows out the candle.

Jonah, concerned with what he heard or did not hear in Lydia's prayer, turned and asked her, "Lydia, if there is anything you want to talk about, we are here for you."

"Thank you, you two are a blessing. And Jonah, Daniel always said you would make a good priest. I think he was right."

Jonah gave a slight bow. "Thank you. Well, we must go. There is much work to be done for the memorial service."

Maria and Jonah leave Lydia's home. Lydia shuts the door then turns and looks down the entry only to find the cold empty house. *I should sell this. Too big for just one person.* She walks down the entry hall and turns into the living room. The seldom used room in the house at one time reserved for drinks and discussions of generations past.

She finds the couch and sits down, staring at the fireplace, memories of Christmas past flood her eyes. The many Christmas trees that changed over time, stockings from two to five, the children in the early morning moonlight opening presents, and Daniel always surprising Lydia with a gift she never felt comfortable wearing: diamond earrings, gold bracelet, or pearl necklace. She would rather give the money spent on gifts for her to the poor or church, rather than for her who felt blessed with all the gifts God already provided.

"I know it's over the top, Lydia, but you are worth it. I love you so much and I guess I am an old school guy that shows my love through expensive gifts." Daniel would tell her when she questioned the cost.

"I'm sorry Daniel, I should have appreciated your symbol of love for me."

"Or maybe the gift wasn't love, but out of guilt for sleeping with that whore." A voice entered her head.

"Why would you want to save Daniel's soul? He should burn for breaking your wedding vows?" She heard another voice.

She stands up and peers around the room to see if she can find where the voices were coming from. Nothing.

It must be my imagination.

Just then, another evil spirit whispers in her ear.

"All the prayers in the world won't help Daniel. He is an adulterer. He is a worm. Let him rot."

Another demon approaches Lydia, this one with a

soft and calming voice. "Lydia, you sacrificed so much for Daniel, and yet he still did this to you. You need to forget about him and live your own life. You still have many years and you are still so beautiful. Now go and find a new man or new men. Enjoy the experience of making love to someone else. Just as Daniel did."

Lydia, troubled by the voices, covered her ears and ran out of the living room, and with quickened pace, returned to her prayer corner with the candle already lit. "I know I blew out that candle." She looked into the flame and was calmed. Then she prayed: "Almighty God, who delivered Your people from the bondage of the adversary, and through Your Son cast down Satan like lightning, deliver me also from every influence of the unclean spirits. Command Satan to depart far from me by the power of Your only begotten son. Rescue me from demonic delusion and darkness. Fill me with the light of the Holy Spirit that I may be guarded against the snares of the crafty demons. Grant that an angel always go before me and lead me to the path of righteousness all days of my life, to the honor of Your glorious name, Father, Son, and Holy Spirit, now and forever. Amen."

At that moment, the hallway lights flickered, then a sound of glass breaking. Lydia stepped out of the bedroom. If she could see, she would see her guardian angel rounding up the evil spirits, binding them, and taking them far away from her.

Calmness and peace rested on her heart.

CHAPTER TWENTY-FOUR

Onward Leo and Daniel climbed.

Which one is the next station? Try to remember. The icon of the Last Judgment is fuzzy now. I must be coming close to the end. Those are terrible. I don't know if I have enough gold.

As they continue through the blackness, Daniel sees two figures up a head. One, a man with a bright light sitting on the sidewalk. Clothes tattered, hair matted down, hands dirty, eyes looking downward. Then Daniel sees a man walk up to him. The man on the sidewalk lifts his hand, putting his palm out. The other man never looks down and walks past him. Daniel feels the sorrow of the beggar in his soul. They come closer and the scene repeats. The beggar with hand out, the man walks by and disappears. A little closer, Daniel recognizes the man. It is him, when he was a young man, walking the streets of Austin.

Leo and Daniel are now at the scene. The beggar lifts his hand, but this time, he lifts his head up and looks at Daniel. "Do you know what it is like not eat for days? The pain in the stomach, the weakness that follows. Have you ever gone so long without water that you cannot even swallow your own spit? Do you know what one dollar could do? How much it would have helped me that day?"

Daniel grieved. "I'm sorry, but..."

"Do not talk to it!" Leo intercedes

"What? Why?" Daniel looks down at the beggar and watches his face transform from the poor, dirty, homeless person into a hideous demon. Eyes piercing, and a crooked smile.

"Angel, this one with you is filled with heartlessness and cruelty. He keeps his money, holds onto a coin like it was a child. So stingy, so miserly."

"Leo, this demon lies. I remember that day passing by that man. I could not have given him anything, as I gave my last dollar to another homeless person down the block. But I did pray for the man that evening."

"You could have done so much more." The demon now shape shifted into a skinny man, with hollow eyes and sunken face. "So hungry, just a piece of bread."

Before Daniel could counter the accusation, the demon transformed again.

"I walked by your house. It was over one hundred degrees. You saw me resting on your lawn under the tree and you kicked me off your property. All I needed was some water and I would have been on my way." Daniel watches the words come out of his chapped and cracked lips, breaking open every time he opens his mouth.

"You could have let me inside, just until the heat of the day subsided."

"These are lies Leo."

Leo was quiet, not answering. Knowing that there was a time Daniel's sins chased him away. He is unable to provide a good defense for Daniel.

"And what about me?" He sees an elderly woman, naked, trying to cover herself to keep some sort of modesty. Her sagging and wrinkled skin hanging off of bones devoid of any muscle. "I was so cold. You had clothes in your closet you never used. Only benefiting the stomachs of moths."

In the distance, a horde of demons approach Daniel and Leo. Daniel looks over at the demon that has prevented them from moving forward.

"Look at me, cold and heartless hypocrite!" The demon is now a man standing, wrapped in chains.

"I was in prison and you did not visit me. I am so alone. I wanted to ask for forgiveness, but I did not know how. My ears were open and longing to hear the word of God, but no one to read to me. My rage eating me from the inside out. I am sorry for what I did. I had no one to hear my confession. Where were you?" The prisoner falls away into the darkness.

Daniel stirs. "I can't do everything." He sighs.

"You could have lent me some money. How hard would that have been? Just one more month and my business would have been back. But you never listened, threw away my letters asking for help."

A voice from the darkness asks.

"Who is that?"

The demon materializes as the old woman who operated a small gift store in one of the many properties his company ran. She had to close her shop for weeks to take care of her dying husband. She asked for leniency, only a month, to get on track, to keep her business.

"You changed the locks and closed my business. I've worked all my life, and I became destitute, so embarrassing to use food stamps and welfare. You not only took my business away, but my dignity." The old woman standing eye to eye with Daniel, eyes clear where Daniel could see the woman at her kitchen table, head in hands, crying.

"You are so cruel." The face of the woman transforms into that of a small boy.

The horde has closed in without Daniel and Leo noticing. They surround the two. The demon that has kept them occupied rises and interrogates Daniel.

"You do not deserve to move forward. All you did was care about yourself. Selfish money hoarder. Just because you keep the commandments, does not matter if you are heartless and have no mercy for your neighbor."

"This is untrue Leo. They make up accusations. They don't know my side. What I did."

"Shut up! You are a nasty, filthy soul. Drag this one to Hades, where he can wait with all the rest of the souls for the resurrection of all the mortals."

"No, Leo, they can't. Help me."

Leo backs away as the demons close in on Daniel.

"Listen to me, you were not there. You did not see what I did. The compassion I had for the homeless, the hungry, those in prison, the sick, the elderly, the thirsty and the naked. I prayed for them, I donated my money to charities, to the church. My charity was working to make enough money so I could give to those that would help. I have a loving heart."

The demons grab at Daniel and try to take him away.

"What about the old woman Daniel, she lost her livelihood, her self worth?" Leo asks

"I helped her. Yes, her landlord locked her out. But once I received her call, I unlocked the doors. I found another space in a building down the street and she opened her business. She worked until she wanted to retire. These demons lie."

Leo moves forward, throwing the demons aside. Stepping on some, crushing others in his hands, pushing them away with his wings. He reaches the leader of the horde, who is still holding onto Daniel.

"Release him now. He is innocent. This soul moves forward."

"Pay up angel. Then I will give him over." The demon's grip tightens.

Leo reaches deeper into his wings, not much gold left. He throws the fiend one gold coin.

The demon catches it and kicks Daniel over to Leo. The horde sees another soul approaching and leave the two sojourners.

They continue on ahead and hear screams of the soul that followed them. It was a swift visit for that particular soul, quickly dragged down to Hades to be with the others who failed to make it through the aerial tollhouses.

"That one must ensnare many souls?" Daniel asks.

"Indeed. Daniel. Indeed. The time you are living in, the people's hearts are hardened. It is a selfish generation. One that is resembling the time before Noah. Fortunately for them, God promised never to wipe away the earth with a flood again."

"It is quite easy to get into Heaven and past the tollhouses if one thinks about it: Have goodness towards everyone, fairness, compassion and give alms." Leo adds

Daniel did not answer.

"What is wrong Daniel?"

"You did not stand up for me at the last tollhouse until the very end. Was I that bad of a person for you to leave me?"

"I was there for you for so many years until you turned away from the Lord and His teachings. I tried, in the only way an angel can, to stop you from leading a sinful life. But I can only nudge you so much. God gave you free will, just as he did with Adam and Eve. Unfortunately, like those two, you ate the fruit from your own tree of knowledge."

"Are the demons the judges?" Daniel asks.

"No. Don't be confused. Christ will judge all of mankind. The demons are separating the souls, and will drag many into Hades. Others get to move on for a taste of their great reward."

The travels to the next tollhouse seemed to take longer. At that time, he wonders about Lydia and their children. How are they? What will they do without him? If he doesn't make it through the tollhouses, how can he live an eternity without her?

I should have told her.

She deserved to know. I am such a coward.

In the distance, Daniel hears moaning and groaning. It grows louder as the two draw near. It's a cave colored in a purple hue. Lights flickering, presenting shadows on the cave wall. The two enter and see the backside of a demon sitting in a chair made of souls. Its head covered by scales, many shedding and falling to the floor. There are sounds of grunts and groans coming out of the chair. Leo and Daniel look above to see what the demon is watching, and it is images of conjoined demons. It is demons having intercourse for the pleasure of the one sitting in the chair.

The images are unsettling to Daniel. So vile and disgusting. Each demon couple having intercourse in various positions, with multiple partners. One demon passed onto a group of demons, each having their turn. The grotesque face of the one being shows pure pleasure. The more they abuse it, the more it feels important.

Daniel feels no love from the images. Just animal behavior.

"Disgusting!" Daniel says aloud.

The head demon, ruler of the cave, laughs.

The laughter grows louder and between laughs, there are hisses, grunts, and snorts. He stands up and turns to look at the two. The scales on his face shedding makes it look as if it is melting.

"You hypocrite. You were as filthy and disgusting as these. When you were bedding women in your youth, you did not differ from what you are seeing now." He says with a serpent like smile.

"I know who, when and where you fornicated. You and those whores. Do you want me to name them?"

Daniel becoming upset. How could this snake compare what he did with what he was witnessing?

"You were on quite a streak in university Daniel: Trisha, Sue, Christina, Kelly, Sadie, Doreen, Alicia, Heather, Helen, Niki, Maureen, Vanessa..."

The demon continues on with his list. *Was it that many?*

"... and finally, Summer. You screwed thirty four different women. You are just like them, but in an attractive package." The demon points at the wall as the demons continue on with their sexual depravity.

"The only difference is, these will never reach

orgasm." The demon snickers.

"Do you want to go one more round before I take you to hell?" The demon morphs into a woman capturing all that Daniel found attractive in the women he was with: thick wavy hair, green and hazel eyes, smooth and tight skin, large breasts, long legs with warm thighs. The temptress closes in on Daniel.

"You filthy creature, back off. Use your tricks on the next soul. This one has confessed to his debauchery. He also warned his children about fornication and its sinfulness. How it can lead to disease, guilt, loss of identity, and child born out of wedlock."

The demon transforms back into its serpent like body, sheets of its scaly skin falling below. Its tongue licks its lips and hisses, "Are you sure he confessed to everything?" The demon slithers around Daniel. It investigates the soul from top to bottom, using its tongue to sniff out the filth of sex. The serpent stops, smiles, and looks to Leo.

"I found something, angel."

Daniel panics. *Here we go, I am done for.*

"What?"

"He likes pornography and gets off looking at naked women, men, and women having sexual intercourse. He lusts after these women and pleasured himself to these images. From magazines to images on the computer. It doesn't smell like he confessed to this sinfulness. Give me the soul!" The demon demanded.

Leo dejected, tired of defending Daniel, struggled to find enough gold to pay off the demon.

The walls of the cave parted, and they continue on.

"I don't understand you humans. Do you know what pornography really is?" Leo asks.

Before Daniel could answer.

"Pornography is the devil's iconography. Everything that is opposite of God's goodness is from the devil."

Leo continues on.

"You humans abuse the gifts of emotions and feelings God gave to you when he made you. Your abuse has led to pain, suffering, and, for many, a miserable existence. Your lack of spiritual strength makes it easy for the demons to attack and win souls. So easy."

They advance their trajectory upward,

"Do you know why you have anger? It's not to use against your neighbor, but against the devil. The pleasure you receive from sex is reserved for the person you marry, the person you love."

"Daniel, how could you not have confessed your viewing of pornography?" Leo asks.

"It's embarrassing. I had every intention to, but I was taken before I could. That, among other sins."

"Didn't your spiritual father tell you that what you confess on earth is invisibly erased?"

"Yes, that is why I started to confess all my sins. I was so close to wiping the slate clean."

"You are lucky to get past this tollhouse. This is where many souls lose their battle. The world below is so vile. So many living in excess. The love of pleasure and fornication. It permeates in everything: in books, movies, music, and songs. The demons have whispered filth into your ears and, with no battling back, have given yourselves up to this sin."

"We need more help." Daniel mutters.

"You have the divine scriptures. From Genesis, proverbs, to the Lord's teaching, it is all there to live a righteous life. What is worse is those that hear and read the divine scriptures and continue to live that sinful life? Now they reach this point and will fail. The demons will drag those souls to the dungeons of Hades. Chained, they will wait in darkness for the second coming of our Lord and Savior Jesus Christ. At that time, the souls will meet the Lord and will receive their just reward."

The angel closes his mouth and waits to hear from Daniel.

"I wish I could go back and let everyone know."

"It wouldn't do any good. Our Savior walked the earth and not everyone changed. He showed himself, resurrected body, and not everyone believed; the Jews, the Romans, the Greeks. They all continued their evil ways. If Christ can't change everyone, you certainly cannot. They will write your spirit off as a dream or hallucination."

"Leo, how long have I been dead?"

"About thirty-nine days."

"My memorial service is tomorrow."

"Yes, it will be forty days. We have one more tollhouse to get past." Leo searches his wings and body. He sighs. "Let's pray you can get through the next one unscathed, as you are out of spiritual gold."

"What is the last one?" Even though he knows, he asks anyway.

"The tollhouse of Adultery."

* * *

"ADULTERY" is written in bold. Lydia reads Daniel's account once again. It is still painful after all these days. But she has to forgive. He will be at that tollhouse tomorrow. She feels it. The demon will come out and accuse him and he will fail. They will drag him away, and it will separate them for eternity.

"Send him to hell." The voice whispers to her.

"Don't let him get away with this. While he was screwing around on you, you were stuck here. He tarnished your wedding crowns." The voice was relentless.

Lydia stood up and tried to walk away from the voice.

"While he was inside her, he was humiliating you. You alone, being so stupid. You believe he loves you the same way you love him? You are a fool. Call the memorial off. Send him to Hell." The voice became more forceful.

Lydia covers her ears and walks towards her bedroom. As she walks she prays out loud "Lord Jesus Christ, Son of God, have mercy on me a sinner. Lord Jesus Christ, Son of God, Have Mercy on me a sinner, Lord Jesus Christ, Son of God, have mercy on me a sinner." As she finishes her third prayer her eyes clear, the colors of her surrounding more vivid. She passes by a mirror and sees the frightening image of a demon the size of a child, riding her back, mouth affixed to her ear and talons grabbing onto her shoulders. The color of heated coal, the demon wakes from a trance and continues on with it's deception. Lydia reaches behind to grab the demon, but her hands pass through it.

"How many times did he sleep with her? All the nasty things they did with each other. Then he came home and went inside of you. He used you too. Make him burn."

"Be quiet! Leave me alone!" Lydia shouted through her tears and sobs.

"He enjoyed her more than he ever enjoyed you. She excited him. You were boring. She was beautiful. You let yourself go. He kissed her with passion. He only gives you a peck on the lips. Cancel the memorial."

Lydia weakened, falls to the floor and rolls on her back. The demon moves on top of her and locks onto her other ear.

"He fooled her, too. Made her an adulteress. She will go to hell. He ruined three lives. Daniel is disgusting. He is below the filth the swine roll in. Send him to Hell Lydia and move on with your life." The demon changed its voice sounding caring and motherly. "Meet someone who will respect you, take care of you, and treat you like the angel you are."

Lydia closes her eyes. She flashes back to when she and Daniel first met, their first date by the lake, their wedding at Christ the Savior. Surrounded by all their loved ones, Daniel was at her side when she gave birth each time, all the moments he held her hand, kissed her, made love to her. Him hugging her with all the good times and holding onto her during the sad times. *A fall to temptation, it is not worth destroying a whole marriage.*

Lydia rises from the floor and enters her bedroom. She approaches her prayer corner. "Lord, Jesus Christ, have mercy on me, a sinner. Almighty God, who delivered Your people from the bondage of the adversary, and through your Son cast down Satan like lightning. Deliver me also from every influence of the unclean spirits. Command Satan to depart far from me by the power of Your only begotten Son. Rescue me with the light of the Holy Spirit that I may be guarded against the snares of the crafty demons. Grant that an angel always go before me and lead me to the path of righteousness all the days of my life, to the honor of Your glorious name. Father, Son, and Holy Spirit, now and forever. Amen."

At that moment, Lydia sees a reflection in the icon of Resurrection, the silhouette of a winged being grabbing a hold of the demon and tearing it off of Lydia's back. Wrapping his wings around himself and the demon, he disappears.

Lydia crosses herself and gives thanks to the Lord.

CHAPTER TWENTY-FIVE

As they continue on, Daniel becomes overwhelmed with fear. Trembling, he knew the upcoming tollhouse would be the end to his travel and the terrible demons would surely drag him into Hell.

Does Leo know what I did? If so, does he have a plan to help me? Is there enough spiritual gold to save me? How can I cancel out my sins? Maybe I don't deserve to move on. Please, God forgive me.

Leo turns to Daniel.

"This is the final tollhouse. Sadly, this is the one where many fail. They do not pass because most from the world below have great lust in their heart and act on it. It is more common now. With the technology to find willing participants, partners from past relationships. The moral decay of your world, some in marriage, agrees to sex outside of marriage. It's an abomination to the sacrament. Marriage is a gift from God," Leo says with anger.

"If marriage was not so important, the demons would not tempt humans, and they certainty would not have this." Leo points ahead. "This is the largest of all the tollhouses."

The cave like structure, larger, with a fiery red glow surrounding it. Demons of all shapes and sizes milling about. The stench of the foul smell becomes stronger as they close in. Daniel sees the demons and tries to hide behind Leo. Some demons are dog headed with mouth full of teeth on top of human like bodies. Others have no eyes, only a tongue flickering from its head. Others run on all fours, surround a soul and tear into it. On the other side are naked souls, bundled together. Tied up in ropes. A pack of demons, smaller than the souls, climb on them and tear at their eyes. Larger ones grab the rope and drag them off to hell. At the other end are demons in human form. Some look like beautiful females, other handsome men. They are practicing how to tempt humans on each other.

As they approach the cave, the demons turn and see the soul and angel. Howls, hollering, barking, yelling and cheering fill the air. Daniel thinks he hears the word "welcome" repeatedly. The demons come out to greet the two. But they stop and wait. From behind, six larger demons approach, break the line of smaller demons. The one in the middle crouches down looks over Daniel and Leo. It licks it's cracked lips with a snakelike tongue, smiles, opens his mouth shows three rows of razor like teeth and growls.

"God established the law of marriage, not you man of dust." The demon pointing to Daniel.

"Marriage is holy. It is a mystery. Where husband and wife become one flesh. Where man will leave their mother and father, with their blessing, to be joined to a woman. In joining her, he made a vow in front of God that he devote himself to her, sacrifice for her, love her forever. You failed, you dirty soul."

"You are a liar, demon. This one has been faithful to his wife."

Leo doesn't know! Daniel's question is answered.

"Man of dirt, tell your angel you failed God, your wife, your children and even your guardian angel."

"Daniel?"

Daniel looks around. He moves away from Leo and tries to find a way to escape the tollhouse.

"Daniel?" Leo asks again.

"You stupid angel. You wasted your time on this adulterer. Hey dirt. There is no escape. This is the end. You will be shredded and burned for eternity."

"Lord, please help me. Please forgive me."

"Daniel, you cheated on Lydia?"

"It is true Leo."

"You did not confess this?"

"I told you I ran out of time. I should have started with it first, but I was afraid to confess it. I wrote it down, but never said it."

"Did you at least confess to Lydia?"

"Never. I was a coward. And I did not want to get divorced."

More demons approach, many covered in a mud like substance and toad like without necks. Large arms and long legs. They wait for the head demon's call to seize him.

Leo looks at the fresh additions to the group of demons.

"When he was on earth, this soul, as a Christian man, did many good deeds. So many that should overcome this sin."

A roar of laughter comes from the demons that have

surrounded Leo and Daniel.

"It was just one woman Leo, I never cheated on Lydia prior. It was something I got caught up in. I have no excuse, just weakness."

A serpent like demon slithers up to Leo. "And angel, the woman he bedded. She didn't know he was married. He made her an adulteress. The Lord will prepare this one for the sword." He hissed.

The toad like demons pushed Leo aside, and close in on Daniel.

"Wait, wait, wait." Daniel cried.

"I am a good man that has failed. I have sinned, but also did some good. I gave alms, fasted, went to church, received the body and blood of our savior Jesus Christ. I have fought the good fight."

The demons laughed and mocked him. "I have fought the good fight. I am a good man. I gave money to the poor."

"Don't mock me," Daniel cried

"You mocked God by having intercourse with that woman who was not your wife." The demon shot back.

Leo moves back from the horde. He has always had disgust for those who committed adultery. As a protector of the bride and groom on their weeding day, he has seen thousands of marriages. When he is present in the church, he can feel the love. Not only the love the bride and groom have for each other. But from the priest, and those in attendance who are witnessing the event.

Angels, like the demons, are not the judge of any person's soul. They can protect it or tempt it.

"Leo, please help me." Daniel screams.

Leo recalls when he stopped guarding Daniel. It was

the moment he witnessed Daniel entering the hotel room with Iris. He could feel the lust in his heart. Sometimes, he would nudge his human in a different direction, but with so many corrupting their marriages, Leo became apathetic, and let the demons win.

This is my fault. I failed to guard the soul entrusted to me. Leo spreads his wings wide open and clears the demons from Daniel and stands between him and the ruler of the cave.

"This soul is good. It must be able to move on. What do you want?"

The demon sniffs the air. "You don't have enough gold to set him free."

Leo feels the weight of his wings, the lightest they have been on this journey. The demon is right all the spiritual gold is gone.

"HA HA HA You don't have any gold, do you angel?!"

Daniel, looking over at Leo, gives him a pleading look. Leo taking time to figure a way out of this.

"Wait demon. Today, in the world below, is his forty day memorial. If he has enough prayers from this service to supply spiritual gold, let us pass. If not, take him to the gates of Hades where he will remain until the second coming and Our Lord will judge him."

"You foolish angel. There is no way he can gather enough prayers to escape this tollhouse. No one prays anymore. They send vibes and thoughts. Pathetic, those fall to the ground. And that little church. It does not have enough believers to break him free."

"Take the deal. It's funny watching the souls have their hope crushed." One of the toad like demon says.

"Well demon?" Leo asks.

"It's a deal angel. We will wait."

* * *

Lydia looks in her closet and eyes the black dress she wore for Daniel's funeral. She decides she doesn't want to wear that one to the memorial service.

Maybe something black with a little color

At the end of the rack is a black dress with purple flower prints. Still in its plastic. It was a dress she bought to wear on their anniversary. She found her black lace head covering.

She lays her dress on the bed, and heads into the bathroom and readies herself for the day ahead. She sees herself in the mirror. "A little makeup, not too much. Be sure to use a tear proof mascara."

She finishes with a brush of the waves in her hair. She has let the gray come through. Daniel always wanted her to stop coloring her hair, told her she would look beautiful with gray hair. It was the one prideful thing she did. She did not have the courage to let it go.

Satisfied with her appearance, Lydia walks over to her prayer corner and says a quick prayer, thanking the Lord for her blessings and for a good day. She crosses herself and walks out of her bedroom, down the hallway past the photos of memories past, and out the door.

Pulling into the church driveway, she sees a crowd gathered about. *Thank you Lord. Only on feast days is there this many people at church.* She steps out of her car, approaching her are Jonah and Maria. They give her a kiss on the cheek and hug her.

"Isn't this amazing Lydia? Look at all these people."

Jonah points at the crowd.

"We have people from multiple parishes. St. Nicholas Antiochian Church, Holy Trinity Greek Orthodox Church, Holy Archangels Russian Orthodox Church, The Ethiopian and even the Egyptian church. Lydia knew the Ethiopians were here as soon as she pulled up. Dressed all in white, over their ebony skin, they are a sight to see. So beautiful in their worship. Around the women, some men were carrying drums.

"Drums?" Lydia asked

Jonah shrugged his shoulders.

At the top of church steps, she sees Father Ephraim, smiling as he looks at the crowd. And behind him, a grinning slender being. Grotesque in appearance, it walks closer to Father Ephraim and tries to whisper something in his ear. He steps forward before the demon can confuse the priest.

On top of the church, like a vulture, is another demon, searching for the spiritually weak. Crouched down, it could be mistaken as a gargoyle. Lydia, searching the crowd, sees more demons, some smaller like the one from last night, on the backs of many locked onto ears whispering temptations, some telling them to leave, to not take part in the memorial service. Some telling them things trying to make them jealous of Lydia.

"She gets all the attention. You should be so lucky." One would whisper.

"Why does her husband need all these prayers?" Another casting doubt.

"Prayer doesn't work. You are so silly being here."

"You are not worthy of sending prayers. God will not hear your prayers. They will condemn Daniel."

The demons work over the crowd with the primary goal of limiting the prayers and trying to move people to doubt and sin.

All of them head inside when the church bell rings. The crowd opens up, allowing Lydia to stand closest to the solea.

Father Ephraim prefers only the light of the candles to shine in the church for evening services. Sometimes the church can remain dark, but tonight, with the number of candles ablaze, the church has never been brighter.

The priest begins the Saturday vespers service. He censes the church and the people. Without realizing it, the smoke from the incense spreads out and clears the church of the demons. All except for the larger one standing in the back. For that one, the angel guarding the church grabbed it, pulled it outside and destroyed with a strike to its head.

The angel enters the church and remains at the back of the altar. Only Lydia can see how magnificent the creature is. Bright wings, alabaster skin, androgynous features. With eyes closed, it seems at peace. But with all assurance, it will pounce on any demon that dares to enter the church.

The choir sings the prayers for the service. Lydia, knowing all the songs from her days in choir, sings along.

The Vesper service comes to a close and Father Ephraim moves from the altar and over to the crucifix. He motions for Lydia to come closer. The choir moves away from their stands and surrounds Lydia and her family. The burning candles cast the glow onto the icon of Christ hanging on the cross. Lydia tries to find comfort in the face of the Savior.

"Dear brother and sisters in Christ. Christ is in our midst."

"He is and always shall be," the congregations answers.

"All memorial services are important for the soul of the reposed. But our brother, who did not leave this church when he passed from this life, needs our help. He needs our prayers. So Lydia and I ask of everyone to sing with the choir, to pray for Daniel, for him to go to Heaven and glorify the Lord with all the angels."

Father Ephraim takes his censer and swings it back and forth, left and right, with vigor. The sweet smoke from the incense filling the air surrounds the congregation, the crucifix and the koliva. After the priest finishes censing the church, the choir begins the memorial service. They sing:

"Blessed are You, O Lord, teach me Your commandments."

Then Father Ephraim prays, "The choir of Saints has found the fountain of life and the door of Paradise. May I also find the way through repentance. I am the lost sheep: O Savior, call me back and save me.

Choir responds "Blessed are You, O Lord, teach me Your commandments.

Father Ephraim, "Of old, You created me from nothing and honored me with Your divine image. But when I disobeyed Your commandment, You returned me to the earth from which I was taken. Lead me back again to Your likeness, so that the ancient beauty may be refashioned."

Choir, "Blessed are You, O Lord, teach me Your commandments."

Father Ephraim, "I am an image of Your ineffable glory, though I bear the scars of my transgressions. Take pity on me, the work of Your hands, Master, and cleanse me by Your compassion. Grant me the desired homeland for which I long, making me again a citizen of Paradise."

Choir, "Blessed are You, O Lord, teach me Your commandments."

Father Ephraim, "Give rest, O God, to Your servant, and place him in Paradise where the choirs of the Saints and the righteous, O Lord, will shine as the stars of Heaven. To Your departed servant give rest, O Lord, overlooking all his offenses. Glory to the Father and the Son and the Holy Spirit."

"Let us devoutly praise the threefold radiance of the one God as we sing: Holy are You, the Father without beginning, the co-eternal Son, and the divine Spirit. Illumine us who worship You in faith and deliver us from the eternal fire. Now and forever and to the ages of ages. Amen."

"Rejoice, gracious Lady, who gave birth to God in the flesh for the salvation of all, and through whom the human race has found salvation. Through you, pure and blessed Theotokos, may we find Paradise."

The choir responds, "Alleluia. Alleluia. Alleluia. Glory to You O God."

Father Ephraim, "With the Saints give rest, O Christ, to the soul of Your servant where there is no pain, no sorrow, no sighing, but life everlasting. Among the spirits of the righteous perfected in faith, give rest, O Savior, to the soul of Your servant, keeping it in the blessed life which is from You, O loving One.

In your place of rest, O Lord, where all Your saints

repose, give rest also to the soul of Your servant, for You alone are immortal. Glory to the Father and the Son and the Holy Spirit."

"You are our God, who descended into Hades and loosened the pains of those who were held captive. Grant rest also, O Savior, to the soul of Your servant. Now and forever and to the ages of ages. Amen."

"You the only pure and spotless Virgin, who ineffably gave birth to God, intercede for mercy and forgiveness of the soul of your servant."

As the service progresses, Lydia's eyes open wide. She looks to her left shoulder and sees black talons squeezing, breaking through her skin.

"Why Lydia, why? He broke your heart when you read his confession. And to think, he would never tell you. Look around. Is he deserving of all of this? If those in here knew what he did, this building would be empty."

Tears well up in her eyes. Jonah and Maria drape their arms over her shoulder.

"Lydia, he's in a better place. He will soon be with all the angels, his parents." Maria trying to assure her, not understanding what battle Lydia was waging.

Unable to move, Lydia continues to be tormented by the demon. "I saw what they did in bed. She did things to him you would never do. She had experience. You did not. They were filthy. He told her he loved her."

Those with closed eyes when looking at Lydia would see a widow hunched over, crying for her husband that passed away. For someone with eyes wide open, like that of an angel, would see she is being attacked by a demon.

Lydia watches as the angel standing in the back of

the altar widens his eyes, spies the demon. He tucks his wings behind his back, then takes long strides toward Lydia. He gives her wink, then ducks down looking eye to eye with the little demon. The angel rips it off of Lydia's shoulders. She winces in pain. And takes it outside, crushes its head, lays it next to the other demon he destroyed.

Father Ephraim continues the service, unknowing of the battle that just took place.

"Have mercy upon us, O God, according to Your great mercy; we pray to You, hear us and have mercy.

Again we pray for the repose of the soul of the departed servant of God, Daniel, and for the forgiveness of all his sins, both voluntary and involuntary."

The choir and everyone responds "Lord, have mercy."

At that moment, Lydia sees light waves move from the tops of the head and the chest of the people streaming upward.

Father Ephraim continues, "May the Lord God grant his soul rest where the righteous repose. For the mercies of God, the kingdom of Heaven, and the forgiveness of his sins."

The choir answers "Grant this, O Lord."

Lydia looked behind her and she could see more light waves from several others in the congregation.

Are those prayers?

Father Ephraim "Let us pray to the Lord."

Choir "Lord, have mercy."

Father Ephraim, "O God of spirits and of all flesh, You trampled upon death and abolished the power of the devil, giving life to Your world. Give rest to the soul of Your departed servant Daniel in a place of light, in a place of green pasture, in a place of refreshment, from where pain, sorrow, and sighing have fled away. As a good and loving God, forgive every sin he has committed in word, deed, or thought, for there is no one who lives and does not sin. You alone are without sin. Your righteousness is an everlasting righteousness, and Your word is truth."

"For You are the resurrection, the life and the repose of Your departed servant Daniel, Christ our God, and to You we offer glory, with Your eternal Father who is without beginning and Your all-holy, good and life-creating Spirit, now and forever and to the ages of ages."

All the people respond "Amen."

Lydia sees light waves emanating from almost everyone in the congregation.

Wow, look at all those prayers. It is so beautiful.

Father Ephraim continues, "Glory to You, O God, our hope, glory to You."

"Lord of the living and the dead, the immortal King and Risen Christ, our true God, through the intercessions of His all-pure and spotless holy Mother; of the holy, glorious, and praiseworthy Apostles; of our venerable and God-bearing Fathers; of the holy and glorious forefathers Abraham, Isaac and Jacob; of His holy and righteous friend Lazarus, who lay in the grave four days; and of all the saints; place the soul of His servant Daniel, departed from us, in the dwelling place of the righteous; give rest to him in the bosom of Abraham; and number him among the saints and have mercy on us, as a good God who loves mankind."

The choir sings "Amen."

Father Ephraim says, "May your memory be eternal, brother worthy of blessedness and everlasting memory."

The whole church, in one wonderful and loud voice, sings for Daniel's soul:

"Eternal be his memory. Eternal be his memory. May his memory be eternal.

Eternal be his memory. Eternal be his memory. May his memory be eternal.

Eternal be his memory. Eternal be his memory. May his memory be eternal."

Lydia is astonished by what God is showing her. Streams of prayers leaving the people and traveling upward to Daniel. The church dazzled with all colors of the spectrum.

With head tilted towards the sky, the angel in the rear of the altar walks out into the middle of the nave and watches in awe.

Lydia looks to Jonah, then Maria and the rest of the congregation and shows them a smile underneath the headscarf. *The prayers are working, keep praying.*

✻ ✻ ✻

Daniel, Leo, and the demon continue to wait. The demon tells stories of all the souls he has imprisoned. He laughs at the ones who make it to the very end and get caught here because of the many affairs they had. "Just like you, Daniel, they will beg, plead and give reason after reason for their transgressions. But it never works. None of them confess their sins. All they had to do was confess and never do it again and their sins are erased and they are taken to Heaven."

Daniel pulls on Leo's wing and motions for him to move closer so he can whisper in his ear.

"How long do we wait?"

And at that moment, Daniel and Leo could see the light waves breaking through the darkness and traveling towards the angel. First little by little, then like a brilliant lightning storm, the waves rip through the darkness all heading towards Leo. The light waves pouring onto Leo, he could feel his wings becoming a little heavier. Daniel watched as he reached underneath his feathers and pulled out several bags of gold.

"Thank you Lord, thank you Jesus." Daniel shouted.

The demon is still confident that there won't be enough prayers to fill his coffers with gold. Stood and gloated. "You still need more prayers."

The light waves waned, the demon's grin grew wider. A new flood of light waves fired through the dark, ending at the angel.

Leo tried to lift his wings, but he couldn't, as all the spiritual gold weighed it down.

Leo took all the bags from the inside of his wings and threw them down at the feet of the demon. The pile, when finished, went as high as his waist.

"There, you sickening creature. Now let us pass."

"No. You are short one coin."

"What?" Daniel says

"In the hill of coins, there is not one that belongs to your wife. These prayers are good, but I want one from your wife."

"Can he do this Leo?" Daniel asks

"Yes, unfortunately."

"What can we do?"

"You are running out of time, angel. We made a deal. You don't have enough gold. The soul is ours." He said, with words garbled in his foaming mouth.

Father Ephraim, "Through the prayers of our holy

Fathers, Lord Jesus Christ, our God, have mercy on us and save us."

The church, with one thundering voice sing "Amen!"

Lydia crying in happiness, believing all the prayers moved Daniel through the final tollhouse and now he is in Heaven. She sees smiles and those hugging throughout the congregation. In the background, outside, she hears the drums from the Ethiopian church mixed in with their chanting.

"Time is up angel, hand the soul over." The demons surround Daniel and take him.

"Leo?" He cries out.

"I am sorry, Daniel. You will have to wait."

The demons take spiritual chains and wrap Daniel from his feet all the way to his neck. Another demon takes a giant lock, puts it between two chain links and closes it.

"Take him down." The head demon grouses.

Lydia walks up to the crucifix. Crosses herself, then prays.

"Dear Lord, thank you for this beautiful service this day. Thank you for the love and support of Daniel. I need you to know that Daniel is, deep down, a good man, father, and husband. Most importantly, he is a Christian who fights, always striving to be as saintly as possible. He was on his way. But You took him too soon. And because Lord, I cannot forgive sins, Lord, I pray you forgive Daniel for his sins, especially for his sin of adultery. Lord have mercy and save us, amen."

All the time Lydia was praying, the angel watched as the light wave left Lydia and traveled up at a striking speed.

"Please, Leo, Help." Daniel cried as he was being

dragged into the ever lasting darkness.

At that moment, Leo felt a jolt of energy. He reached into his wing to find one large coin. Holding it between his fingers, this one larger and shinier than the rest.

"Here demon, now release Daniel."

Still holding the coin, Leo sees in its reflection the lock on the chains breaking, then falling to Daniel's feet. Leo takes the coin and throws it to the gate keeper.

The demon, full of anger, bitterness, and spite, grabs the coin, eats it and lets the two pass.

Lydia lifts her head from prayer and catches the angel in her eye. The angel breaks from an expressionless face, nods and smiles at Lydia. At that moment, she knows Daniel escaped the tollhouses.

CHAPTER TWENTY-SIX

A bright light, more brilliant than the sun, shredded the darkness. The angel grabbed hold of Daniel and they advanced upward at impossible speeds. Daniel glanced at Leo, his face shining, head tilted up, bathing in the radiance.

The upward journey came to a stop. The two now found themselves at the gates of Heaven. Rejoicing, they made it through the tollhouses.

The gates of Heaven, made of crystals filled with starlight and fire, stretched far and wide. *Is this the heavenly kingdom of Jerusalem?*

As they look at the gates with awe, a being with a face so bright, filled with sweet happiness, greeted Daniel and Leo. "Welcome, how joyous. God has given approval for another soul to pass through the tollhouses." The being embraced Daniel. "Go through the gates. Your just reward awaits."

"Who was that Leo?"

"That was the good thief. He is the first one encounters when they reach the kingdom of Heaven."

They pass through the gates and the first gift of Heaven is a scent of the sweetest fragrance, never matched in the world below. As they continued further into Heaven, an airy expanse opens up. More beings, too many to number fill the area. All bright, with shining faces. Several of them see the angel with Daniel and they rejoice, running over to greet them. "With God's approval and mercy, we add a soul to the kingdom of Heaven."

At that moment, a group started singing a song filling Daniel's soul with joy. They joined the two as they continued deeper into Heaven. Radiant beings passed by, the first the color of rose and violet, the second white as light and the third like gold. Passing through radiant beams of light, containing a myriad of colors, hues of God's glory.

Songs of wonder filled the space they entered, a throne made of multicolored beams of light reaching upward. Above it was the Cherubim, six wings, many eyed singing "Holy, Holy are You." At the base of the throne, hundreds of angels singing the praise of God.

Daniel instantly feels the awe and fear before the greatness of God. "I am not worthy." He says to Leo. Trembling, Daniel prostrates before God. Leo nods and stops Daniel. "The Lord loves you and he wants for you to see more, then we will take you to a place of rest."

Daniel lifts his head towards the Lord. *I am safe. I can feel God's love.* Leo pulls him away and they continue on to an area that is paradise, where Adam and Eve might have been placed in the beginning. Milling about are beings radiating with many colors of divine light. "These are the Saints." Leo whispered to Daniel. Unnoticed, they pass through paradise, and over the hill is an enormous city. The inhabitants of this area comprise the apostles, martyrs, prophets, hierarchs, teachers of Christ and all the righteous.

Turning to the right, a new area opens to Daniel. It's the home of Abraham, Issac, Jacob and his twelve descendants. Sitting on a throne is Abraham, surrounded by Christian children illuminated by holy baptisms. The area is full of wonder and ineffable glory.

"Everything the church taught was correct." Daniel states to Leo.

"Yes, and for those that listened and followed the Lord, like you, are here, in Heaven for eternity. It is so much worse for those that turned away from the Lord. I must show you where you would have been if you chose to live a life of sin without repentance."

Daniel followed Leo, and they began their descent into hell. The first area was the dungeon, the place that held all the souls from Adam and Eve to Moses to John the Baptist. Here is where Christ, in His passion, defeated death by His death, creating a way for all the righteous souls to make it to Heaven.

They proceed further. The stench emanating from the area of hell sickens Daniel. "Look and behold the miseries from which the Lord rescued you by the prayers of your brethren and, most importantly, your wife. It's a place where the suffering and torments and pain cannot be described."

Daniel hears the cries of "Woe, woe, woe." The light of Leo that guided Daniel through the darkness of the tollhouses now illuminates the shadow of death, exposing a sea of souls, devoured own sins. Wailing, crying a gnashing of teeth.

They hear laughter from behind. It is coming from the salivating mouths of demons, dragging five souls and throwing them into the valley with the millions of others. They turn away from the valley and proceed to a pit filled with fire. The flames shooting high. Daniel sees the horror of souls inside the flames being tossed up, then dropped back into the fiery pit.

The cries of the sinners fill all the caverns of hell. Daniel sees God is merciful. The pious journey over the right roads laid down by Him with His commandments.

"No one pities them, no one comforts them, they beg, and no one listens to them, no one prays for them, no mercy for them. Be thankful that your priest taught salvation, saved by repentance, true confession, and pure knowledge of Our Lord and Savior Jesus Christ. It is time to move away from here." Leo takes Daniel under his wings and they leave hell. Daniel looks over his shoulder, as the light of the angel fades on the souls of the damned shouting and crying. Not one asking for forgiveness.

Leo guides Daniel to his final resting place. A place filled with ineffable joy, happiness, delight and wonder. At the edge of the airy expanse and outside the land of paradise is where the souls of Christians who led the righteous life remain until the Last Judgment.

"This is your new home in paradise, Daniel. You will be here until the second coming, then you will reunite with your resurrected body to live in eternity in God's kingdom."

Daniel, recalling his prayers to his guardian angel, opens his mouth and says, "Leo, my heavenly companion, thank you for not abandoning me, a sinner. And protecting me from the evil demons that overwhelmed me through my weakness. You held my weak hand and guided me on the path of salvation. You were my guardian and protector of my soul and body, overlooking all the things by which I have grieved you. You guarded me in the world below, at night from the influence of Satan, that I would not fall into sin. You interceded for me on earth and through the tollhouses so that the Lord would grant me forgiveness of my sins and help me be worthy of His goodness. You have done well for this miserable soul. Because of your help, I now have a home in God's wonder."

"You are now in a place filled with God's love. It's time for me to protect the newly baptized." Leo wrapped his wings around Daniel and hugged him goodbye.

"Wait, what about Lydia? Will she be able to find me? Will we ever be together again?"

Leo smiled and disappeared into the earthly realm.

CHAPTER TWENTY-SEVEN

"I see crosses on the hill. They are so beautiful."

"What is that, mom?" Paulina asks.

"Look." She points her aged and frail hand towards the window.

"Crosses, all over the hill. Bright and beautiful. There are so many. Some tall, some small, you have to see them. What about you, Father Jonah, can't you?"

They all turn and glance out the window, but only see the orange yellow sun descending behind the dusty hills.

She looks about the room and sees her children, they are now old. With them are her grandchildren. She sees the eldest, the boy who could pass for her husband.

"Have I ever told you, you look like your grandfather?"

"Yes grandma, many times." He smiles.

"He was so good looking, a wonderful man, husband, and father. Taken away from me too early." A tear fell from the corner of her eye.

"One day, Mom, you will be with him again." Simeon reassuring her.

"I pray so. I just wished he lived long enough to see all

of you grown up. He loved you all so much."

"Just think of all the stories you can tell him when you see him again." Liev said.

She wants to speak, but she needs to catch her breath first.

"My children, when I go, continue on. Remember that this life is short, temporary. Don't let the devil fool you and keep you from your salvation. Do what is necessary to earn your place in the Kingdom of God. Go to church, read the scriptures, repent, give alms, love your neighbor and most important confess yours sins to your priest."

They all, in hushed voices, say "yes." Except for one voice, a voice she never heard before saying "Amen."

She struggles to sit up in her bed. Opening her eyes wider, Lydia sees an angel in the back of the room. Face illuminated, he smiles at her.

"Children, my time is coming to an end. Please pray for my soul when I pass from this life."

"Mom, if there is an expressway to Heaven, you will be on it." Simeon says.

"No one knows for sure. I did the best I knew how. Just please pray for me."

Liev takes her hand and strokes it. He's disturbed by the feel of bones underneath her paper thin skin. "I love you Mom," is all he can say.

At the back of the room, she finds the angel. He nods.

Tears stream down her face. She knows her time is at hand.

"I need to close my eyes and rest a bit." She lays back on her pillow.

Her son continues to hold her hand. He feels a slight squeeze. Paulina watches her mother's eyelids close tight. Her breathing becomes heavy, then slight, the time between each breath decreasing.

Father Jonah stands, walks past the grand children sitting in chairs surround Lydia's bed. He opens his weathered book of prayers handed down to him from Father Ephraim and starts to pray over Lydia. She hears the comforting words of the Lord. The warmth of her son's large hands wrapped around her small hand gives her comfort.

She tries, but is unable to open her eyes one last time. She feels the warmth from her son's hand recede and the sound of the beautiful prayers becomes more distant, fading and then silence.

Eyes open wide, the angel standing in the corner greets her. "Servant of God, Lydia, I am your guardian angel. My name is Leo. I am your guide."

Lydia's soul rises out of her temporal body. And grabs onto Leo's extended hand.

A voice from above fills the aerial realm. The voice full and loud.

Leo bows down. Lydia bows.

"Sons of darkness flee! Flee and hide yourselves from the force of light of righteousness. Angel, take Lydia, bring her here and put the demons to shame."

Leo stood up straight, puts Lydia within his wings and moves them at other worldly speed through the tollhouses, never deterred by the hideous demons. All of them hiding in the depths as Leo and Lydia pass by.

They come to the end, breaking the darkness with glorious light. The two finding themselves at the gates of Heaven.

As with her husband, Leo takes Lydia through the expanse of Heaven, where she spends time speaking with the Saints and Apostles, having all of her questions answered. She comes to the abode of the patriarchs. She finds Noah, who tells her about building the ark, the 150 days at sea with all the animals and landing in Ararat. And walking off the ark to a transformed world. And back further in the area of the patriarchs, she found Adam and Eve. They told her of paradise, the temptation of the serpent, and the time after being expelled from the garden. Lydia wished to stay and hear more from them, but Leo told her it was time to move on.

Leo took her to the depths of hell. She tried to hide her face in the wings of the angel. The torments, crying and wailing were more terrible than she imagined. "Please take me away from here, Leo." She asked of him.

✻ ✻ ✻

In his time in Heaven, Daniel has never missed the world below, only longing for his wife. But in the company of goodness, love and joy, he never has the feelings of sadness, anger, and despair. The slight moments of happiness on earth are a sample of true happiness found in Heaven.

Since his arrival, Daniel has been a part of the group that greets arriving souls. Every time a new soul arrives, they all jump for joy, as they know there are those on earth that still believe in the Lord and Savior Jesus Christ. Another soul with the fruits of the spirit. Love, joy, kindness, goodness, faithfulness, gentleness, and self control.

Daniel hears the choir sing one of their beautiful

hymns, showing a new soul has arrived. Daniel looks past the souls and, with awe, he sees the angel Leo standing in the midst with his wings wrapped around his body. He spots Daniel and, with a glance, he tells Daniel to approach him.

Daniel, full of excitement, moves swiftly across the expanse to meet Leo. As he approaches, the souls make a path for Daniel, while others move behind the angel. To watch what is about to unfold.

"Leo, where have you been? I missed you." Daniel says with gladness.

"I had a beautiful soul that they assigned me to guard. Now that mission has come to an end." Leo unfolded his wings to reveal the soul of Lydia.

Daniel shouts with joy and wrapped his spiritual arms around his wife.

"Lydia! I love you."

"I love you Daniel!"

The choir, joined by thousands of other souls, sang in celebration for the reunion of husband and wife.

The End.

EPILOGUE

The coldness of the hospital room surrounds him. The brightness of the artificial light bouncing off the white walls strain his eyes. He asks to have lights dimmed, but the nurses and doctors do not oblige. They can barely hear his request through his oxygen mask.

He knows his time is at hand. It is just a matter of days, or hours. What will get him first, the multitude of aggressive tumors taking over his body or the failing of his bitter heart.

He closes his eyes, visions of himself swinging the censer, smoke from the incense blessing the icons of Christ, the Theotokos and the icons of God: the people standing and praying at Sunday's Divine Liturgy. His heart fills with joy administering communion to the faithful. He sees himself from behind giving a sermon after the gospel reading. Those in attendance intently look on.

A tear falls out of the corner of his eye and lands on the cheap cotton pillow case. How he loved baptisms and weddings. Bringing new life and new couples into the Kingdom of God. Submerging the infant into the water three times, anointing the child with oil, placing crowns on the heads of the new king and queen of their home. The way God intended.

I loved being a priest.

Another sharp pain pierces his chest. He winces. *More morphine please.* Too weak to move, to get up and have a drink of water. The embarrassment of having to ask for help to go to the bathroom or lift a small plastic cup of water and put it to his lips. No need for the bathroom anymore. The body is shutting down and has not had to use the bathroom in days.

Blurred vision he sees a figure entering his room. He braces the best he can. "Yes, Father, what is wrong?" The attending nurse asks. She puts her hand on his, bracelet with a cross charm dangles, shining gold from catching the light of the artificial candle. He weeps, "My race is finished, I did not fight the good fight, I did not keep the faith."

The nurse squeezes his hand. She feels his forehead, and it is warm. She takes the wet cloth to cool him down. Then she removes the oxygen mask and moistens his lips with petroleum jelly.

"Water." He asks for. She takes the blue cup with white straw and brings it closer to his lips. He struggles to turn his head and bring his lips to the straw, but he uses what little strength he has to extend his neck to reach and take some sips. The freezing water covering his tongue and hitting the back of his throat. He wonders if he will be like the rich man, looking up into Abraham's bosom, pleading for his thirst to be quenched. If he is the rich man, who is the Lazarus?

"Father Ephraim." He whispers.

"Did you say something, Father Lazarus?" The nurse asks.

He slowly moves his head side to side, indicating no.

Another stabbing pain in his chest, and then again into his spine. He quietly prays for mercy. The nurse pats his hand. "My shift is up and I have to leave. My replacement will be here soon to take care of you."

He hears the squeak of her shoe as she walks out of his hospital room. He turns his head and stares at the entrance to his room. Waiting to see who her replacement is. He prays that it is a woman. The male nurses do not have the kindness and patience for the dying.

Outside of his room, he sees the tip of a shadow on the hall floor. This must be the person.

The shadow grows longer, but the footsteps are silent. The shadow closer and rises from the hospital floor and materializes at the doorway. It takes a moment for the demon to be fully recognizable. Father Lazarus shutters in fear. The demon grows lanky. It's as dark as midnight. Large almond-shaped eyes open, no color, just mirror like with enough reflection for Father Lazarus to see what he looks like: a frail, living skeleton with fear all over his face. The demon grins, showing its shark like mouth full of tiny razor teeth.

The demon walks toward the priest and falls into pieces with each piece turning into another demon. They surround the bed, peering down at him. The priest closes his eyes and mutters the Jesus prayer under his breath. "Lord Jesus Christ, have mercy on me a sinner." He opens them and the demons, now double in number, chatter in indistinguishable language, some laugh, others howl and bark.

"We have a priest." He hears one say to the other.

"It's almost time" his friend says to him.

Father Lazarus struggles to stay alive. Everything Father Ephraim taught is coming true. His eyes open wide, with the final realization that he will not make it through the tollhouses.

If one with true eyes looked into the hospital room, they would witness a horror show of demons on the verge of attacking the soul of a priest.

Father Lazarus, with heart beat increasing ever faster, breathes rapidly. He knows it is time. The demons crowd even closer around him, each one trying to be the first to attack the soul at the moment of the priest's death.

"I was a good priest. I don't deserve this. I should be with the saints." He tries to scream. But his mouth won't move and there isn't enough air in his lungs to vibrate his vocal chords.

His heart continues to pound. He feels it swell, the pain crushes his chest. Eyelids are forced open. His last vision on earth are of the monstrous demons. His first vision when he opens his eyes on the other side is that of the same demons. The large demon rips his soul from his body and throws it to the horde, where they rip it apart over and over until they are instructed to take the soul straight to Hell.

Father Lazarus, alone in the realm, no angel to guide him, to battle for him, to defend him from the demons, only sees the demons as they drag him into Hell where he will remain until the last judgment.

MEMORY ETERNAL

"For the remission of the sins of those who have departed this life in blessed memory, let us pray to the Lord."

"For the ever-memorable servants of God, for their repose, tranquility and blessed memory, let us pray to the Lord."

"That He will pardon them every transgression, whether voluntary or involuntary, let us pray to the Lord."

"That they may present themselves blameless before the dread throne of the Lord of glory, let us pray to the Lord."

"Lord have mercy on us and save us."

"Amen."

- Supplications from the Orthodox Memorial Service.

Memory Eternal

THANK YOU

I hope you enjoyed the book! Please support my writings by leaving a review on Amazon.com.

I am an independent author who chooses to self-publish. Self-publishing allows me creative control of the stories I write and explore the subjects I am interested in. It is the most democratic way for authors, ignored by the large publishing houses, to share their stories.

The drawback of being an independent is that I proofread and edit my stories (to save money and allow me to publish more books). With that said, there is the possibility of errors in this book.

If you find any, rather than posting a negative review please contact me via my website www.cebass.com.

ACKNOWLEDGEMENT

I have struggled with the question of life after death since the passing of my father twenty-seven years ago. To help me try and understand, I found The Soul After Death by Father Seraphim Rose (Memory Eternal) and what I read has stuck with me ever since. His book is not embraced by the whole Orthodox community.

When it was time to write this book, soon after the passing of my mother in 2021, I researched other writings to find what happens after we pass from this life. The sources I found most healing to my soul and answers to my questions include:
The Orthodox Study Bible
The Departure of the Soul: According to the Teaching of the Orthodox Church
- St. Anthony's Greek Orthodox Monastery
The Soul After Death: Father Seraphim Rose

These three sources are wonderful for those that wish to delve further into what the church father's say about the aeriel tollhouses.

And as always, please reach out to your spiritual father to discuss and build a relationship. Do it today, not towards the end of your life. Because we do not know the hour we will be called home. Your spiritual father is a guide to help you on your journey through this life, so, God willing, you may spend your eternity in God's kingdom.

ABOUT THE AUTHOR

C. E. Bass

About the Author

C.E. Bass is an independent author who publishes under the imprint Ark Doves Press. An Orthodox Christian, C.E. writes faith driven novels from a biblical world view, to inspire and help the reader navigate through the ever-changing world. His stories delve into a variety of genres, from suspense to romance, drama and adventure.

C.E. shares his life with his wife, and their two sons, in the great state of Texas.

C.E. is a member of American Christian Fiction Writers (ACFW) and the Central Houston chapter of Inspirational Writers Alive!

For more information on C.E., and upcoming writings, please visit www.cebass.com

Made in the USA
Middletown, DE
30 May 2023